Along the Guadalquivir

by
Joseph R. Costa

This book is dedicated to
my brother Bill (Guillermo in Spanish)
who was killed in Viet Nam in 1969
while serving in the Marine Corp

For the convenience of readers, distances are expressed in English units rather than the Spanish units of the time.

- JRC

Pronunciation
Guadalquivir (gwa-DAL-ki-veer)
Andalusia (an-da-loo-SEE-a)
Guillermo (gee-YAIR-mo)
Mencía (men-SEE-a)

ISBN-13:9798652731373

Contents

Foreword iii
Main Characters iv
Ch.1 Mateo 1
Ch.2 Battle at Sea 7
Ch.3 Guillermo 12
Ch.4 Neighbor 23
Ch.5 Señorita 27
Ch.6 Pascual 33
Ch.7 Mencía 39
Ch.8 Cousins 49
Ch.9 Luisa 59
Ch.10 Trouble 72
Ch.11 Trickery 80
Ch.12 Wrath of God 91
Ch.13 Happiness 100
Ch.14 Curate 113
Ch.15 Reform 125
Ch 16. Garden 132
Ch.17 Dying Brother 142
Ch.18 Neglected Estate 153
Ch.19 Setting It Right 162
Ch.20 New Crop 170
Ch.21 Brothers 185
Ch.22 Her Story 198
Ch.23 Trader 204
Ch.24 Rescue 214
Ch.25 Compadres 224
Ch.26 Sebastian 231

Ch.27 Conclusion 244

List of Characters...247

Foreword

In the late sixteenth century, the two young men of our tale are friends, living on an upper-class family estate, situated north of the Guadalquivir River in Andalusia, a section of southern Spain heavily influenced by its Moorish past.

In those times, the Catholic Church dominated the culture and laws of the Spanish kingdom, which had forced all non-Catholics to leave many years before.

Despite the massive treasure of silver arriving on the Spanish treasure fleets each year from the New World, Spain was not a flourishing country. Banditry, crime, and poverty were commonplace. It is a time of civility and piety, as well as villainy and wickedness.

Main Characters

Mateo & Guillermo - The true friends
Don Lorenzo & Doña Antonia - Mateo's parents
Miguel - Guillermo's father, Don Lorenzo's Overseer
María - Guillermo's mother

Mencía - Mateo's date and then true friend

Pascual - Local highwayman, Don Lorenzo's friend
Sebastian - One of Pascual's men, Guillermo's friend

Luisa - Mateo's love
Don Francisco & Doña Isabel - Luisa's parents

Don Carlos & Doña Catalina - Mateo's cousins
Don Diego - Mateo's uncle

Ch.1 Mateo

WITH A SIGH OF THANKFUL RELIEF, Mateo pulled up his horse at the entrance of the family estate. Sitting in his saddle and smiling, he happily viewed the familiar hills, meadows, oaks, and dwellings. Now late June, he was, at last, home after over fifteen months away in the Indies (Spain's name for the New World) with no means of communication with his family.

The family estate had not changed a great deal during his time away, but things never change here. The well-worn earthen road into the estate stretched out before him. Several white-washed, tile-roofed houses of the estate workers could be seen along it. His parent's main house was back farther in the oaks and not yet in sight. He could hardly wait to see them, so he spurred his horse forward.

Up ahead at the first of the houses, he noticed Juana, the wife of one of the longtime workers, hanging out clothes. When she looked up, as she always did when she heard someone approaching, she saw him and burst into a happy smile, putting her hands together in happiness. She excitedly said something to her young son Pedrito, who jumped up with a startled look and raced off barefooted down the road.

As Mateo neared, Juana hurried out to him and excitedly said, "Don Mateo! Oh, thank God! You are back! How wonderful! Your parents will be so happy!"

"Good day, Juana. How nice to see you again."

"Oh, the Don and Doña, how happy they will be. I have sent Pedrito to run ahead to tell them."

"There is no need for it. I will be there soon enough."

Up the road meanwhile, he could hear Pedrito crying out as he ran past other houses, "Don Mateo is back! Don Mateo is back!"

"Our prayers for your safe return have been answered," she said with emotion.

"Thank you, Juana. I hope everything is well here?"

"Yes, Don Mateo. Your parents are well, and I am so happy for them that God has returned you safely. Yes, I am so happy that I think I am going to cry."

She began to sob, wiping her eyes with her apron.

"I am glad to be back and hope all is well with your family," he said, reaching down and patting her on the shoulder.

"Yes, yes, we are well," she replied, still sobbing.

"Well, I must not keep my parents waiting and should keep moving."

"Yes, Don Mateo. Oh, it is so good to see you back."

"Thank you, Juana. It is indeed good to be back."

As he gave his horse a nudge to start it forward again, he could see women and children running toward him to welcome him home. As he continued along, he happily exchanged greetings with them. A group of well-wishers were soon gathered around his horse, and he got off to shake hands and thank them for their kind welcome home.

Minutes later, his mother and father rode up at a gallop. Pulling to an abrupt stop, they jumped off their horses and raced to hug him. He embraced them both happily as the crowd around them cheered and cried.

That night, Mateo's parents held a celebration banquet to which all on the estate were invited. The parents and son were very popular with its workers. The celebration lasted late into the night, and the work on the estate the next day suffered from a slow start.

Late the next morning, Mateo sat with his parents at their breakfast table as they snacked on cakes and sipped wine.

(Note: In those times in the late 1500s, decades before the Pilgrims landed at Plymouth Rock, coffee from Africa was known in only a few cities in Europe and still unknown in Spain. Portuguese traders had told of a drink called Chai (tea) in China, but it was also as yet unknown in Spain. Any get-togethers or meals with friends or family usually included some form of wine, which was the preferred drink of upper classes. When in season, they might also enjoy locally grown fruit drinks like orange juice. The lower classes also drank wines, although the lesser-quality affordable ones. Spaniards did not care for beer. Well water or collected rainwater were sources of drinkable water, but wine was considered safer to drink if the quality of the water was unknown. Being hard to keep unspoiled, milk was a special purpose drink for the sick and young. As a result, you may notice wine mentioned herein numerous times.)

"And now it is time to see what gifts I have brought back for you." Mateo announced, putting down his wine glass.

"Father, this one is for you," he said, pulling something wrapped in a cloth from a satchel.

"Mateo, your safe return is gift enough. I have no need for further gifts."

"I know, Father, but here, it is for you."

After a moment of hesitation, Don Lorenzo took it, smiled, and unwrapped the cloth to find an ornately decorated pair of silver spurs. He beamed with delight at the sight of them and proudly showed them to his wife and the nearby servants.

"Look at these magnificent spurs, made of silver from the mines of the Indies!"

He moved his chair back from the table with great enthusiasm and put them on his boots. Then getting up, he strode around the room, looking at them proudly.

"I plan to wear these on all special occasions," he declared as he paraded about, "not to dazzle people with their shine or value, but because I want people to notice them and ask me how I got them. I will tell them my son Mateo, of whom I am enormously proud, was an officer on a treasure fleet galleon. They were his gift to me from the Indies!"

"Lorenzo, I know you are excited, but do not clomp around so much inside with them," chided his wife, Antonia.

"Ah, yes, my dear, yes, the floors," he said, sitting back down highly contented and taking them off.

"Mother, you are next," said Mateo as he reached in his satchel for a small gift box and handed it to her. She opened it and gasped when she saw an ornate necklace with matching earrings, made of silver and amethyst.

"Mateo, they are magnificent!" she said with astonishment as everyone gathered around to see.

"Here, I will put them on you," said Mateo.

After doing so, his mother hugged and thanked him. She hurried to a nearby mirror to inspect them. Everyone crowded around her examining, touching, and admiring their beauty.

It took several minutes before the hubbub over the necklace subsided enough for Mateo to next say, "I also have a piece of jewelry for you too, Father."

"What? More? But I have no need for jewelry, Mateo."

Mateo with a smile took his father's hand and plopped the cloth-covered gift onto it. Sighing, Don Lorenzo took the cloth and carefully unfolded it. Inside, he found a small golden snake with a head and outstretched tongue on one end, curved body, and a bulb on its tail.

Examining it closely and then passing it to his wife, he said, "It is very nice, Mateo, but what is it?"

"I was told it is jewelry once worn by the high-ranking men of the native civilization there in the Indies. It is solid gold."

"And how is it worn?"

"I understand that men of their civilization first cut a slit in their upper lip. They push it through from the inside, and the bulb keeps it in place there on their lip."

Both his father and mother gasped, which drew a laugh from Mateo. After a moment of examining it, his father said, "Well, it is an interesting piece of native artwork, which I greatly admire, even if I shall not wear it properly."

"I thought you would think so, and I am sorry, Mother, for my startling you so with its history."

"You forget, Mateo, you are no longer with your soldiers."

"Yes, Mother, I am sorry. To make amends, I have this added gift for you," he said, bringing out a small, long ornate box from his satchel.

"Do I dare open it?"

"Yes, Mother, it is not crude. I think you will like it."

Opening it hesitantly, she looked inside.

"A hand fan from the Indies," she said with delight.

"Not quite, open it out," said Mateo.

When she opened the fan out, she examined with awe the elaborately painted designs and scene of people in a garden on its black silk background.

"My goodness. How beautiful the artwork is. Look at the people. So this is how the natives of the Indies appear?" she asked, admiring it.

"No, Mother. Those are the people of Cathay. It is a silk fan from Cathay," Mateo told her with a laugh as the servants came close to admire it too.

"Cathay? You went all the way to Cathay, Mateo?" his father asked in astonishment as he craned to see it.

"No, Father, traders bring such things from Cathay across the great Pacific Ocean to the west coast of the mainland there in the Indies, and then they carry the goods cross-country by mule trains to Veracruz on the east coast where our fleet stops. I visited one of these traders, and he showed me this. I thought you might like it, Mother."

"I have never seen such a beautifully decorated fan before. We will have to be careful with it. It is very delicate. What a wonderful surprise. Thank you, my son."

For some time, they continued to admire the presents, talk about them, ask about how he found each one, and so on. Wine and cheese were brought in for snacking. After much talk, his mother gave him a serious look and, grasping his hand, began a topic that had come up many times before.

"These presents are wonderful, Mateo, but you know I would rather have grandchildren than gifts from the Indies. What would we have done if you had been killed by a storm or pirates and had left us with no grandchildren? You must stay home for a time and start a family for our sake."

"Do not worry, Mother, I have no immediate plans for soldiering again. Before leaving, I told my senior lieutenant I do not plan to take part in the voyages next year."

"Thanks be to God, Mateo."

"But I feel I should warn you, Mother. If you pester me too much about meeting the daughter of this neighbor or the niece of that official, I may return to sea," Mateo said with a smile.

"But, Mateo, you do not give them a chance. Take the friends of our neighbors, the Andujars, for example. We met them a few months ago, and they have a lovely daughter Angela, who is like an angel as her name implies."

At this, Mateo's father broke in, "Please, Antonia, you are already doing just what the boy says will drive him away to sea again. You should give him a chance as you say. And besides, I have heard this Angela is perhaps not so angel-like."

"All right, my husband. All right, my son. I will try to restrain my womanly desire to have grandchildren, but it will be difficult for me. I am surprised that you, Lorenzo, are not on my side. Perhaps you do not want grandchildren for the continuation of the family line?"

After a thoughtful pause, Mateo's father said, "You make a good point, Antonia, my dear." And then turning to Mateo, he said with a serious expression, "Yes, Mateo, on second thought, perhaps you should marry this girl, Angela."

After a moment though, he smiled, and they burst into laughter. In between laughs, Mateo's mother, with a cross look, threw her napkin across the table at her husband as they and the watching servants enjoyed a moment of levity.

Ch.2 Battle at Sea

HIS MOTHER'S CONCERNS for her son were well founded. Only a month earlier, Mateo's galleon, the lead ship of a returning treasure fleet, had been under attack.

"Fire as she bears, men!" called Mateo, repeating the captain's orders.

"Fire as she bears!" acknowledged the gunners under his charge on the main deck.

Boom, boom, boom, boom, boom, boom went the six cannons as they belched smoke and their gun carriages jumped backward. More booms could be heard from the cannons on the deck below and from the cannons of the enemy English ship.

Mateo ducked suddenly, in a purely reflex reaction, as a cannon ball flew past his head and crashed into the gear behind him. After a moment recovering his wits, he faced around and shouted to his gun crews to keep their heads down, get the cannons reloaded, run them back out, and keep firing.

Don Mateo de Cordoba was outfitted for battle in his steel helmet, leather armor, pistol, and saber. He was a young lieutenant in charge of one company of soldiers onboard the lead galleon of the "New Spain" treasure fleet. Each year this fleet sailed from Spain to the northern reaches of the Indies and back. His heavily armed galleon and a second one in the rear of the fleet were responsible for protecting the tight, slow-moving formation of seventy ships and their valuable cargos.

Soon their cannons were firing a second round as he paced back and forth along the deck encouraging the gunners.

Crack! Crack! Two enemy cannon balls struck the high wooden gunwales near one of the gun crews and sent large wood splinters flying that severely wounded two men. One man had a foot-long sharp splinter through the side of his neck. The wounded men were quickly carried below for treatment and other men took their places. Musket balls and crossbow bolts were also pinging nearby in the wooden structures. One of the musketeers on their forward castle was hit and fell over the railing to the main deck. Shouted orders, the booming of cannons, musket fire, and the sounds of the sea filled the air.

Mateo could hear the captain shouting sailing orders and the ship began to turn. The sails and rigging had already suffered damage in this battle with English privateers, but the ship could still maneuver.

The captain shouted down from the after castle, "Lieutenant, man and ready the guns on the right side!"

Mateo acknowledged the order and directed the gunners to shift to the cannons on the other side. Soon they were firing on a second English privateer ship. The third one was also working to get within range.

As they fired on the right side, one of the enemy cannon balls came through a gun port and struck the cannon as the crew was reloading it. One man was nearly torn in half by the ball and a second one lost an arm. The dead and wounded were taken below, and with heroic effort, the cannon was made ready again for use.

The ship again began changing course, and the captain shouted down, "The ship on the left is attempting to close us to board. Man and ready the guns on the left side. Load them with shot!"

The crews were shifted, and within minutes, the cannons were ready. Mateo watched as the ship neared. On the English ship, the fighting blood of the men on deck was high. Their grappling hooks were ready for throwing over to snag on the Spanish galleon and bring it alongside for boarding. As they shouted wildly and waved cutlasses in a fury, Mateo's captain gave the order to fire. The grape-sized shot pellets from the guns swept across their decks, decimating the exposed men on the deck of the enemy ship. The English ship seemed to shudder in response.

And yet, as the captain gave orders to change course, the English ship returned cannon fire, damaging sails and rigging. One shattered wooden spar and its sail came crashing down onto Mateo who was struck a glancing blow and buried under the wreckage.

Under the heavy weight of the canvas and wood debris, he could not move or breathe. He felt no obvious pain but could not tell if he was seriously injured. He thought of his father and mother back on the family's estate in Andalusia and wondered if he would see them again.

The nearby gunners scrambled to clear the debris from him and were relieved to find he was alert although shaken.

"Lieutenant, are you injured?"

"Help me up, please."

After they helped him to his feet, Mateo rubbed his neck, moved his limbs, and shook off dirt.

Taking a breath, Mateo said, "I am fine." Looking about, he added, "All right men, I am fine. Get this gear cleared away and get back to your cannons. Get them reloaded. Both sides."

As they returned to their cannons, he gathered himself and looked out across the water at the nearby enemy ships, which ordinarily would never dare to attack and board a galleon with its many cannons and soldiers. How did his ship get into this predicament?

It was an ill-timed sickness, possibly from bad meat, which suddenly incapacitated nearly half of the men onboard. Until the day before, their return voyage to Spain had gone quite smoothly. Since sailing from Havana, favorable weather, winds, and currents had pushed the fleet on relentlessly. They had not encountered any of the dreaded, terrible storms that sometimes broke unexpectedly on ships in the Indies. A second yearly treasure fleet, called the "Tierra Firma" fleet, had left Havana right after their own departure. This second treasure fleet, heavily laden with silver from Peru, was somewhere behind them.

The timing of the illness was most unfortunate. They had just reached the vicinity of the Azores Islands, a favorite spot for privateers to lay in wait for the returning Spanish treasure fleets.

These English, French, or Dutch privateers were, in effect, pirates sanctioned by their governments to attack and bring back Spanish treasure, for which they received prize money.

When the five English privateer ships had appeared on the horizon, only half of the galleon's crew was well enough to fight it. He and his soldiers were assigned onboard for use in boarding and capturing other ships. But with half of the crew sick, his soldiers were being used on the ship's cannons. Gun crews had been hastily reformed and trained on them. He himself had been put in charge of the cannons on the main deck.

As Mateo encouraged the gunners at their work, he wondered, "Where was the fleet's second galleon, the María Erizelda? God grant that it is at full strength and making short work of the other pirate ships."

Looking over the gunwale, he spotted it several miles astern of them, pursuing the fifth privateer ship after having already damaged and driven off the fourth one.

His sergeant, now on one of the gun crews, saw him looking and said, "She looks busy, sir, and will be no help to us anytime soon."

"No, perhaps not," replied Mateo.

"These heathen English seem intent on boarding us. We will have to show them of what mettle we Spaniards are made."

"Yes, Sergeant, I suppose they noted our weakened state and thought it worth the risk to try for the king's fifth below. It would be a pretty penny in prize money for them." (A fifth of the silver returning on the treasure fleet belonged to the king and was carried on the escorting galleons.)

"Well, let them try, Lieutenant. We have plenty of fight left," said his sergeant.

"Ship closing on the right! Man and ready the guns on the right side! Fire as she bears!" called down the captain.

In a burst of activity, the men hurried to finish readying the guns and soon they were firing and taking fire. More men were wounded by flying splinters, more damaged rigging fell, and more men on deck were felled by musket balls. But their cannon fire had damaged the other ship and it now posed less of a threat.

"Only two more ships to deal with," thought Mateo to himself. "God, give us the strength to prevail."

During their next engagement, one of their cannons exploded when fired, killing three of its gun crew. After clearing the damage and getting the dead and wounded below, they again exchanged fire with a closing privateer. The captain was able to turn away in time to avoid being boarded, but with the damage to their rigging and sails, they were losing maneuverability.

Mateo looked again for the María Erizelda, which was still busy and far away. Looking out at their attackers, he saw that the two remaining English ships were maneuvering to close his ship and board it. At seeing this and steeling himself for the upcoming fighting, he noticed two more ships upwind on the horizon with full sails and approaching fast.

"Two new enemy ships," he thought to himself, "They have sealed our fate."

Their ship had already narrowly escaped being boarded. But now, with their galleon's maneuvering capability impaired and more enemy coming, their situation was looking desperate. Being boarded was now only a matter of time. Mateo and the others would soon be fighting hand-to-hand to repel the boarders.

At some point, they might be overwhelmed, and the captain forced to surrender. Should that come to pass, Mateo, if still alive, would become a prisoner and probably be taken to England where he would be imprisoned until his family could pay a ransom for his release and return.

With determination, Mateo called out, "Soldiers in the gun crews! Stay at the guns and keep firing. But if they board us, be ready with your cutlasses and bucklers to repel them. God willing, we will succeed."

With saber raised, Mateo added with spirit, "We must teach them some respect for Spanish steel!" And the men cheered.

Ch.3 Guillermo

AFTER THEIR DELIGHTFUL time at the breakfast table, Mateo's father put on his new spurs and wanted to take Mateo out for a ride around the family estate from which he had been away for so long. They got their horses at the stable but decided to walk the horses for a time so they could talk more intimately. It would be a good opportunity for Mateo to tell his father about the battle in which he had fought and almost been killed. His mother, he thought, had best not hear or she would worry too much about him in the future.

As they walked, Mateo told him about his close brush with death during the attack by the English ships, how they had fought hard despite the shortage of available men. The two English privateers they had been fighting were on the verge of capturing them, but the two rapidly approaching ships turned out to be two Spanish galleons, arriving just in time and forcing the English ships to flee.

The English privateers had been previously raiding shipping along the Spanish coast. With such a threat to the returning treasure fleets in the area, a squadron of Spanish galleons had been sent to the Azores to meet and help protect the returning fleets. After splitting up to find the approaching fleets, two galleons of that squadron were by chance heading toward their location when they heard the sounds of battle over the horizon. Knowing the fleet must be under attack, they rushed ahead to help. Fortunately for Mateo's ship, favorable winds enabled these rescuers to make good time and speed toward them. Meanwhile, their rear escort galleon had succeeded in chasing off the other two English ships and was also working its way to help Mateo's ship.

One of the English ships attacking them had managed to close, get grappling lines over, and board them. There had been hand-to-hand fighting briefly before the Spanish were able to cut their lines and get free of them. Mateo had suffered a cutlass slash on one arm, and a bullet had grazed his shoulder. After this failed boarding attempt, the English ships looked at the approaching Spanish galleons and had no choice but to break off their attack and flee. It had been a narrow escape.

The fleet's Captain-General aboard had regained his health enough to transfer from their ship to another galleon, which took over as lead ship of the treasure fleet. The fleet was slowed, and a galleon stayed close by to assist them and protect their valuable silver cargo. In a day, their ship was sufficiently repaired and their crew supplemented to enable them to continue with the fleet.

Meanwhile, the second returning treasure fleet behind them had caught up to and joined their fleet. The two fleets then continued their voyage together with the enlarged escort.

With its temporary repairs, their ship was fortunate not to have encountered any violent storms or heavy seas during the remaining voyage. Without further incident, they anchored in the Guadalquivir River at Seville two weeks after passing the Azores.

Mateo's father listened with great admiration to his description of the fighting at sea. He was proud of his son Mateo, as he had been of his other two sons. They had sought adventure several years earlier as soldiers fighting rebels in the Spanish Netherlands. It had been God's will and their lot to die there, one in the fighting and one from disease. Don Lorenzo and his wife had been devastated at the time. And now, after hearing of his only remaining son's near brush with death, the words of his wife echoed in his ears. He feared now more than ever the possible loss of his one remaining heir.

"I must confess, Father," said Mateo earnestly, "that I do appreciate now that I have neglected my responsibility to continue the family line. In the midst of the fighting when things looked darkest, I felt a deep regret about it."

He paused and looked at his father, who looked back with emotion.

"You warm my heart, my son. Your mother and I are immensely proud of you and know you will soon, we pray, find a wife who will bless us with grandchildren," said his father, embracing him.

They began to walk again, and looking up, his father said, "Ah, here comes Miguel."

Approaching on horseback was Miguel, the overseer of the family estate. For many years, he has been the Don's loyal and dependable right-hand man, an important part of the extended family on the estate. Miguel had watched Mateo and his brothers grow up, and his own son Guillermo was Mateo's best friend.

"Good day, Don Lorenzo, Don Mateo."

"Good day, Miguel. And how are things today?"

"Fine, Señor. I was coming to see you about the pepper seeds that Don Mateo brought back from the Indies."

"Ah, yes, the pepper seeds," said Don Lorenzo. "How very smart of you to think of it before Mateo departed. Just imagine! Soon we shall grow our own pepper seasoning and no longer rely on expensive black peppercorns from the Orient."

"I hope so, Don Lorenzo. It was a friend of mine who had tasted and told me about them. He said they were quite spicy and flavorful. The peppers from the Indies are still quite uncommon here. If we can grow them, much money can be made selling the seed as well," said Miguel with enthusiasm as he got down from his horse to join them.

"Miguel," said Mateo, "I did not wish to bore you with talk of gardening last night, but I brought other seeds as well."

With raised eyebrows, Miguel said, "Really? I cannot imagine any other plants there could be as valuable as peppers, but I am interested in hearing what else you have brought."

"I brought the seeds of a plant called maize (corn), which has large yellow seeds growing in clusters on tall stalks. When I was in Veracruz in the Indies, I visited a maize plantation where I saw how it was grown. From the maize seeds, the natives make a flat cake, which is a staple food for them."

"Cakes from vegetable seeds? That will be most interesting to see," remarked Miguel.

"I also brought things called beans, which are edible seeds that grow in pods like peas. Lastly, I brought the seeds of two other plants, which grow large edible bulbs. One plant grows the bulbs on its branches and the other grows the bulbs on its roots. They are called tomato and potato."

"Possibly, I have heard of these foods in my travels. Do such things taste good to eat?" asked Don Lorenzo.

"Yes, I thought so. The natives in the Indies have cultivated and eaten these foods for centuries. It is quite funny that some Spaniards there refuse to eat them for fear they will turn into Indians."

"And does this happen?" asked Miguel.

With a laugh, he replied, "No, I have no worry on that count. My only worry is about our soil. They grow these plants in fertile soils. I hope ours is rich enough to grow such plants."

"We will prepare a large plot of our best soil with manure for fertilizer. I do not know if these other plants will be of value, but we shall make our best effort with the peppers. Pedro, our best man with garden crops, will be in charge," Miguel said with resolve.

"Already Miguel has a plan!" Don Lorenzo said happily to Mateo.

"Good, I made notes from my trips to their plantations. I will pass them and all I saw on to you. Come to the house later, and I will give you the seeds and the notes."

"Many thanks, Don Mateo."

"I only hope, Miguel," said Mateo grinning, "that your beloved children with limbs will not become jealous of your interest in these new plants."

"Ah, you mean my almond trees," Miguel said, laughing. "No, I cannot forget them. As you know, I have great affection for each and every tree. While I do not have names for each one, they are like my children as you say."

"We enjoyed a fine almond crop last year while you were gone," Don Lorenzo said with satisfaction. "The shipments of almonds to the merchant in Cordoba went very well and the prices paid were most satisfactory. Guillermo handled it."

"He is away just now taking his mother to visit her sister. I am sure Guillermo will be disappointed that he was absent when you returned, but he will be back soon," said Miguel.

"So you have put Guillermo in charge of shipments to the almond merchant," Mateo said, amused.

"Yes, we have dealt with Señor Cruz for years, but Guillermo seems to have a way with him."

At this, Mateo had to choke back a laugh. Both his father and Miguel looked at him curiously.

"Why do you laugh, Mateo? You must share the joke with us," said his father.

"Father, we have actually had few difficulties with the old merchant since Guillermo went along on the first shipment the year before."

"I had not noticed, although it seems true enough."

"An incident that took place on the trip may deserve the credit. I have previously not burdened you with the knowledge of it."

Looking puzzled and seeing a similar look on Miguel's face, Don Lorenzo said, "We are curious to hear, Mateo. Please tell us more."

Smiling, Mateo began, "Well, Guillermo accompanied me on that trip. When we arrived at the market in Cordoba, we nosed around, looked at the prices for nuts, talked to people, and determined a fair price for our almonds was twenty reales per hundredweight. Before going to see the merchant, I told Guillermo to let me do the talking, for he was a tricky sort, and experience in dealing with him was essential to success.

"When he saw our wagons arriving, the merchant sighed and slumped, saying, 'Oh, Mateo, bad timing. I do not know if I need more almonds. But, alas, since you have come, show me what you have.'

"Once inside, the merchant sampled from a sack, made his normal disparaging remarks about the nuts, trying not to show he was actually impressed with the quality. He went into a long tale about the inferior quality of the shipment, the glut of almonds in the market, and of his financial woes. He told us that he, regrettably, could only offer eleven reales per hundredweight.

"He was up to his usual tricks. We knew the quality was good, and his talk of a glut was a fabrication. I told him the almonds were worth twenty, and we would take no less. After another extended denial and further description of his sad state of affairs, he said the best he could offer was twelve. We told him we would take the almonds to someone else.

"As we turned and started to leave, he stopped us and said 'thirteen.' That, he said emphatically, was the absolute best he could possibly do. He started again to tell us how he had so many almonds already and of all his financial difficulties.

"Before I knew it, Guillermo was throttling him and had the point of a knife close up under the merchant's whiskers.

"With a firmness and voice beyond his young years, he told the merchant, 'Enough of your games, Señor. The almonds are worth twenty. Do you want them for twenty or not?'

"With a look of terror, the merchant glanced over at me, but my surprised look and silence gave him no comfort.

"He sputtered, 'There is no need for such mischief and haste! Ouch! You are cutting me!'

"Guillermo asked him firmly, 'Yes or No!'

"Well, in short, he wanted our entire load and agreed to our price. Only then, did Guillermo release him and say, 'Good. Then fetch your cashbox and a receipt! And in the future, Señor, there is no need for such games. They only waste time.'

"The merchant rushed off clutching his throat with a fearful look. At first, I was going to interfere, but his approach was working marvelously, so I did not.

"After that trip, the merchant welcomes us when we arrive. We tell him our price and the weight. Instead of his old antics, he thinks for several moments, looking up in the air and stroking his beard. Then he says 'done' and gets his cashbox."

Mateo paused here at the end of his story and was amused by the faces of his two listeners.

"You look bewildered, Father."

"The merchant has never complained to me of the incident," Don Lorenzo said bemused. "I wonder he still wants to deal with us."

"Our almonds are a unique and valuable commodity for him. They are already shelled with broken and shriveled nuts removed, lightly roasted so they do not become worm infested later. His other almonds, still in shells, come mostly from the southern coast. Inside the shells, the almonds themselves may be wormy or shriveled. Ours are much more valuable to him."

Chuckling, Mateo continued, "The last time there, we gave him our price. After considering it and saying 'done,' he looked at us curiously and said, 'You two are quite right again about the value of the almonds. How did you know? If you ever tire of your life there on your family's estate, you shall come work for me.' He even had his pretty daughter bring out small glasses of a sweet liquor, and we toasted.

"He seems to trust and esteem Guillermo like no other. I am not sure what he might have in mind, Guillermo marrying his daughter and taking over for him? I do not know. It is quite astounding. The old Jew is not a bad sort, even though he is a ruthless and tricky businessman."

As an afterthought, he added, "I should correct myself and say, the old 'converso.' I do not mean to imply he is not a true convert and get him into trouble with inquisition officials."

(Note: The Spanish kingdom was dominated by the Catholic Church which was intolerant of all other religions. Many years before, royal edicts had expelled from Spain all Jews and Moors who refused to convert to Christianity. The converted Jews (conversos) and converted Moors (moriscos) who remained in Spain were of particular interest to the Spanish Inquisition, which sought to rid Spain of all heretics such as Jews and Moors only posing to be converted to Christianity. Any accused of not being true converts faced arrest, torture, and burning at the stake.)

With a look of amazement, Don Lorenzo said to Miguel, "These sons of ours, Miguel, they never cease to amaze. Your Guillermo is quite the young man. When will he return from your wife's sister?"

"My María only planned to spend a few days there, and they are due back today in the late afternoon."

"I greatly look forward to seeing him again," said Mateo happily.

"When he hears of your return, he will be overjoyed and come straight to see you, I am sure. He talked of you often when you were gone and wanted badly to go with you when you left for sea. But he was then only sixteen years old, still too young. Since you have been late returning, he has not been himself. Taking his mother to visit her sister was our attempt at a diversion for him."

"I understand completely for I, too, became worried for my son's safety as the days passed."

"As you saw last night, Don Mateo, everyone on the estate is delighted at your safe return," said Miguel.

"And I am equally delighted to be here and see them," replied Mateo. "I thanked God for our safe return to Spain by visiting the Cathedral de Santa María in Seville after our arrival. When fearing for their lives in storms at sea, the frightened mariners promise God to give Him thanks at that church if He spares them. I still gave my thanks there, even though I saw no terrible storms and made no such promise."

"It is right for you to have done so, my son."

That afternoon, when Guillermo and his mother came up the drive of the estate in their carriage, young Pedrito saw them and called to them that Mateo was back. Guillermo handed the reins to his mother at once and jumped on his horse tied to the back. Moments later, he leaped from his horse at the main house, where he rushed inside and enthusiastically welcomed Mateo back. They were most excited to see each other again and talked for hours until it was time for dinner, for which the Don and Doña asked him to stay.

The sun had already set when Guillermo came home from his visit with Mateo. He found his father, Miguel, out back on the patio enjoying the cool night air after one of their normal hot sunny days in late June.

"Come sit down, my son, and enjoy this fine night with me," he said, beckoning him to the chair next to him. "It is clear out, and the stars are bright. The moon should be rising soon."

"Yes, it is pleasant out. I saw two or three shooting stars on the way," he said as he sat down beside his father.

"Did you have an enjoyable time seeing Don Mateo again? He is quite a fine young man and to think of him returning safe and unharmed from such a voyage. Thanks be to God."

"Father, it is so good to see Mateo again. I feel as if a brother has returned, and he seemed as happy to see me. He told me such things about his voyage."

"Guillermo, I know you and Don Mateo are close friends, but you must remember to be respectful of him and his parents."

"When I am with them, they treat me as one of their own. How can I act otherwise? I am respectful of them just as I am respectful of you, Father."

"Yes, Guillermo, they are uncommonly good people and have always shown a special interest in you. I still marvel that they included you in Mateo's tutoring. Thanks to them, you have learned to read and write our Castilian tongue and Italian, plus mathematics and other arts. An unusual gift and quite to your advantage."

"Mateo trains me with the saber, and I go with them on their hunts. Yes, they treat me much like a son and a brother. Their goodness to me is most uncommon and sometimes puzzling for me. As if preparing me for something, but I do not know what it might be. To be the estate's overseer when you retire? Others here are better suited than me, and learning the arts is not needed for an overseer. It would seem to be something bigger."

"Guillermo, they have lost two sons. There is perhaps a void in their hearts you are helping to fill. I would not be surprised for…," here Miguel hesitated, "I do not know if I should tell you this, but you much resemble those sons when they were your age."

Guillermo gazed at his father thoughtfully for a moment as he considered this.

"But never mind that," his father continued. "You are nearly grown now. By and by, these things will work themselves out, and you will find your way in the world. It does not grieve me that you should feel like their son. Just do not take advantage of their good hearts and remember you are still my son too."

"I will remember, Father. You and mother have always been good to me. As for the future, I plan to go with Mateo whenever he leaves again for sea. I want to be at his side in any fighting and give my life if I must, to save his. His survival is important to this family and to the continuation of their line. I have no such concerns. Perhaps, that is my purpose in life."

"No! No! I am sure such is the intention of no one! Least of all Don Mateo! I think he will be pleased for you to join him, but not so you can sacrifice yourself for him. As for the Don and Doña, I believe they would greatly mourn your loss just as they would the loss of Don Mateo."

After reflecting a moment and sighing, Miguel continued, "Yes, I admit Don Mateo needs to find a wife and have children. If only so you will not feel the need to sacrifice yourself for him! Perhaps I made a mistake in warning him about several local young ladies who his mother had put forward for him. He might have a wife and offspring by now."

"On the other hand," Miguel added with a laugh, "he might also be miserable and unhappy, but at least the Don and Doña would have heirs!"

"No, you did him a great service, Father."

Thinking and smiling, Miguel asked, "And what about you, Guillermo? Perhaps it is time you should consider such a pleasant thing as a wife?"

Stirring uncomfortably, Guillermo answered, "No, I have no need for a wife yet, Father. I suppose you and Mother desire grandchildren too, but you will have to wait. I can admire a pretty face, a graceful figure, and a soft hand as much as any other young man, but it is what lies beneath their ornate hair combs of which I am wary, namely the minds of these calculating creatures. When I observe their poses, looks, and movements, I get an uneasy feeling of being hunted. Without provocation, I am the object of their guile and schemes for my entrapment. When I turn and see them looking at me, I wonder what plots they are hatching."

"Guillermo, you are a handsome lad. Why should they not look at you?"

"Still, Father, I would prefer to see innocence or kindness in their eyes rather than wheels turning. For now, I am content to admire their charms and beauty from a distance and not to get entangled with any."

"Alas," said Miguel with a sigh, "it seems your poor mother must do without grandchildren running about for quite some time."

Peering about, he continued in a hushed tone, "Speaking of Mother, Guillermo. She and I both think you have grown to be an honorable and good young man. We are very proud of you, but if you could only be a little more pious! For your mother's sake? She worries about your soul. You must at least maintain appearances, for her sake!"

At hearing this, Guillermo replied with a laugh, "Yes, Father, I will try for her sake as well as yours."

"You are a good son," he said, patting Guillermo on the arm.

Ch.4 Neighbor

SEVERAL DAYS after Mateo's return, a curious incident happened on the family's estate. A sad and dignified gentleman rode up in the afternoon on his horse to the front of the main house. An astonished household servant recognized him and rushed to tell Don Lorenzo, who was in his study.

Opening his door, she told him excitedly, "Don Lorenzo! It is Don Felipe! Don Felipe just rode up!"

"What! Are you sure?"

"Yes, come see!"

With a look of disbelief, Don Lorenzo rose quickly from his chair and hurried from the room. When emerging from the front door, he looked with surprise at the stately gentleman standing by his horse, his face lined deeply with sadness.

Don Lorenzo was touched at the sight and said with emotion, "Felipe, it has been such a long time. I have greatly missed my dearest friend."

"Lorenzo, my dear friend, I have come to say I am sorry and hope you can forgive me."

And with that, the two men came together, embraced, and began to weep. The servants stood back watching in silence.

After a minute, Don Lorenzo drew back and said, "My friend, you have no need to ask for my forgiveness. Come, let us go inside to my study. We will have some wine and talk, like in the old days."

Don Felipe smiled weakly and nodded. The two men then slowly walked inside together with their arms around each other's shoulders. To his housekeeper, Don Lorenzo said, "Rosa, please bring us wine in the study and set another place for dinner."

"Yes, Don Lorenzo." Then she added, "Don Felipe, it is so good to see you again."

Looking up, Don Felipe gave her a weak smile. The two men went into the study and closed the door. They sat down in comfortable chairs, and the wine was brought in.

"I cannot tell you how much it gladdens my heart to see you again, Felipe. Your absence has weighed heavily upon it."

"I am terribly sorry to have caused you such grief, my friend Lorenzo. Let me explain what has happened."

They both took a sip of wine, and Don Felipe began.

"When I heard your son, Mateo, has recently returned safely from the Indies, it caused me to think again about us and what happened. It stirred up such emotions in me that I went to church to pray for guidance. While there on my knees before the railing of the altar, praying and lighting candles for my son as I have done many, many times before, I looked up. The sunlight coming through the large stained-glass window behind the altar was producing streams of colored light in the dusty air inside the church. I have often seen such rays of light in our church, but today, they seemed to be telling me something. I stared at them for some time. When I looked back down at the candles in front of me, I realized somehow that I had been wrong in blaming you for the death of my son."

Don Lorenzo had been listening with great emotion and now pressed his hand on his friend's arm.

"I have been wrong in blaming you and not speaking to you for all these years, Lorenzo. What happened was not your fault. I ask for your forgiveness in having wrongfully blamed you and caused you pain."

"Felipe, I have forgiven you long ago and knew someday we would be friends once again."

Years of pain and sorrow were thus ended, and the two neighbors were fast friends again. Before going to dinner, they talked for hours without mentioning the cause of their years of distance and silence. It had happened six years before.

But the start of it was even earlier when one of Don Lorenzo's cousins, one whose family estate was north of Andújar, required more room for raising bulls for the bullring. Don Lorenzo agreed to put several of his cousin's bulls on the back hills of the estate. These hills were ideal to keeping them away from people to maintain their wildness. He was surprised to find bull raising such a lucrative yet easy enterprise. So he purchased one of his cousin's bulls and got into the business of raising bulls himself, even though he had little interest in the sport and rarely went to see a bullfight. In his years of raising bulls, he went only once to see how his bulls fought in the ring. He was surprised to discover they fought well and were highly regarded, despite the fact he did nothing to encourage it. His cousin's bull apparently had been excellent breeding stock.

Don Felipe, his best friend and neighbor, had a son Lucas who was fascinated by Don Lorenzo's bulls and developed a keen interest in the sport of bullfighting. When old enough, he went to train in the sport and, after a time, became known in their region of Spain. It was only a matter of time before one day his son would be in the ring with one of Don Lorenzo's bulls.

That day came in the bullring in Cordoba six years before. On that day, Don Lorenzo and Don Felipe sat together happily in the stands in great anticipation of the event, witnessing his son Lucas dispatching one of Don Lorenzo's bulls. The rest of the crowd was very excited too. Their fight was to be the highlight and culmination of the day's pageantry and fighting.

When the time finally arrived, Don Felipe's son was mounted on his horse, armed with a lance for killing the bull, which was the bullfighting style of the day. The horse had a covering over its eyes, so it could not see how dangerously close it was to the bull, thereby enabling the rider to get closer to demonstrate his bravery. Because of this, the horses were frequently gored and nearly as many horses were killed as bulls, which was another reason Don Lorenzo had no taste for the sport.

On this day, his son showed great bravery and skill as he attacked the bull, lancing its bloody back repeatedly. After one particularly successful pass and a deep painful looking wound, the bull stood enraged. Snorting and flinging up dirt with its hooves, the bull glared at its attacker.

The son spurred his horse to get into position to make another attack on the bull's side. But the bull charged in a rage, and the horse, hearing its pounding hoofs, hesitated in fear. The son whipped the reins and spurred the horse furiously to make it move, but without success.

The bull plowed into them, burying its horns deep into the belly of the horse and knocking it over on its side. As the bull continued to charge over the top of the downed horse and rider, it flailed its horns wildly as it attacked the rider shoving him along head over heels through the dirt, leaving him lying in a bloody heap.

As quickly as they could, the picadors distracted the bull and got him away as people rushed to the aid of the injured bullfighter in the dirt. Don Felipe ran to his son, fought his way through the crowd, and found him dead.

He was staring down at his son when Don Lorenzo came up beside him. Seeing the boy dead, he put his hand on his friend's shoulder and said, "I am so terribly sorry, Felipe."

His friend flung his hand from his shoulder, gave him a look of hatred, and said nothing. Don Lorenzo could only walk away sadly and leave his friend to his grief. His neighbor had never spoken to him since that day. It also was the end of Don Lorenzo's pastime of raising bulls for the bullring. He sold them all the next day.

Ch.5 Señorita

ONE MORNING during his first week back, Mateo brought out another surprise for his parents.

"Mother, Father, I have been saving something special for you, my esteemed parents. This morning, you are to be treated as royalty," he told them.

"Such foolishness, Mateo. What are you up to?" said his mother, waving him away.

"No, really, Mother. Today you will have for breakfast a drink that I understand is a favorite of our royals. It is called cocoa or chocolate."

"Another new plant from the Indies, my son, do tell," said his father enthusiastically.

"It comes from the seeds of a tropical plant there in the Indies. The native civilization cultivates the plant and drinks a frothy concoction of the seed's powder mixed with water. It is very tart if you do not add sugar or honey. I tried the drink there, and it has a most remarkable flavor. I brought back a small bag of the seeds and made powder from some of them this morning. I also borrowed sugar from the kitchen."

He proceeded to mix the powder, sugar, and water as they watched. As he stirred the frothy mixture, he said, "I am not sure of the proportions. Let me sample it first to see."

He took a sip and said, "I think it needs a little more powder and sugar."

He added more and, tasting it again, said, "Umm, this seems correct. Here try it, Mother, my queen."

With a concerned look, she passed the cup to her husband and said, "I think the king should try it first."

His father took the cup and cautiously took a sip. He smacked his lips, pondered the taste a moment, took another small sip, and said, "Most interesting flavor. I should imagine it will become quite popular."

He gave the cup to his wife. She examined the contents, frowned, and then took a sip. Her eyes lit up, and she took another sip. Mateo and his father laughed at her sudden interest.

"It is quite delicious. I have never tasted anything like it. I feel like a queen," she said. "We must let the others here sample a bit but shall save these seeds for special occasions."

"Can this plant be cultivated here, Mateo? Should we try planting the seeds here? Think what profit could be made from growing them."

"No, Father, the plant needs a tropical climate unlike ours, and these seeds have been prepared for use. Either cured or baked, I am not sure. So they would not grow regardless."

"A pity," said his father. "I am sure this drink would be quite popular if more of these seeds were available."

"Let me try another sip, dear. Pass the cup to me please," he said to his wife, reaching.

"No, I am sorry, but this cup is mine. I have no intention of giving it up. Make another cup for your father, Mateo."

She then turned to the housekeeper nearby and said, "Rosa, taste a sip of this. You will not believe it."

It was not long before Mateo began in earnest the task of supplying an heir to the family. His mother had two good prospects for him. The first was the girl Angela who she had previously mentioned, and the second was a girl named Leonora, the daughter of a friend of a neighbor. This girl lived an hour or more away and was known to have a lively interest in men-of-arms, soldiers such as Mateo. Even without having met this second girl, his mother was excited about her and thought she might be the long-sought mother of her grandchildren.

To Mateo, they sounded less promising, so he went to find Miguel to see what intelligence he could learn about these two potential brides. He found Miguel and Guillermo rebuilding a stone fence near their house. They took a break from their work when they saw him approach.

After their greetings, Miguel said, "Don Mateo, have you come to make us another sample of your cocoa, I hope."

"No, Miguel," he said, smiling, "I come on a mission of the utmost importance."

"By the look of you, I would say your mother, the good Doña, has proposed a girl for you to meet."

"Precisely, Miguel. I have relied on your advice in the past and hope I still may."

"You may, Don Mateo, although I fear that I may be doing a disservice to the family and its prospects by passing on to you what I may have heard."

"No, Miguel, think how the family and its prospects would suffer from an unfortunate and unhappy marriage."

"You make an excellent point, Don Mateo. I promise to advise you as best I can."

Meanwhile, Guillermo sat down on a stump, listening and feeling sorry for his friend.

"And who is the girl she proposes?"

"There are two. The first is named Angela from nearby."

"I believe she is talking of Señorita Angela Suárez."

"Yes, she is the one. Mother says she is exceptionally beautiful and angelic much like her name."

After a pause and sigh, Miguel told him, "I have never met the young lady but hear from servant talk that she is both an exceptional beauty and an exceptional actress, skilled at her art. When needed to play the perfect angel, she performs her role beautifully. But to her servants, she plays the devil. An unsuspecting suitor may not see through her veil of angelic goodness. It is a veil that I suspect she will also remove when she removes her wedding veil."

Mateo listened in silence, and said, "Goodness."

"Better pass on her," Guillermo said with a chuckle.

"It would seem so. I hesitate to continue but must. The second one is a girl named Leonora. She is the daughter of a friend of a neighbor and lives an hour or two away. I do not know in what direction."

"No, I am sorry, Don Mateo, but I know nothing of her and cannot advise."

"Well, you have been most helpful as usual, my friend. I suppose I will have to venture forth with this second girl on my own, trusting in God and my own judgment."

"It would seem so. I will pray for you that she is a gentle lamb without guile."

Afterward, Mateo and Guillermo were talking by themselves.

"Guillermo, what am I to do?" asked Mateo with a sigh. "You remember the Italian play we read, *Giulietta e Romeo*. I have sought my own Giulietta for some time, but without success. What chance have I of ever finding her? Yet, I must marry."

"I am not one who should offer advice in such matters, Mateo, but I must say that these loves portrayed in books are perhaps too romanticized and not very realistic. You do have a tendency for such things, like the stories of valiant knights, damsels, and monster slayings that you enjoy reading in *Amadis of Gaul*. They are in the same vein. They may be entertaining to a degree, but you cannot take them too seriously."

"Perhaps you are right, but I still have this hope of finding her. I have not given up yet. I know my mother means well, but I do not think such arranged meetings will produce her."

Only three weeks after the day of his return home, Mateo was getting ready to meet the young girl Leonora, for whom his mother had such high hopes. While waiting for the arrival of their dinner guests, he was not feeling optimistic. But he would try to make the best of it. He might even enjoy himself. What could go wrong?

The neighbors and their friends with the daughter Leonora arrived on time. After introductions and drinks beforehand, everyone sat down to dinner. She was a pretty girl who had expressed a great willingness to meet Mateo, a soldier back from war, so to speak. Dinner went well, and Leonora showed great interest and admiration as Mateo told the attendees about his voyage with the treasure fleet to the Indies. In turn, he found her attractive and pleasant enough.

It was suggested they take a stroll in the garden after dinner, with Leonora's duenna following behind at a distance, of course. A long-standing custom was for young girls to have these matrons called duennas assigned to chaperone them and ensure all the appropriate social proprieties were being properly observed during courtship. The stroll outside in the garden would be an opportunity for them to get better acquainted.

Not knowing how such things normally proceeded, Mateo complimented her on her appearance as they strolled and said what fine weather they were having. But she quickly switched to the topic of her interest.

"Mateo, I have such great admiration for you soldiers. So brave and willing to die for the King."

A little embarrassed by her unbridled enthusiasm, Mateo said, "Well, dying for the King is a fate we try to avoid if possible."

"Yes, but soldiering is so romantic. Marching proudly in parades with your swords, banquets thrown by the local towns, handsome uniforms. Why did you not wear your uniform tonight? I so admire them, the bright colors, the epaulettes, the sashes, the plumes, the medals, and the bright buttons."

Mateo started to speak, but Leonora continued, "Next time, you must wear your uniform. I have always wanted to be seen on the arm of a handsome soldier in his uniform. It would make the other girls very jealous. So you must wear yours next time. Oh, and your sword too! My parents shall invite you to dinner, and I will invite my friends so they may be green with envy!"

Mateo kept walking beside her, unsure what to say, finally deciding that truth was best.

"Señorita Leonora, I am sorry to tell you this and perhaps disappoint you, but I own and wear no bright or flashy uniform."

Leonora stopped and faced him with a look of great disbelief and disappointment. He looked at her and then back at the duenna who appeared alarmed, suspecting something inappropriate had taken place.

With a laugh, he explained, "I am a soldier aboard ship, and you would probably find our uniforms drab and common. Marching, formations, parading, and pageantry are part of the life of land soldiery. Flamboyant and colorful uniforms are more important to them. They wear the bright uniforms with sashes and plumes you admire so."

"They told me you were a soldier!" she said with an annoyed look.

Now amused by her folly, he went on, "I am, but soldiers on ships wear a dull light green uniform with very little ornamentation to distinguish the officer from the men. They are meant for long voyages and battles at sea, not parades. But I am a soldier none-the-less. I have been in battle, and I am sorry to tell you this, but there was nothing at all romantic about it."

"Well, what good are you! You are of no use to me!" she exploded.

She then proceeded to stomp off toward the house with the duenna all upset and hovering over her, asking what happened. But the girl marched intently on without speaking as Mateo calmly watched her, barely controlling his urge to laugh.

When she arrived back in the house in a fury with the duenna trailing in confusion, the others stared in shock. What could have possibly happened out in the garden?

"Leonora, what has happened?" wailed her mother.

Leonora only blurted out, "He is no soldier!"

Then turning, she stomped out the front door to their carriage. They were all standing in confusion by now. The neighbors and their friends looked about open mouthed, put their drinks down, and hurried after her.

Needless to say, Mateo's first attempt at snaring a bride had not gone well.

Ch.6 Pascual

THE NEXT MORNING, Mateo and Guillermo were erecting archery targets made of hay-filled sacks with a red dot, about one foot across, painted in the center. Guillermo laughed a great deal as Mateo told him about his date.

The night before, when Mateo explained to his mother what had happened, she did not find it quite so amusing. She had put much effort and expense in hosting the dinner only to find the girl did not deserve it. Leonora was nothing more than a silly frivolous girl. His mother was embarrassed that she had presented her to Mateo as a promising candidate. Why should he ever believe her again? Much time would be needed for her to recover from her anger at the neighbors who recommended this empty-headed girl.

Mateo tried to soothe her ruffled feathers, telling her that she was not at fault and making light of it. But his mother was in no mood for humor. She already had a second candidate in mind and did not wish to waste her time again.

With their archery targets in place and still in high humor, Mateo and Guillermo stood back thirty yards from the targets and got out their archery gear. They strung their bows, loosened up, and pulled arrows from their quiver.

Mateo had practiced archery with Guillermo before leaving for his voyage. From his recent experience on ship, Mateo knew archery skills were still something of value.

Warfare at sea still involved ships coming together, one boarding the other and overwhelming its defenders. The cannons tried to cause death and damage before closing. But once together, many of the same weapons of land warfare were still a main part of the battle: muskets, crossbows, arrows, sabers, pistols, clubs, and knives. The arrows of a skilled archer were one of the lethal weapons valuable in the melee, only skilled archers were becoming a rarity in these times of improving firearms. Such were the details of modern shipboard warfare that Mateo told Guillermo to impress upon him the continued importance of archery skills.

"We only had four archers among our soldiers, and they were all sick and unable to take part in our battle. We could have used them. Have you seen a musket, Guillermo? They are bulky and heavy."

"I have seen them in Cordoba, and then only a soldier standing guard with one at a building. They stand there at attention with it by their side, one end resting on the ground. I have never seen them do anything with them."

"Muskets can shoot a large ball a great distance and pierce armor. I grant them that, but with poor accuracy. Quite heavy and awkward, the long barrel must be supported when aiming and firing them. Reloading them safely can take up to a minute.

"From what you say, they do not impress me as very useful," commented Guillermo.

"They are useful in warfare if fired in mass by a unit of musketeers at a group of the enemy. But in their current state of development, they are not as useful for individuals. In these times of cannons, pistols, and muskets, I believe there is still value in having and practicing archery skills."

Satisfied that he had impressed upon Guillermo the importance of their practice, Mateo then refreshed him on the basics of aiming and shooting, as Guillermo watched attentively.

"It has been some time since I have shot," said Mateo, "but I will go first."

He took his position and let fly five arrows in steady succession. All of them imbedded in the hay bag target near the red dot, but none within it.

"Well, I am definitely in need of practice. Well, Guillermo, your turn. You try it."

Guillermo stepped up, took his position, and let fly with five arrows in rapid succession. Mateo watched with growing surprise as, one after another, the arrows struck within the red dot. After the last arrow, Guillermo lowered his bow and calmly looked over at Mateo. They looked at each other for a moment and then burst into laughter, finally collapsing to the ground in spasms. After a time, Mateo managed to look over and say, "What an idiot I am. Me instructing you!"

Hearing their laughter, others came, and the joke was shared. When they were able again to resume their practice, they managed to shoot four more rounds before Mateo wanted to give his shooting fingers a rest. While they were shooting, Guillermo told him how he had learned.

One hot day last summer, he had been riding home from the south, sleepily plodding along unaware that he had reached their friend Pascual's place along the road.

Pascual and his men were not actually criminals and highwaymen. For many years, they had lived there by the road, where they expected people to pay them for the privilege to pass, much like a toll. Occasionally, it became necessary to get rough with people who did not know them and refused to pay. It would do unhappy travelers no good to complain to the local constable about it. Pascual had an informal understanding with him. He allowed them to do it, and in return, they would support him, when needed. For example, Gypsies were considered incurable thieves and a plague upon any area they visited. If a Gypsy caravan appeared in their area, Pascual and his men would run them off for the constable. If the constable needed information, Pascual and his men were good at laying low, watching, and learning things for him. The constable could also rely upon Pascual in times of emergency. The arrangement was beneficial for all, except perhaps for the travelers along the road.

Don Lorenzo and Pascual were good friends as well. Each trusted and knew he could depend on the other if ever one needed help. Don Lorenzo regularly visited Pascual, bringing supplies and gifts. Pascual, in turn, felt protective of Don Lorenzo's family, his estate, and its traffic along the road.

Guillermo knew them well and when passing would always stop to say hello. However, that day on his way home, he was riding along half asleep. As a joke to wake him up, they shot an arrow into a tree knot close by his head. Waking with a start at the sound of the arrow whizzing by and seeing the arrow stuck in the center of the tree knot, he was amazed.

"Who shot that arrow!" he said, jumping from his horse and walking determinedly toward Pascual and his men.

"Who shot that arrow! I want to learn to shoot as well!"

Coming forward and laughing with his men, Pascual said, "Young Guillermo, it was Sebastian, of course. He is our best shot. I had him shoot so you would not get hurt."

Turning to Sebastian, Guillermo said, "Teach me how to shoot better, Sebastian. I plan to go to sea with Mateo next time. So I want to learn to shoot and practice here with you."

Sebastian was smiling ear to ear, flattered by the attention of the highly regarded young man.

"Guillermo, you are not just trying to avoid work on the estate, are you?" joked Pascual.

He smiled at Pascual and then again to Sebastian, "Teach me how to shoot better, Sebastian. I will pay if necessary."

"There is no need for pay, young Guillermo. We can start right now if you wish."

Thus began his archery training. He and Sebastian went back to their camp, through the huts, campfires, wives, children, chickens, and dogs. They prepared an archery range and Sebastian showed him the proper technique. Guillermo would visit them regularly to practice and improve.

Hearing this story, Mateo said with enthusiasm, "Guillermo, we must go to their camp tomorrow. We can bring some sausage and wine with us for them. We must tell them what happened today. They will enjoy the humor of it, Sebastian especially!"

"Yes, Mateo, let us do it."

At Pascual's camp the next day, they told Pascual and his men the story of Mateo's archery instructions on the previous day, and they all enjoyed the story immensely.

Pascual and his men had heard only a brief description of Mateo's voyage to the Indies when they had greeted him warmly on his journey home. They now wanted to hear more details of the voyage to the Indies, and especially about the battle with the English ships, a part that most interested them. They sat glued to every word as he spoke. After hours of merriment at the camp, Mateo and Guillermo regrettably needed to leave and return home.

On the way home, they were in high spirits as they rode at a leisurely pace. Looking at Mateo riding beside him, Guillermo asked, "Mateo, we are true friends. Are we not?"

"Yes, Guillermo, the truest."

"And there must be no secrets between true friends."

"Quite true."

"Then I say we must tell each other something we have never told anyone else. It will prove we are true friends."

Mateo considered this for a moment and said, "Very well, my friend. I shall begin. You know the silver spurs of which my father is so proud, the ones I brought him from the Indies?"

"No, Mateo! You did not!"

"Yes. I am sorry to say I did. I actually bought them in Seville after our ship returned."

"Ooh, I cannot believe it," said Guillermo, laughing.

"Yes! The ones in the Indies were atrocious, of such inferior quality that they would never suit. The great interest there is in making silver coins and ingots, not spurs."

"Well, you did the right thing then, Mateo."

As they continued riding, Mateo said, "So, Guillermo, now I have told you a secret. It is your turn to tell me one."

"Mateo, are you sure you wish to hear it?"

"Yes, we shall have no secrets from each other."

"Then I shall tell you. My secret is I have killed a man."

"What?" Mateo looked at him in surprise, suddenly sobering.

"Yes, you know Manuel who tends the south oak meadows. While you were gone, his sister and her children came to live with his family. You probably have not heard about them yet. She had lived with a brute of a husband in a nearby village. He was a cruel drunkard who beat her regularly."

"The lowly coward!" interrupted Mateo.

"My thoughts exactly," continued Guillermo. "After one particularly bad beating, she took the children and escaped to her brother's house here on the estate. That is when I became aware of it. I went to the village and confronted him in his house. I called him a spineless coward for beating women and children. I told him if he ever set foot on our estate, I would kill him."

"Bravo, Guillermo! Well done!"

"He did not share your opinion, Mateo. Instead of saying 'Bravo! Well done!' he called me a 'bold young whippersnapper' and came at me with a knife. I killed him with mine and left him there on the floor of his house. I am told that when the villagers found him two days later, they were glad. They whispered to one another that it was the Wrath of God. They reported no crime, buried him, and no more was said about it."

Reflecting, he added, "I suppose it makes me an instrument of the Wrath of God."

"Manuel's sister had no desire to return to the village," continued Guillermo. "She is good at bread making and now works at the main house. So, all has turned out well."

Mateo had been listening in amazed silence. Finally, he said, "Guillermo, I am truly proud to be the friend of such a man as you. You did the right thing too."

With that, he turned back forward and continued to ride deep in thought. A minute later, Mateo started to chuckle to himself and shake his head.

"What is it, Mateo? Why do you laugh?" asked Guillermo, laughing too.

"You tell me a secret about fearlessly confronting a villain, of being an instrument of God…"

He chuckled again.

"And I tell you a secret about deceiving my father about spurs! It is too funny!"

Ch. 7 Mencía

MATEO WAS FOND of jesting with Miguel about his love of his almond trees. When he spotted the overseer checking the crop one day, he got down from his horse and went over to him.

After their exchange of greetings, Mateo said, "And how are your children doing today, Miguel?"

"Ah, I was just checking the progress of the nuts. The hulls of the nuts are splitting and starting to dry out. The almonds are good size, not small and shriveled. We should have a good crop to harvest in early September. This tree is a favorite of mine. It produces well every year, and I am pleased to say it is heavy with nuts this year," he said as he patted a branch tenderly.

"How did you develop this affection for them, Miguel? I have always meant to ask."

"I got it from your grandfather Hector, your father's father, God rest his soul. He was a good man, like your father and like you. All the more reason this lineage of good men should continue," he added with a chuckle.

"Yes, I know about continuing our line, but what about my grandfather Hector and almonds?"

Smiling, Miguel continued, "Your grandfather was the one who first had a passion for almonds and brought them here to the estate. When soldiering as a young man, he spent time at Málaga on our southern coast. Almonds have been grown on the hillsides there for centuries. The pretty white blossoms of the almond trees are God's first announcement of the coming spring. Seeing these blossoms for the first time, your grandfather became interested and watched as the nuts grew. At harvest time in late summer, he sampled their sweet taste and very much wanted to grow them here, even though they are not commonly grown in our area. He brought seedlings to the estate and planted them. With much care and experimenting with different varieties and locations over the years, you see how he has succeeded. I was only a boy at the time but developed my own regard for them. Seeing this, your grandfather took me under his wing and taught me all he knew. I have such wonderful memories of him. As I say, he was a very good man. It is unfortunate that he died before you were born."

"I am sorry too. Father also speaks highly of him. And you have cared for his trees ever since," Mateo said with a smile.

"Yes. Your father is more interested in our oak meadows and our black pigs that feed on the acorns. They are the well-known and more common product of our area."

"Quite true. During the dry summer, Father prays regularly for the start of fall rains for the oaks. He delights when the pigs fatten on a heavy crop of acorns on the ground under them."

"Your father prays for rain as early as possible in the fall and I pray the rain holds off until after the almond harvest. God must receive many conflicting prayers."

"Miguel, you must admit these acorns are important to us."

"Oh, yes, quite so, Don Mateo. The acorns impart a flavor to the cured hams of our black pigs that is highly prized. They are a lucrative product of our estate. People in this area boast that our cured hams are the best in Spain. I think the flavor is marvelous, but I prefer the hams to be cured at least four years instead of the normal three. Then the meat is less raw and more like cooked. My María and I have four hams curing in our attic at home, our next four Christmas Eve dinners."

"Cured ham at Christmas Eve dinner was one of the things I regrettably missed last year in the Indies, and to which I greatly look forward this year."

"Yes, I can imagine," said Miguel with admiration.

Three weeks after his first failed attempt, Mateo dutifully agreed to attempt a second encounter with a girl and her duenna. This time, the potential bride was the daughter of a friend of a city official. Not being from the immediate area, Miguel was unable to advise.

The girl named Mencía was pretty enough but said little during dinner and only gave Mateo an occasional glance. Mateo's mother looked with concern at the girl and was not hopeful that this second experiment would be successful either. She just hoped for no repeat of a scene like the last time.

After dinner, Mateo and the girl went for the customary walk in the garden with her duenna following behind. They strolled for a time separated by a proper distance without saying anything. Mateo glanced at her. She did not seem meek or bashful. She seemed to not be talking because she had no desire to. It would be ridiculous for him to break the silence with a remark about what nice weather we have been having lately. He thought perhaps an honest inquiry might be more appropriate.

"You seem unhappy. Did you not like dinner?"

Without looking at him, she replied without emotion, "I must be honest with you and say that I was forced to come to this dinner to meet you, a potential suitor."

"Are you in love with someone else and are being forced into an arranged marriage?"

"No, nothing like that. It is just that I have no need for men. I pity the man who should be chosen to marry me. He would be miserable indeed."

A little surprised, Mateo replied, "I admire your honesty. I hope I have done nothing to offend you. If so, I assure you that had no intention of doing so and apologize."

For the first time, she looked over at Mateo. After eyeing him for a moment, she returned her gaze forward.

"No, you seem to be better than most. But, in general, men offend me with their arrogance, dishonesty, weakness, and laziness. If you have any good sense, you will not invite me back for dinner."

The girl suddenly fascinated Mateo. He had never met one like her before. He said with a laugh, "On the contrary, I want very much to invite you back, but as a friend, not for this silliness we do now. I find you most fascinating and unique. I have a great interest in knowing you better. My friend and I regularly practice archery. Perhaps you would like to join us?"

She looked at him and smiled, "I would like that very much. I am rather good at archery. You will not be offended if I shoot better than you?"

"You have not seen my friend shoot. You would be hard pressed to beat him. What other interests have you?"

"Well, of course, I enjoy horseback riding but not in a skirt and sidesaddle. I wear riding pants and boots and go on long rides sometimes. You may not believe this, but I saw a man throwing knives in a traveling show one time and took it up."

"Fantastic!" said Mateo, delighted. "My friend and I would love a demonstration! You must come back next week."

"It would please me a great deal."

When they came back inside, they were talking and laughing like two friends. Everyone stared at them in amazement. A moment later, the duenna came in behind them, frowning and shaking her head. While it may have been better than the first attempt, it still was not the outcome for which his mother had hoped. She told herself she must keep trying.

Several days later, Mateo and Guillermo were waiting in front of the main house when Mencía rode up and alighted from her horse. Smiling, Mateo said, "Good morning, Mencía. It is so good of you to come."

"Not at all, for I have very much looked forward to coming," she said, smiling back.

"Mencía, I would like to introduce you to my good friend Guillermo."

Coming forward and bowing curtly, he said, "A friend of Mateo's is a friend of mine. I cannot tell you how much I have looked forward to meeting you and seeing your knife throwing demonstration."

"It is true, Mencía. He has talked about nothing else," added Mateo.

"I hope I shall not disappoint," said Mencía as she turned and quickly hurled a knife that stuck solidly in a wooden hitching post fifteen feet away.

Guillermo looked astonished and said excitedly, "Mateo! We must convince her to teach us!"

Mencía was pleased with their reaction and promised to teach them. Guillermo retrieved her knife from the post and examined it with great curiosity as he walked back. The knife was a single flat piece of metal eight inches long, shaped like a strong blade at one end and a slightly bowed handle at the other. The metal was thick enough to give it weight and good force when thrown. It had stuck solidly in the post.

They walked with Mencía to the stable where the stablemen took her horse. In an open area beside the stable, they set up several wooden targets. She had brought a number of these knives. Taking three of them, she stood so the three targets all faced her at different distances, from four to six paces. They watched in great anticipation and silence as she stood facing away from the targets. She then quickly turned and threw the three knives in rapid succession. Thunk, thunk, thunk, embedding a knife squarely in the center of each target.

Mateo was speechless, but Guillermo excitedly said, "Bravo, Mencía! That was fantastic! Let us see it once more!"

She retrieved the knives from the targets, stood back, and again repeated the demonstration with the same result. Guillermo and Mateo could not believe it and came forward laughing to congratulate her.

"How much time is required to learn such skill?" asked Guillermo.

"It is not difficult to learn to throw the knife and embed it in a target at a fixed distance. It is more difficult and takes months of practice to learn to adjust the throw to make the blade hit and embed at different distances. Here, I will first show you how to hold the knife."

With that, their knife throwing training began.

Later inside the house, as they sat at their breakfast table, eating a snack, Mencía told them more about how she had learned knife throwing.

"As I mentioned the other night, I first saw it in a tent in a traveling show. I watched with fascination as the performer threw knives at an assistant standing against a wooden background. Suspecting the knife throwing was trickery, I paid to see his act over and over. I concluded the show was real. He was actually throwing the knives that traced a pattern around the outline of his assistant, just inches away from her. He noticed my intense interest and asked me how I liked his show. I told him I wanted to learn how he did it. He took it as a great compliment and agreed to teach me.

"Between his acts, he instructed me in 'the art of knife throwing,' as he called it. He said the knife throwing in his act was easy, throwing from only four paces and always the same distance. Within an hour or two, I could do it with reasonable accuracy. Then he showed me what was needed for the much more difficult skill of embedding the knife at different distances. Such skill was not needed for his act, so he had not tried to perfect it and said he was only marginally good at it. I went back again the next two days while he was in town. By the third day, he marveled at my skill, saying I had already surpassed his own. In the end, he had to move on with the traveling show. When he left, he gave me two of his knives and told me that he was exceedingly proud of me. I thanked and paid him generously for his help. I have been practicing ever since."

"Quite a story, Mencía," Mateo said, shaking his head in awe. "And where did you acquire your knives? They look finely made with a saber-like finish."

"From a knife maker in Cordoba. After showing him one, he said he was familiar with such knives. He had made a similar design, which he showed me. I asked him if I could try it. When I embedded it into a piece of wood five paces away, he was impressed and said the knife looked to be the perfect balance and weight for me. I agreed and he made a dozen for me."

"Perhaps we should gain a little skill with your knives and then see this knife maker. He may suggest some adjustment to the design for us," proposed Mateo.

"I agree," said Mencía.

Sitting on one side of her, Guillermo leaned forward, as he clapped her on the shoulder, saying, "Mencía, my friend, you are fantastic!"

Sitting on the other side, Mateo clutched her arm and enthusiastically said, "I concur whole-heartedly. Thank you, Mencía, for sharing this incredible skill with us."

Just then, Mateo's mother entered the room. She stopped and looked at them with a stunned expression. Seeing her shock, they quickly took their hands from Mencía and began to laugh.

"Do not worry, Mother," said Mateo. "We are fine. She is here as our friend and does not require her duenna."

For four straight days, Mencía came, and they practiced knife throwing for hours each day. Mateo's father came with his friend Don Felipe to watch them several times. They were completely amazed at this young knife-throwing girl.

During one of these practices, Mateo asked her about her parents. Did they not object to her coming here to be with two young men without a duenna?

"After our dinner together," she told him, smiling, "my mother saw it would be useless to continue. Her notion of me wearing an evening dress and ornate hair pin, with a duenna in trail, to a dinner party to find a suitor was one doomed to failure. She also feared it might end badly. Knowing of my interest in knife throwing, she worried that a suitor might offend me in some way and be pinned to the wall by knives."

After their laughter, she added, "They have accepted that normal customs do not work for their oldest daughter, yet they still love me."

"They sound like fine people. We need to have them over for dinner again but without the duenna," said Mateo, smiling.

"She is already gone."

"And your sisters, do they have knives too?" asked Guillermo, chuckling.

"No, Margarita is fourteen, and Cristina is twelve. By all outward appearances, they are two normal Andalusian girls. But, while I have developed an interest in knife throwing, Margarita has developed an interest in music and playing the guiterna (an early form of Spanish guitar)."

"How did she become interested?"

"Our uncle was once a traveling minstrel and came to live with us several years ago. After hearing him play, she wanted to learn and can now play beautifully. She and Cristina began singing together. Someday you must hear them. They are quite remarkable."

"Like their big sister," said Mateo, smiling.

One morning for a break, the three of them went to see Pedro so that Mateo could talk with him about the seeds from the Indies. From outside the stone fence around his garden, they spotted him inside, bent over and looking through the leaves of a large spreading plant.

As they passed through the gate, Mateo called, "Pedro, how are you today?"

Looking up, he straightened and greeted them, "Good day, Don Mateo, Guillermo, and to you Señorita Mencía."

"Good day, Pedro."

"So are you finding any cucumbers, Pedro," asked Mateo.

"Yes, there are many small ones, but if I look hard enough under the leaves, I usually can find some big ones to pick."

"Pedro, are your carrots ripe? Can I pull one out to show Mencía?" asked Guillermo.

"Guillermo, I have seen carrots before."

"Perhaps on the dinner table, Mencía, but have you pulled one from the soil?"

"No, I suppose not."

"Yes, be my guest, Guillermo. They are in that second row," said Pedro, pointing.

"Are you sure you know how, Guillermo?" asked Mencía in jest as they walked over.

Standing with Pedro and chuckling, Mateo looked about, admiring the garden.

"You have a fine garden, Pedro. Beside these cucumber plants here, I see onions, turnips, carrots, peas, chickpeas, and oh yes, lettuce and spinach. You are the right man for growing our peppers."

"I wish we could have started growing the new plants this year, Don Mateo. But it is summer, and we must try a spring planting first. It is our best chance to succeed in growing them. I am looking forward to it. We can experiment a little, but we must be careful not to waste the precious seeds."

"You and Miguel can work that out. I will tell you everything I know of what I saw there in the Indies."

"We may have to find a better place for a bigger garden than here," suggested Pedro, "a place where water can be brought by a ditch perhaps."

"We should consider it," mused Mateo. "Watering a large garden by hand would be much work. The oaks, almonds, and olives are watered by God, as they say. We Spaniards are not as good as we should be at making systems for irrigating our lands. I am not sure why. The Romans and Moors before us were far better at it, and many of their water projects have fallen into disuse."

"One of my wife Juana's friends mocks the notion of ditches bringing water to irrigate a new garden, saying that if God wanted water to flow to gardens here, he would have done it long ago Himself."

"Regardless of Juana's friend, the peppers are important, and we must make our best effort to grow them. And, Pedro, you have not seen these other plants. They are important foods in the Indies and may become valuable foods for us here in Spain. They are called maize, beans, potato, and tomato. I fear they need much water, and we may be forced to grow them at Uncle Carlos' estate by the Guadalquivir River where irrigation water is more available."

"I am interested in these other plants too, Don Mateo. You must let me, at least, try to grow a small amount here too, even if I must water them by hand."

"There is no need to ask, Pedro. We want our best gardener to try growing them here too, of course."

The next day, all three friends rode to see the knife maker in Cordoba. When they stopped at Pascual's camp to say hello, Mencía and her knife throwing demonstration were a huge hit. Pascual had his two best knife-throwers compete with her. When she easily beat them, he and his men howled with delight and laughter. They were so enthralled with her that the three of them were hard-pressed to get away and continue. After a long ride, they arrived that night at the home of Mencía's aunt and uncle on the outskirts of Cordoba, where they stayed the night.

The next morning, they visited the knife maker where Mateo and Guillermo demonstrated their knife throwing for him. He suggested minor changes for their knives, a little more length, a little more weight. He could have a dozen ready in three weeks. With business completed, they were soon on their way back to the family estate. Their arrival at home was so late at night that Mencía spent the night there in a guest room in the main house.

Mencía came every other day, and they continued to practice their knife throwing, but Mateo and Guillermo wanted to hold off with intensive training until they got their own. Along with knives, they practiced their archery. They discovered Mencía shot very well, and they began to practice regularly. At their request, Sebastian came several times to shoot with them and give pointers to help their technique. Over the next weeks of practice, their archery skills were honed to a fine point, so to speak. All three were excellent archers like Sebastian.

Ch.8 Cousins

SINCE THEY WERE working on their archery and knife throwing skills, why not also work on saber and cutlass skills? A retired cavalier Don Tomás, who was a friend of Mateo's father, lived nearby in town. It had been normal in the past to invite him out when Mateo and Guillermo practiced. He enjoyed taking part again in his old pastime, passing on his knowledge and telling stories.

Don Lorenzo would have a stableman take a horse to him, and later they came riding back together. Happy to be out on a horse again and away from his house in town, Don Tomás went smiling into the main house to visit with Mateo's parents for a time. Later, he came out with Don Lorenzo to see how the saber practice was going.

When he saw Mencía practicing with a cutlass, he proclaimed, "No, no, no, this is not right. A young girl wielding a cutlass? I am sorry, but I am old fashioned. The martial arts are not something for the fairer sex. It is a dirty business, a *man's* business."

Hearing muffled laughter, Don Tomás looked around curiously and asked, "What is it? Did I say something funny?"

Mateo looked at his father and nodded in the direction of a nearby wooden post. His father smiled and nodded back. Meanwhile, Guillermo had walked past Mencía who stood with her cutlass five paces away. He had slipped three knives to her unseen as he passed.

Don Lorenzo said, "Tomás, my old friend, I have something to show you over here by the wooden post. It may surprise you."

Going with Don Lorenzo to the post and looking about, he said, "I see nothing, Lorenzo. What do you mean?"

Then turning around, he saw Mencía toss her cutlass aside and throw three knives in quick succession that imbedded, thunk, thunk, thunk, into the wooden post just a foot away.

The surprised look on his face was priceless and everyone burst out laughing. Don Tomás looked at the knives in the post and wagged his finger at Mencía who smiled broadly. Don Tomás joined in the laughter, which after a time subsided enough for him to say, "Well, I certainly deserved that, did I not?"

Looking at Mencía with admiration, he added, "I am quite impressed. Where did you find this warrior princess, Lorenzo? She is marvelous. Yes, quite impressive. I freely admit I was wrong in her case."

Bowing to Mencía, he added, "But you must forgive me, young lady, for I pictured you as one of our normal young girls which you most certainly are not."

With his interest now up, he became more active than normal in their training session, instructing them in slow motion on attacking and defending, showing them various techniques to improve their skills with both the cutlass and the saber.

Afterward, he told Mateo's father, "Lorenzo, my friend, I have never enjoyed a training session so much. These three are the best students I have ever trained, and I hope you will invite me out again very soon. The girl is marvelous, a warrior like the other two. I have never been so impressed."

When three weeks had passed, the three friends rode together again to Cordoba to the knife maker. The knives were ready as promised, and after inspecting them closely, Mateo and Guillermo were satisfied and ready to try them out. The knife maker was impressed with their ability and thought the knife design was well suited for them. As they gathered up their new knives and paid the man, they were already impatient to get home and practice with them. Shortly, they were on their way, arriving back home late at night.

Mateo wanted to accomplish as much practice with their new knives as possible before stopping to work on the almond harvest in a month. The early August sun made the afternoons too hot for practicing their skills, and he did not like asking Mencía to make an hour ride there and back from her home several times a week just to practice in the morning. So Mateo decided it made more sense for Mencía to stay at their estate for several days during the week to make the most of the mornings.

His mother resisted the idea at first but finally agreed to have her move into a guestroom. Doña Antonia liked Mencía personally, but the Doña had a difficult time accepting Mencía's close friendship and activity with her son and Guillermo, which was far removed from normal customs and proprieties of young Spanish girls.

During her stays, they practiced their knife throwing every morning and sometimes archery too. Twice during the month, they invited Don Tomás back for saber and cutlass training. He was tickled to come back and instruct them again. After their saber training, they showed off their archery skills for him. When Guillermo consistently hit bullseyes from sixty yards, he could not praise him enough. He told them that he considered his participation in their training to be the highest honor of his life.

In late August, Guillermo began spending more time helping his father with preparations for the almond harvest in September, so the training sessions were scaled back. By then though, they had already developed their knife throwing skills and could thunk, thunk, thunk their knives in targets without error up to twenty feet away.

In September, the almond harvest began. They used the time-tested methods they had evolved over the years, which may have been unique to their estate. Nut samples taken from the trees told them the almonds were mature and dry enough for the harvest to begin.

The almonds hanging on the branches were a hard brown shell with a pale withering hull clinging to them. The nut itself was inside these shells. Harvesting involved using poles to knock the almonds from the tree onto tarps spread underneath. Children were tasked to pick up any stray almonds landing beyond the tarps. From the tarps, the almonds were dumped into wooden bins. The empty tarps were then spread under the next tree, and the process repeated.

The bins full of almonds were hauled back to a storage area where the shells were removed from the mixture of shells, hulls, twigs, and leaves. Next, a heavy roller was used to crack the shells, one heavy enough to just break the shells without breaking the nuts inside. The broken shells were piled in big mounds on long tables, around which women and children of the estate sat and picked the nuts from the broken shells. The nuts were then put on trays and baked a short time in ovens to dry them a little more and kill any worm eggs that might be on them. Finally, the nuts were laid out to dry more and then put in sacks in which they would be sold to the merchant.

As a major work and social event during the year, everyone on the estate took part in the long tedious, labor-intensive process. Miguel supervised the work while Rosa supervised the feeding of everyone. Mateo, his father, and Guillermo helped wherever help was needed, even sitting with the others and picking nuts from shells. Mencía came to help as well.

Everyone worked hard for they knew the importance of the crop to the estate and their continued way of life on it. When the work was completed after three intense weeks, a celebration dinner and dance was held at the main house for everyone.

Later in early October, Don Lorenzo was chatting outside with Miguel when he felt a sudden cold gust of wind. Don Lorenzo looked up and saw the sky beginning to cloud over. He felt another gust of wind, and breaking into a smile, he looked excitedly at his overseer.

"Miguel, I can smell it. It is going to rain!"

Miguel was looking up and smiling too, "I can smell it too. Our prayers will soon be answered. I see the dark clouds coming. Let us pray it is a good storm with lots of rain and that God will provide many more after it. A good wet winter would be a blessing. I should check to see if anything needs to be put inside or covered before the rain comes."

"Good thinking, Miguel. I will help." With that, they both climbed on their horses and rode off.

The rains began in October to the happiness of Mateo's father. With the rains came the promise of a good crop of acorns. Mateo, Guillermo, and Mencía talked about hunting wild boar, but every time they prepared to set out the next day, it poured down rain. After two failed attempts, they gave it up.

Mateo and Guillermo visited Mencía at her parent's house and spent a nice lunch and afternoon with them. While their daughter may have crazy interests in throwing knives, shooting arrows, and fighting with sabers, it was a modest consolation for her parents that, at least, she was doing it with these two exceptional young men.

Olive harvest takes place in the November-December timeframe. A sizable number of olive trees grew on the hillsides of one area of the estate, sectioned off by the high stone fences to keep the black pigs out. When ripe, the olives were knocked with poles from the trees onto nets much like with almonds. Making the oil from the olives is an ancient and messy process.

For many years, Don Lorenzo had an arrangement with a neighbor with an olive processing facility. Each wagonload of olives he delivered to the neighbor was considered equivalent to a given amount of oil. The neighbor gave him back enough olive oil for use on the family estate and sold the rest for him to an olive oil buyer.

In early November, the olives were not yet ready for harvesting when a letter arrived from Don Lorenzo's cousin inviting Mateo and his parents to visit them. The cousin, Don Carlos, owned an estate west of Cordoba near the Guadalquivir River. It seemed to Mateo and his father an excellent opportunity to investigate the possibility of growing the new plants there. They would take seeds and notes to Don Carlos, so he could try his hand at growing the plants next spring. They were sure that he would, at least, be interested in attempting to grow peppers.

Miguel assured Don Lorenzo that he and Guillermo could manage the olive harvest. Consequently, Don Lorenzo decided they should accept the invitation. However, he stipulated to his wife, they absolutely must be back in early December, so he could see his black pigs begin to root around for acorns under their oaks.

Hearing this, his wife, Antonia, looked dumbly at him a moment, rolled her eyes, and said, "Please, Lorenzo, do not be ridiculous."

Later in the month, they were prepared to leave. Guillermo and Mencía attended a farewell dinner the day before their departure. Mateo had been specifically invited on the trip and felt obligated to go. He would have to say goodbye to his two friends for a time but promised to return as soon as possible.

Mateo and his parents made the day and a half trip to Don Lorenzo's cousin, spending a night at an inn on the way. The lodging was typical of inns in those days. Its building, courtyard, and stable were fully enclosed by a high wall with a large wooden gate, which was closed and secured at night. They had paid for better rooms there. Two government officials and their wives were also staying and joined them for dinner.

A number of muleteers were staying as well. For less money, they could eat their dinner in a common dining area and sleep in a large common bedroom, or out with their mules in the stables, protecting their goods. One could not really escape the smell of the stables in the place. Staying with relatives when traveling was preferred, but sometimes inns were a necessity.

Late the next morning, their carriage arrived at the family estate of Don Carlos and his wife Doña Catalina. Don Carlos was the cousin of Mateo's father and similar in age. Being so much younger, Mateo had always called them Uncle Carlos and Aunt Catalina, although they were cousins. Their children were grown and gone, a daughter in a convent in Cordoba and two sons in the Indies, seeking their fortune.

His aunt and uncle had heard nothing from their sons in seven years. During his voyage to the Indies, Mateo had inquired about them in every port he visited, without learning anything. On his return trip home after the voyage, he had visited with his aunt and uncle to report that he had been unsuccessful in discovering any news of their sons. They had been hopeful for news, and poor Aunt Catalina had cried miserably when he brought back none.

Eager to get home after his long service on the treasure fleet, his earlier visit had been only a brief stop. The purported reason for their current invitation to visit was to hear more about his trip, but Mateo suspected the real reason was Aunt Catalina had some local girl in mind for him to meet.

Mateo suspected correctly for on the second night after their arrival, his aunt and uncle held a dinner party, to which a neighboring couple and their daughter named Inés were invited. She again was a pretty girl, but Mateo happened to see her as she passed a small mirror on a wall and thought she looked at herself a little too much.

After a pleasant dinner, it was time for Mateo and Inés to take a stroll in the garden with her duenna following.

"Do you like my hair?" was the first thing she said.

Her hair was pulled tightly back into a bun with a large ornate hair comb called a peinete sticking from the top. A thin black veil called a mantilla, in turn, covered the peinete and hair, draping down over her shoulders. Such was a traditional look in Andalusia, their section of Spain.

Peering through her mantilla at her hair and trying to sound enthusiastic, he said, "Yes, it is very becoming, and such a very ornate and beautiful peinete in it."

"It is made of tortoise shell, very expensive."

Not knowing what to say, he said, "Oh, how interesting. It does look very nice."

"Some people say I have beautiful eyes," she said turning and staring at him.

Looking in her eyes as requested, Mateo said, "Well, your eyes have a beautiful almond shape, but I cannot see their color very well here in the dim light of the garden."

When the duenna behind them cleared her throat loudly, Inés quickly turned her head forward again, and Mateo did the same.

"They are light brown in color with subtle green sparkles."

"I am sure they must be very beautiful," offered Mateo.

"I take very good care of my skin. I wear no makeup on my cheeks, and they are as soft as baby skin. You may touch them if you wish."

"No, I do not think I should. I am certain that the duenna would not approve."

"What do you think of my nose?"

Getting desperate, Mateo tried to change the subject, "Before we talk of your nose, I was thinking how fine it must be living on an estate here along the Guadalquivir River. It must be most enjoyable. What are the people who work on your family's estate like?"

"I do not know," she replied indifferently. "They are obedient enough, I suppose. It is tiresome meeting them when I am riding. They are always bowing or tipping their hats, and I have no interest or time for such things."

Now frantically thinking of a way to get away, he said, "I see. Well, they are probably just trying to be respectful, I suppose. Getting back to your nose, I must say that it is certainly a most lovely one, a true work of art that must be carefully protected. I feel a chill in the air and think we should go back inside. I would not want you to catch a cold and cause that beautiful nose of yours to swell up."

"It has not started to swell already, has it?" she asked with alarm.

"No, it is still quite beautiful," he said, and her look of alarm turned into a delighted smile at the compliment.

"But we cannot be too careful," he added as he graciously took her arm, politely turned her around, and started back toward the house.

Now facing the frowning duenna, he released her arm but resolutely kept walking, desperate to get back inside.

"Your nose is really quite beautiful," he said trying to think of things to say. "I think very highly of it. So symmetric and finely shaped. The nostrils are just right. Yours is truly one of the loveliest noses I have ever seen."

"Do you really think so?" she said excitedly. Then she dejectedly added, "But just *one* of the most beautiful, not *the* most beautiful. Whose nose did you think better?"

Mateo somehow managed to get back inside without incident and quickly found the girl's father.

"Ah, Señor, regrettably, your lovely daughter and I had to cut short our stroll in the garden because of a chill in the air, not like in the tropical air of the Indies where even the nights are warm and humid."

"Do tell," said the father with interest, wanting to hear more.

Mateo knew that any mention of the Indies would draw him into conversation with the father. Although talking about his voyage had grown quite old for him, he was willing to do anything tonight to not be alone with the girl with green sparkles in her eyes. He still continued to politely show her attention as he told about his voyage, but he thankfully had no more conversations about noses or eyes or even ears or teeth.

When the guests departed, he politely said goodbye to the girl and her parents. As their carriage rolled away, he quietly sighed with relief.

Turning to him, his aunt asked brightly, "Well, Mateo, what did you think of Inés? Is she not a lovely girl?"

Mateo had to ponder a moment before replying, "She is a lovely girl, yes, but too good for me. She seeks a different manner of man than me. She requires one who heaps compliments, and I am inept at such things. I appreciate your interest, Aunt Catalina, but I am afraid that Inés and I are ill-suited for each other."

Turning with a frown to Mateo's mother, his aunt said, "Oh, well, Antonia, it did not work out. Perhaps Mateo is being too choosy."

"I think you may be right, Catalina. He reads silly stories written by silly Italians, *Giulietta e Romeo.* They have confused his thinking. He expects too much."

"You are right, Antonia. Perfect wives can no longer be found. We are the last two," she said with a giggle.

Ch.9 Luisa

MATEO'S AUNT AND UNCLE had previously received an invitation to a dinner party to take place three days after their own. When they sent their regrets that they could not attend because their cousins were visiting, they received a reply saying the cousins were welcome to attend as well. In considering this, Don Carlos thought it might prove interesting for his cousins to get a taste of the affluence of one of their prominent citizens, so they accepted.

When Mateo entered the fine oak paneled dining room on the night of the party, he saw well-dressed people clustered in groups about the large table elaborately set for dinner. The host, a middle-aged, proud man with a serious expression, came to greet them and seemed a little surprised at seeing Mateo. He must have expected the visiting cousins all to be similar in age to Don Carlos.

"El Señor Don Gaspar Jimenez, I would like to introduce you to el Señor Don Lorenzo de Cordoba, his wife Doña Antonia, and their son Don Mateo. They are my cousins visiting from north of Cordoba," said Mateo's uncle in introduction.

Shaking hands respectfully, Don Lorenzo said, "It was indeed gracious of you to invite us as well."

"It is my pleasure," replied the host with reserve.

"Don Gaspar is one of the largest landowners in these parts, greatly respected by all," said his uncle.

"His house and this dining room are certainly impressive. I have seen none better," said Don Lorenzo.

"Thank you. Let me introduce you to some guests," he said, eyeing Mateo. Then turning, he beckoning them toward a group on one side of the room.

When entering, Mateo happened to notice a fine-looking girl in a group on the other side of the room. She was strikingly beautiful but seemed to be distracted and not paying attention to the young man beside her.

After more introductions and small talk, the time came for being seated for dinner. The host showed them their seats at one end of the table. Grace was said, and the meal was served.

Mateo had asked his parents, aunt, and uncle to please not mention his trip to the Indies. It could only necessitate the telling of it yet another time. They all promised not to mention it, but in his pride in describing his nephew to his acquaintances seated with them, Don Carlos forgot himself and accidentally let it slip.

Any stories or experiences from outside one's own small sphere of existence were always of great interest. The others were instantly fascinated and wanted to hear about his voyage and the Indies. The more he told, the more captivated and animated they became. They were soon telling the people next to them about the handsome, brave young man and his voyage to the Indies onboard a treasure fleet galleon.

Mateo became aware that the host seemed displeased by the attention he had generated. So Mateo finally had to beg the forgiveness of the others, saying he feared he was disturbing the dinner and must hold off further discussion of his voyage until after dinner. They agreed not to pester him further, so long as he would continue with his stories later.

When things became less lively around Mateo, the host seemed more satisfied and animated in his own conversation. During his glances down at the host, Mateo noticed the beautiful girl had been seated near the host and the young man who was his son. Mateo also noticed she had looked his way several times and no longer had the distracted look of before. She now looked hopeful and radiant as she politely joined in conversation at that end of the table.

After dinner, the guests adjourned to a living room where cheeses and fruits were laid out for dessert. As the mingling and conversation continued, Mateo noticed the host seemed unusually protective of the beautiful girl, keeping her continually surrounded by a fixed set of friends.

The tales of the Indies were again in demand, and the listeners seemed particularly interested in the pepper seeds he had brought back. They began to pepper Don Lorenzo, so to speak, with requests for them. Did he have any with him here? Could he possibly spare just a few? The best he could offer was to share some seeds next fall if the first crop was successful, which seemed to please and soothe them to some degree.

Finding that he could not get this beautiful girl from his mind, Mateo asked his uncle about her.

"Her name is Luisa. She is the daughter of a neighbor and friend. He and his wife are also guests here tonight. I introduced you to them earlier, Don Francisco and Doña Isabel."

"Why then, Uncle, was *she* not your dinner guest the other night, rather than Inés?" asked Mateo incredulously.

"She is the most coveted girl in the area. Our host wants her for his son and believes she is promised to him, regardless of the truth of it. He is a determined and influential man, not one to be crossed lightly."

"And what about the son?" asked Mateo.

"I do not know. He seems indifferent to the idea, which is incredible to me. I have watched her grow up, and she was always a delightful child. She blossomed into a beautiful girl, which now seems to be to her detriment."

"Uncle, I must rescue this damsel, quite the same as a knight errant in the tales from *Amadis of Gaul*."

His uncle thought this very funny and replied, "Real danger may also exist here. You may have to slay our host with your pike."

"Uncle, could you do me the honor of introducing me to her?"

"Let us attempt it, although it may earn me the wrath of Don Gaspar."

They discretely began to make their way across the room, talking briefly with this couple and then another, looking at the trays of cheeses. As they were approaching the group around Luisa, Mateo saw Luisa was watching them.

When almost there, the host Don Gaspar suddenly stepped in their path and said, "Young Mateo, tonight I have heard no other talk but of your voyage to the Indies. Come, let us stroll over here, sample our fruits, and you can then tell me about it yourself."

"Don Gaspar, you are exceedingly kind, but it really was nothing. However, if you wish to hear of it, I will be happy to gratify you," he said after deciding it would be exceedingly ungrateful if he were not to indulge his host. As Don Gaspar led him away, he noticed the disappointed look on Luisa's face.

For the rest of the evening, Don Gaspar kept Mateo in tow, listening in feigned interest to his stories and taking him to all groups, except Luisa's, to introduce him and hear the stories repeatedly. Seeing further efforts to meet the girl named Luisa this evening would be futile, Mateo thought it best to leave. He was able to signal his uncle and father with subtle gestures suggesting they should go.

Catching his drift, they came over to where Don Gaspar had Mateo. Putting his hand on Don Gaspar's arm, his uncle said, "Forgive us, Don Gaspar, but regrettably we must leave. My wife must have her rest."

Don Lorenzo added, "We thank you again for inviting us, Don Gaspar. We have enjoyed ourselves immensely, and the attention you have paid to my son has been most flattering."

"No, it has been entirely my pleasure, and I am so glad you could come."

After several more "thank-yous" and "goodnights," they left, but not before Mateo was able to cast a quick glance at Luisa who gave him an ever so subtle smile.

On the trip back to their house, the others marveled at the wonderful night and how Mateo had been the center of attention. Mateo, on the other hand, paid little attention to their talk and was thinking of this girl Luisa.

Early the next morning, he saddled his horse with a determined look. Without delay, he was off at a quick pace to visit the estate of Luisa's family. His uncle offered to take him later, but he told his uncle that he wanted to go early before

Don Gaspar had a chance to step in front of him to divert him once more, so to speak. Upon arrival at the main house of Luisa's family, he knocked on the front door. After a short wait, a servant opened it.

"Good morning. I was regrettably unable to meet Señorita Luisa at the dinner party last night and have come to pay her a visit. Please inform her that I am here."

"And who shall I say is calling?"

"El Señor Don Mateo de Cordoba."

The woman nodded as if expecting the name, showed him in, and asked him to please wait. The servant left but returned shortly and led him to a doorway where he saw Luisa sitting in a chair in a quaint sitting room.

Luisa got up to receive him. Now wearing an attractive blouse and long skirt, with her hair pulled back simply, Mateo thought she was just as radiant and beautiful as she was the night before when elegantly dressed. She stood expectantly in silence as he approached. When she raised her hand for the proper greeting, he felt intoxicated.

Barely knowing where he was and forgetting himself, he kissed her hand and said, "Giulietta, at last we meet."

Amused and smiling, she replied, "I take it then that you must be Romeo."

This reply totally surprised him, and he suddenly awakened with a laugh, "So you know the story of Giulietta and Romeo too?"

"Yes, and though it may be pleasant to think of ourselves as Giulietta and Romeo, you must recall they came to a bad end."

He had only admired her from a distance the night before. Now up close, he found her to be more beautiful than ever as well as intelligent and witty. He looked into her eyes and saw warmth and honesty as well as a twinkling of mirth.

Taking both of her hands in his, he told her, "I have dreamed for a good while of finding my own Giulietta and think I finally …"

"Wait," she interrupted, "Before you continue, you sweet boy, you do not know me well enough yet to know that. What do you know about me, other than how I look? We have only admired each other from across the room. Perhaps I am arrogant, selfish, frigid, a terrible nag, or bray like a donkey when I laugh. You know very little of me. You must come to visit me while here. I would like it very much. I am fond of you too. If you still think me Giulietta afterward, then I will know that Romeo's love has credit and is not just a passing fancy."

Surprised and laughing, Mateo said, "Luisa, you astonish me with your beauty as well as intelligence and good sense. I confess that you are right. I act like a silly boy. You must forgive me and allow me to redeem myself in your eyes. I desire very much to visit with you if you will allow me. Perhaps I could come back this afternoon at a more seemly hour."

Before she could answer, Luisa's parents entered, and her father asked, "Luisa? You have a visitor so early?"

Mateo turned around somewhat embarrassed and stood facing them as Luisa replied, "Yes, Father. A new friend."

"Ah, Mateo from the dinner party last night," he said, recognizing him.

"Good morning, Don Francisco and Doña Isabel. How kind of you to remember me. It was indeed my honor and pleasure to meet you both last night."

"It would be hard not to remember you. You seem a fine able young man and back from quite an adventure!"

"I thank you, sir."

"And what brings you here so early, Mateo, my boy."

"I apologize for the early hour but came to finally meet your daughter. I was unable to meet her last night, despite having a keen desire to do so."

"Perhaps then, Luisa, you should invite your new friend to join us for a little breakfast. I confess an ulterior motive of wanting to hear more about his voyage to the Indies," said Don Francisco enthusiastically.

Turning to Mateo with a playful smile, Luisa asked, "Would you do us the honor, kind sir, of breakfasting with us?"

With a little bow and smiling, he replied, "It would give me, fair maiden, the greatest of pleasure."

"Excellent," said Don Francisco.

Looking about and seeing the housekeeper, Doña Isabel told her, "Costanza, we are having a guest for breakfast. I will get the boys up. I know they will want to hear the stories too."

They enjoyed a light but splendid breakfast, and the parents were quite taken with Mateo. Luisa's two younger brothers, Domingo who was twelve and Gabriel who was ten, listened intently as Mateo told about his voyage. They got so animated at one point that Mateo had to calm them down, saying, "Boys, boys, you must remember, such a voyage is not all excitement on the high seas and visits to exotic ports. There are also rats, fleas, smelly ships, cramped quarters, hot sun, bad food, disgruntled men, and lonely separation from loved ones."

"Thank you, Mateo, for saying that," said Doña Isabel with a sigh. "I thought for a moment the boys were going to ride to Seville this very minute and sign up."

Then noting the animated face of her husband, she added, "And their father too."

When leaving afterward, Mateo asked Don Francisco if he might call on his daughter again this afternoon.

"Yes, by all means."

Then deflating a bit, Don Francisco turned to his wife and said, "Isabel, I suppose it means you must arrange for that horrid woman again. We must have a duenna and show respect for our old customs and proprieties."

When back at his uncle's, Mateo told Don Carlos about his visit and his uncle congratulated him.

"Bravo, Mateo. She really is a lovely girl, and her parents are friends with whom we socialize occasionally. I think we shall invite them to dinner tomorrow so they can become friends with your parents."

"That would be very nice, Uncle. I am going back this afternoon again."

"Mateo, I must mention it again that Don Gaspar will not be pleased to hear of your visits. You must watch yourself."

On the way to visit Luisa in the afternoon, two rough looking men stood with their horses by the entrance of her family's estate. When he neared, they stepped into the entrance road to block his way. Mateo stopped his horse in front of them.

"You must be this Mateo fellow who I hear my boss Don Gaspar complain of," said one man in a surly tone. "Your visit to Señorita Luisa upset him, and we do not like to see him upset. I think you should stop. Then he will no longer be upset."

"I will do as I please, now kindly move out of the way."

Eyeing Mateo's belt and saddle, the man said with a grin, "Brave words for an unarmed gentleman." Pulling a knife from his own belt and holding it up in a threatening manner, he warned, "I advise you to reconsider. If not, my knife and I can maybe persuade you, and it would be a shame to get such nice clothes all bloody."

Mateo threw his concealed knife with great speed and force, embedding it deep into the shoulder of the man's knife-wielding arm. He screamed with pain, dropping his knife and looking up in surprise. The other man was equally surprised and backed away when he saw Mateo pull out a second knife.

"Perhaps not," Mateo said firmly. "Now go! Before I become angry and embed a knife in each of your throats."

They backed off with awed looks, mounted their horses, and rode off. As he watched them go, Mateo dismounted, tossed the man's knife in nearby high grass, and then rode on.

On his way up the drive to the main house, he considered whether he should mention the incident to Don Francisco and decided it would be of no value to do so.

He enjoyed himself as he visited with Luisa and her family. They had already installed a duenna. When he and Luisa went for a walk in the garden, she followed at a distance.

"You did not have a duenna here before my visit this morning?" he asked.

"We did have a duenna before. When I was fifteen, Father installed one here to be my chaperone when young men visited. A few young men visited at first but then none. At church, I would see young men glancing my way, but they never came to visit.

After six months, the duenna told Father her services were not needed, so she left. Father could not understand it and asked his friends about it. They told him that Don Gaspar had warned everyone to keep their sons away, because he had an arrangement with Father for me to marry his son. Father denied it and complained to Don Gaspar, but to no avail. So we have, by necessity, been forced to live with it for now, in hopes he would tire of his notion with time."

She paused and added with a smile, "Or that someone would someday come to rescue me. The local young men do not seem to be up to the task."

From the prescribed, respectable distance away, he smiled back at her and said, "It has become my mission in life if you will allow me."

That night at his uncle's house, they got an unexpected visit from Don Gaspar. On entering and hastily greeting Don Carlos and the others, he asked to speak with Don Mateo in private.

When they were alone in the study, Don Gaspar said, "I have heard of the unfortunate incident on the road today and wish to assure you I had nothing to do with it."

"No?" asked Mateo.

"No, of course not," he said, looking sidelong at Mateo. Then he continued, "You see, my young friend, my men, they are so loyal to me that they do such things without my direction, thinking it will please me. They know how it upsets me to see young men paying visits to Señorita Luisa when she is promised to my son. I regret that I must tell you this, but I fear it may be extremely dangerous for you to continue to see her. It would be most unfortunate if something were to happen to you. My men very much want to please me, and I do not know if I can control them always."

"Perhaps your two men today will tell the others what happened, and they will think better of any further attempts at interference."

"Hmm, yes, that knife that we pulled from his shoulder was most interesting," he said, bringing the knife out from inside his coat and examining it.

"Is this also something from the Indies?"

Ignoring the question, Mateo told him, "Luisa is not promised to your son, and I will continue to visit her if it pleases me. It is not me, but you, Don Gaspar, and your men, who are warned. I also have friends, one named Guillermo. Any harm to me would unleash his wrath and vengeance upon you and be your death sentence."

Don Gaspar looked this bold young man over for a moment. Then trying another tack, he said, "Perhaps it is a matter of money. I can pay you whatever sum you want."

Seeing Mateo's icy look in response, he said, "No, I suppose not."

"I remind you again to be warned," said Mateo.

Regarding him with admiration and shaking his head, Don Gaspar said, "God, I wish my son were like you. What we could accomplish! But alas, he is not."

Tossing the knife on a chair, he added, "Nevertheless, *he* will marry Luisa and not you, my young friend. So keep that in mind."

That said, he turned and exited the room. After saying hurried farewells to the others, he left the house. Mateo's father and uncle came in to ask what happened.

"I told him I will continue to visit with Luisa if it pleases me, and he told me his son will marry Luisa, not exactly what one might consider good or proper conversation."

The next evening, Luisa and her parents were invited to dinner at Don Carlos' estate. Mateo's and Luisa's parents got on most amiably and enjoyed a lively, friendly conversation during dinner. Don Lorenzo talked enthusiastically about raising pigs and invited her parents to visit their estate to see the pigs foraging for acorns.

"Lorenzo, for goodness' sake, can you not think of anything but those pigs!" his wife told him with embarrassment, causing everyone to enjoy a laugh at his expense.

After dinner, it was time for the walk in the garden with the duenna following. They walked to the three-tiered fountain in the center, listened to the bubbling of the water, and gazed at the shimmering lights on the water reflected from the nearby lamps. The plants, the decorative tiles, the religious statues, and the stars above added to the romantic setting of the garden.

"It is lovely out here tonight. Not too cool for late November," said Luisa from her proper distance away.

"Yes, it is lovely out here but not as lovely as you, my sweet. I wish I could hold your hand. No, that is not enough. I want to hold you in my arms."

"Goodness, Mateo. You rogue. What would the duenna say if she heard?" she chided him in jest.

"How many times must we perform this ritual? Walking in the garden at a prescribed distance, when I long to hold you and, heaven forbid, even kiss you."

"Shush, she will hear you," said Luisa, looking back at the duenna.

"This is our fourth time together, Luisa. I do not need a fifth or a twentieth. I know you are my Giulietta. I am in love with you and want us to be married. It is not the infatuation of a silly boy. Indeed, I am a man who wishes to carry you away from here and make you happy for the rest of your life."

Luisa looked at him from her proper distance and said, "I, too, am in love with you, Mateo. I admit I have been from the first."

"What!"

"Yes, I only wanted you to be sure. I was just testing you."

"Is this kind of unnecessary testing to be a regular practice after we are married too?" he asked, smiling.

"No, but I must know something before I can truly be sure that you love me."

"What is it, My Sweet?"

"I must know what you think of my nose?"

Mateo laughed and then struggled to control it when the duenna gave him a stern look.

Luisa laughed too and added, "Doña Catalina told me about Inés asking that. How funny!"

As they started walking again, Luisa said, "Yes, Mateo, my Romeo and knight-in-shining-armor, I will marry you. It would make me most happy if you would come to breakfast tomorrow and afterward ask my father for my hand."

At breakfast the next morning, Mateo gazed across the table at Luisa and could not believe his good fortune. As he told the boys more about the Indies, he tried hard to act normal and not disclose to her family that something momentous was about to occur. He had not told his own family either. His uncle seemed to know, but not wanting to ruin the surprise for Mateo's parents, had not mentioned it to them.

After breakfast, Mateo asked Don Francisco if he might speak with him in private. Luisa walked with them to the double doors of his study and when closing them, she said, "Yes, Father, I do."

He looked at her in puzzlement as she closed the doors.

"Most curious," he said as he turned back to Mateo and went to pour a glass of wine.

After a sip, Don Francisco said chuckling, "And now, my boy, what is it you wanted to tell me? Some interesting or gruesome detail of your voyage, which the ladies or the boys should not hear?"

"No, Don Francisco, it is that I am in love with your daughter. She is the girl of whom I have dreamed and for whom

I have searched for some time. I love Luisa deeply and am asking you now most respectfully for her hand."

Her father listened in surprise and finally said, "This is all quite sudden! You have only met! And does she…"

Here, he broke off, first looking mystified, then shaking his head and chuckling.

"The clever girl," he continued. "As always, she is far ahead of me. I was about to ask if she reciprocates your love and wishes to marry you, when I realized she has already told me so, when she was closing the doors."

They both laughed, and then her father spread his arms out. Mateo happily approached and hugged him. "Yes, Mateo, I give you my blessing to marry my Luisa," he said happily, "but you must come to visit us regularly."

"Yes, we will."

"What about your parents? Are they aware of any of this?"

"No, Don Fran…," he started to say. But then stopping to correct himself, he said, "but I should call you Father. No, Father, they will be as surprised as you."

Don Francisco smiled brightly and said, "I am so very glad to hear you call me that. It warms my heart to have my Luisa marry such a fine young man as yourself. If you could only know how I have dreaded the thought of my Luisa married to Don Gaspar's son. He is an idler who cares not a fig for my Luisa. Don Gaspar only wants her for his son because he must have the best of everything to feed his vanity. And once he sets his mind on something, he is not easily deterred from it. For her sake, I have withstood his pressures thus far!"

Don Francisco had become incensed talking about Don Gaspar and his son, but now he calmed down and smiled.

"But thanks be to God, it will not be that idler on the altar with my Luisa. It will be you, Mateo, and I am very pleased."

He hugged Mateo and motioned toward the door, saying, "And now, perhaps we should tell the others."

Ch.10 Trouble

THE DOORS OF THE STUDY opened, and Don Francisco and Mateo appeared, elated and smiling.

When her father saw Luisa waiting outside the study, he declared, "Luisa, my child, you are to be congratulated."

A servant nearby understood at once, gasped, and began giggling and clapping.

Luisa happily came forward, hugged him, and kissed him on the cheek, saying brightly, "Thank you, my wonderful father, I knew you would consent."

"You are always much ahead of me, my child," he said, beaming.

Then pointing to the smiling Mateo beside him, he added, "Do you not think you should also hug your husband-to-be? I will allow it just this once before the wedding."

They hugged, and then a commotion of congratulations and prayers of thanks began. The duenna was now there and sternly motioned for the couple to separate, which they did. Hearing the commotion, Luisa's mother came to investigate.

"What is all the noise I am hearing?" she asked, entering the room.

At seeing his wife, Don Francisco announced happily, "Isabel, my dear, I have consented to the marriage of this fine young man to our Luisa."

She gasped in surprise. Then she happily hurried to hug her daughter. "I suspected something when Mateo asked to speak alone with your father. Your father probably hoped to hear more stories of blood and gore. Thank goodness, he had the good sense to consent!"

Feigning pain, Don Francisco said, "I am wounded, my dear." To his daughter, he said, "Luisa, my child, when you are married, please be kinder to Mateo than your mother is to me."

Luisa's brothers and other servants were coming in now, adding to the congratulations and hubbub. Don Francisco called for a carriage to be brought out. They would go at once to Don Carlos' estate to announce the wonderful news to Mateo's parents. The boys were to stay behind until the adult formalities were out of the way.

When they arrived in front of Don Carlos' main house, they exited the carriage and started for the door when Don Carlos came out laughing.

"Could it be possible? You all look so happy. I sense the heavens are about to open and shower us with blessed news."

"Yes, Carlos, my friend, a veritable thunderstorm of it! We have wonderful news for Mateo's parents. Where are they?"

"His father is inside, and his mother is out back in the flower garden with my Catalina. Let us find them," he replied.

Then patting Mateo enthusiastically on the back, he said, "Congratulations, my boy! Bravo, Mateo. Bravo! You came. You saw. You conquered, as they say!"

Kissing Luisa's hand, he said, "Congratulations, my dear. I know this boy and know you will be very happy."

Kissing her mother's hand in his happiness, he told her, "Isabel, my dear, with your glow of happiness, you appear more like Luisa's sister than her mother."

"Enough of your flattery, Carlos, you devil, let us go inside," she replied with a big smile.

They all merrily started for the door and saw Mateo's father coming out to see what was happening.

Don Carlos called to him happily, "Lorenzo, I think you are about to be very surprised and pleased. But I must allow Francisco to tell you."

Don Lorenzo looked in wonder at the approaching happy group, which included his son and their daughter. He cautiously said, "Francisco, my new friend, I have an inkling of it but dare not hope for such wonderful news. For if your good news is a new colt born in your stables, I will be crushed."

Coming together, Don Francisco stood before him, beaming with happiness, and announced, "Fear not, Lorenzo, my new friend, not only have I had the recent honor of meeting you, but now I also have the honor of informing you that I have consented for your son Mateo to marry my daughter Luisa."

Don Lorenzo looked in astonishment at him and at Mateo. Smiling and nodding, Mateo said, "Yes, Father, it is true."

Speechless and still too shocked to believe it possible, he went to Luisa, took her hand, and kissed it. He felt one of her fingers and then pinched himself.

"Yes, you are quite real, and I am awake, not dreaming. It is all too wonderful to be true," he said, looking up.

Turning and tearfully hugging his son, he had difficulty saying, "Mateo, my son, you have made me very happy."

All were watching and touched. But soon, they were heartily congratulating him, celebrating, and heading him for the door.

Having regained his senses on the way in, Don Lorenzo warned them, "We must be careful telling my wife, Antonia, for she will surely faint. If she sees the whole group together so happy, she may guess and fall to the floor. She may not suspect if she sees only Don Francisco at first. I will have her sit down, and he can then tell her."

"If you think that best, Lorenzo," said Don Francisco, amused.

With the others out of sight and listening in an adjoining room, Don Francisco waited by the door to the patio. Dons Lorenzo and Carlos found their wives outside and brought them in the house. Each of the women carried roses from the hothouse.

When they saw Don Francisco, Doña Catalina said, "Oh, Francisco, I did not expect to find you here. How are you today?"

Coming forward, he kissed her hand and said, "I am well, Catalina, and you look lovely today as always, just like the flowers you carry."

This, of course, pleased her and made her smile. Then turning his attention to Doña Antonia, he kissed her hand and said, "Antonia, it is a great pleasure to see you again. You are also much like the pretty flowers you carry."

Doña Antonia smiled too.

"My, you are high spirited today, Francisco," said Doña Catalina, eyeing him.

Don Lorenzo then interrupted by saying to his wife, "Antonia, my dear, would you please come over to this chair and sit down."

"For what reason, Lorenzo?"

"I have a surprise for you. Believe me, dear. It will be best," he said, leading her over to a chair.

"But I should put these roses in water! Can it not wait?"

"No, dear. Please sit down for your own sake."

"What is it, Lorenzo? This had better not have anything to do with your pigs!" she said as she sat.

"No, dear, it is not about pigs. We have good news to tell you, my dear."

When Doña Catalina saw Don Francisco step forward, she guessed what was happening and gasped, dropping her flowers.

"What is it, Catalina?" asked Doña Antonia, looking over at her in surprise.

Then turning back at Don Francisco, she looked up at him as he announced, "Antonia, I have the distinct pleasure and honor to inform you that I have consented for your son Mateo to marry my daughter Luisa."

After an initial open-mouthed look of shock, her eyes rolled back, and she slumped forward dropping her flowers. Don Lorenzo's attempt to catch her had been too slow and they both tumbled to the floor.

"See, I told you," he said, laughing.

The others rushed in from the adjoining room creating a great uproar of laughter and attention for the passed-out Doña Antonia. As someone ran to bring smelling salts, they were able together to get her back up onto the chair.

A few whiffs of the smelling salts quickly awakened her. Soon, she was tearfully and happily celebrating, and thanking God with the others.

At one point, after admiring Luisa for a time and thinking how beautiful her grandchildren would be, she began to sob into her handkerchief with happiness. Fearing she might require catching again, her husband came over and put his arm around his sobbing wife.

"I thought, Antonia, you would be a little happier about it," said Don Lorenzo in jest.

She waved him away with her handkerchief, which helped her collect herself. She then went to the couple and gave Luisa yet another hug.

"I am sorry for all my blubbering, dear. I am so very happy for you and Mateo."

"I am so glad," said Luisa.

She turned and hugged her son, saying, "All my prayers have been answered, Mateo. She is a dear sweet girl."

"I finally found my Giulietta, Mother," he said, smiling.

"Bah! She is an angel, Mateo. Far better than any Giulietta in your silly books," she said, smiling and rapping him on the chest.

A few moments later, Doña Catalina came to Mateo and told him, "You see, Mateo. I wanted to find you a wife and succeeded after all."

The boys were sent for, and everyone celebrated the glad news over lunch at Don Carlos' house. As wedding plans were discussed, they tried not to think about Don Gaspar who upon hearing of the planned wedding might try to interfere. And he definitely would hear about it, if he had not already.

Church rules required that before the wedding could take place, it must be publicly announced at masses on three Sundays or holy days of obligation in the parish churches of both the bride and groom, which also were the only churches where the wedding could be held. Before agreeing to perform the service, the officiating priest must ensure the participants were in good standing with the church by seeing documentation of their baptism, communion, and confirmation. Original documents would be needed for the purpose, or in cases of great distances, a verified copy would be made for the officiating priest.

They discussed the wedding into the evening. No one wanted a lengthy engagement. Advent season would start soon and last until Christmas Eve. It was four weeks of praying and solemn reflection, fasting six days a week, and meatless Fridays and Saturdays. Advent was hardly a time for a wedding celebration, so the wedding would be held two days after Christmas.

As was normal, the wedding would take place in the bride's church. Mateo must bring his religious documents to the priest here, who would be officiating. Don Francisco would invite many friends. Being the last week of November, sufficient time remained for all the necessary preparations to be completed.

They decided to meet again at Don Francisco's tomorrow for breakfast, when they could talk more about the wedding, as well as get better acquainted. With such sudden happiness and excitement, everyone doubted if they could sleep that night. But there would be much to do tomorrow, so Don Francisco reluctantly took his family home.

An hour after Don Francisco and his family arrived home, the household was still abuzz with news of the wedding plans when Don Gaspar arrived and sternly requested to speak in private with Don Francisco.

Don Francisco greeted him cordially, showed him into his study, and closed the doors.

"It has been reported to me that you plan to marry Luisa to this young man Mateo de Cordoba."

"Reported to you by whom? It has not been announced?"

"How I heard is of no consequence. Is it true?"

"Yes, it is. The announcements should begin in church soon."

"But you cannot do this. She is to be my son's wife. We have an arrangement!"

"No such arrangement exists, Don Gaspar. I think I have made that point clear in the past."

"I will not allow it! I have many gold pieces. I will pay you whatever sum you desire. I must have her for my son!"

"You offer a dowry for your son. Such a thing is most unusual, Don Gaspar."

Slamming the desk with his hand, he said fiercely, "I will *not* allow it! She *will* marry my son!"

Then he stormed out.

At breakfast the next morning, Don Francisco told about Don Gaspar's interview. Mateo wanted to put an end to his meddling by going there and challenging him to a duel if need be. Don Francisco advised against it. He did not think Don Gaspar honorable enough to duel without some treachery involved.

They decided instead to hold the wedding sooner during Advent to minimize the time available for any attempts by Don Gaspar at disruption. They looked at a calendar. If arrangements with their priest could be made speedily, this Sunday, only five days away, could be the first announcement and the following weekend could be the second and third announcements, since that Saturday was a holy day of obligation, the Feast of the Immaculate Conception.

The wedding could then be moved up to the afternoon of the Monday after the third announcement, the tenth of December. Little time remained for the ride to get Mateo's documents from his parish priest, the ride back with the documents to make the arrangements with Luisa's priest here, and a third ride back to Mateo's parish to return his documents and give the wedding announcement to their priest to read at mass on Sunday.

They quickly discussed it and decided to do it. They also decided that the wedding would be "family only," so their friends would not suffer Don Gaspar's wrath and intimidations not to attend. All was settled. Mateo said he would ride at once to get the documents. Don Francisco called to have Mateo's horse readied, and within fifteen minutes, Mateo was galloping off. The trip was a long day of riding, but Mateo was traveling light, so his horse was able to keep up a fast pace and only needed to rest a few times.

Mateo arrived at the family estate late that evening and rode first to the overseer's house. Hearing the gallop of an approaching horse, Guillermo and Miguel came outside to find a tired and dusty Mateo pull up on his wet horse.

"Mateo, you ride hard. What has happened? Why are you back so soon?" asked Guillermo.

"Guillermo, Miguel, I have much to tell. I am going to the main house to clean up and have some food. Guillermo, I need you to ride back with me tomorrow."

"Has something happened? Are your parents well?" asked Miguel anxiously.

"My parents are fine, Miguel. Come to the house, if you would, and I will fill you both in."

"Thanks be to God. You had me worried for a moment that something had happened to them," said Miguel with relief.

With a smile, Mateo replied, "No, Miguel, something has indeed happened, but to me, not to them. I am pleased to inform you that your services advising me about young ladies will no longer be required."

"What! No! Mateo, you are to be married!" exclaimed Guillermo with delight. "I do not believe it!"

"Congratulations, Mateo. I am very pleased to hear it," said Miguel happily.

"But there is some trouble about it. I must see the priest in the morning to get my religious documents and hurry back with them. I need Guillermo to return with me. Come see me at the house," he said as he reined his horse around and rode off.

"We will be there shortly," Guillermo called to him as he and Miguel hurried inside to put on their boots and tell Guillermo's mother the wonderful news.

Ch.11 Trickery

THE NEXT MORNING, Mateo met with his priest and got the necessary documents. Shortly thereafter, he and Guillermo were off. The day before when passing Pascual's camp, Mateo had told one of his men to tell Pascual he could not stop but would be back tomorrow to say hello and give him news.

On the trip back, he and Guillermo stopped briefly. Pascual greeted them warmly as they came into his camp.

"Mateo, Guillermo, welcome. It is good to see you, but you seem troubled and rushed."

"Pascual, it is good indeed to see you as well," said Mateo. "You are perceptive as usual. We are visiting my father's cousin west of Cordoba and a family member is to be married. Ordinarily, a marriage is a happy event and not cause for concern, but a wealthy neighbor wants to prevent the marriage and may create trouble. We are not sure of the assets he can muster, so we may be in need of your assistance."

"It would be my great honor to provide my great friend, Don Lorenzo, with any and all help he may require," declared Pascual, beaming with happiness.

The listening men cheered to second this sentiment.

Guillermo told them, "I offered, but Mateo does not want me to put an arrow in this neighbor and be done with it."

The men laughed, and Pascual said, "Seriously, Mateo, send a rider with a message if assistance is needed, and we will come right away."

"Thank you, Pascual. I knew we could count on you."

"And who is the family member getting married?" asked Sebastian, standing beside Pascual.

Breaking out in a big smile, Mateo said, "He stands before you, my friends. I am to be married."

This set off a wild melee of cheering and congratulations. Pascual embraced him happily. Mateo and Guillermo then had to work their way, laughing and smiling, through the cheering happy crowd to their horses. After mounting, they sat beaming and waving for a moment as the others cheered, before spurring their horses and galloping off.

After leaving Pascual's camp, they rode hard. Guillermo insisted on riding in front, saying that he did not like eating dust. Actually, he was thinking that if Don Gaspar planned an ambush, he wanted to be the first into the fray as well as the first to be targeted. But his precaution proved to be unnecessary.

At dusk, they arrived back at Don Carlos' house where they cleaned up and ate. Word was sent to Don Francisco of their return. Arrangements had been made to meet with the priest at church the next morning.

Although Don Gaspar had caused no trouble during his absence, Mateo had to hold Guillermo back. He was all for an immediate visit to Don Gaspar's estate and a confrontation similar to the one with the abusive husband of Manuel's sister.

The next morning, Guillermo rode with Mateo to Don Francisco's to accompany them to the church for their meeting. Entering the house with Mateo, Guillermo was introduced to Don Francisco and his wife who were as impressed with Guillermo as they had been with Mateo.

When Luisa entered the room to meet him, Guillermo gazed in disbelief at the beautiful girl with the welcoming smile. Then he began to chuckle and shake his head.

"Guillermo," asked Mateo, laughing too, "why are you laughing?"

"Mateo, I am sorry. It is just that so many times in the past I have laughed at you about your romantic silliness and your talk of finding a Giulietta. And now, I find the laugh is on me. You have done it! I cannot imagine a more perfect girl for you, and I congratulate you. Please introduce me."

To Luisa who was amused by these two amiable friends, Mateo said, "La Señorita Luisa Guiterrez, I would like to introduce you to my true friend, el Señor Guillermo Ramos."

Kissing her hand, Guillermo said, "Truly a pleasure. I feel as if I know you already, Giulietta."

"And Giulietta has also heard much about Romeo's true friend," she replied, smiling.

On their way to the parish church to see Luisa's priest Father Benito, the three of them rode on horseback alongside the parents riding in a carriage.

Guillermo had his archery gear along and told Mateo, "I dare anyone to interfere with this wedding and pity anyone foolhardy enough to try. He will pay dearly. Regrettably, we did not have time to bring Mencía with us. Her skill with arrows and knives might also prove useful in our efforts."

Overhearing this as she rode beside them, Luisa gave Mateo a questioning look.

"She is a friend. You will get to meet her," he explained.

The meeting with Father Benito went well, and after examining Mateo's religious documents, he agreed to officiate the wedding on the date set. He wrote a wedding announcement notice for Mateo's priest to read starting on the upcoming Sunday in two days. They came outside and told Guillermo all was arranged.

"Things seem peaceful enough here for now. Let me take your documents and the wedding announcement back to our priest. I will be back soon, perhaps with Mencía," he said.

They agreed, and within minutes, Guillermo was off. Not knowing what plans Don Gaspar might have to interfere, they would be cautious until Guillermo returned, and then decide what added precautions might be warranted.

Late the next evening, Mateo and Luisa happened to be outside when Guillermo and Mencía came riding back. Luisa as well as Mateo looked with amazement at Mencía in her equestrian outfit with a broad-brimmed round black hat. She was a pretty girl who exuded strength and confidence. Even after a long ride, she was quite becoming in her hat, short jacket, vest, blouse, riding pants, and knee-high riding boots.

"This is Mencía? The one good with arrows and knives?" asked Luisa in surprise.

"Yes, she practices with us back home. She is a remarkable girl," Mateo said with a laugh.

"I can see that. Her outfit is quite charming, and I adore her hat (a Cordoba Sombrero like the one worn by Zorro). I have not seen one like it before. I must ask her about it."

Later, Mateo, Guillermo and Mencía met as Luisa listened in. "I think it makes sense for Mencía to stay close to Luisa, posing as a companion," suggested Mateo.

"Should anyone attempt to abduct Luisa, Mencía can perform her 'traveling show knife throwing act' upon them," said Guillermo with a chuckle.

"I do not have a dress with me for posing as a companion," Mencía said, looking at Luisa.

"I have some dresses you could wear," said Luisa, then added, "But, Mateo, is all this really necessary?"

"Only precautions, my dear."

"Mateo, I still say that you should let me put an arrow in the chest of this villain and be done with it!"

"Guillermo, he may be a villain, but he has not done anything yet to deserve your arrow. You must not kill him, but perhaps you should watch him. That is a good activity for you."

"Agreed," said Guillermo.

"Also, Don Francisco thinks Don Gaspar may have spies here on his staff. We should root them out if possible."

"Of what level of violence do we think this Gaspar is capable," asked Guillermo, "and at what point can I just put an arrow in him?"

"Don Francisco tells me that a large number of men work on his estate. They are farm and ranch hands he browbeats regularly. He tries to use the hardest ones for henchmen, but they are not particularly good at it. I met two of them."

"Mateo, what happened?" asked Luisa.

"It is hardly worth mentioning. When they threatened me, I put a knife in one of their shoulders, and they decided to leave."

Luisa gasped, but Mencía and Guillermo beamed.

"Bravo, Mateo. Your training is coming along nicely," said Mencía, chuckling.

Mateo continued, "Gaspar has ties with a local band of highwaymen but his use of them is subtle. It seems unlikely he would come with a bunch of men to carry Luisa away. He is more apt to try to dispose of me somehow, so I will be careful."

"Ah, there it is! That is the answer to my question! If he makes such an attempt, then I will put an arrow in him," declared Guillermo, slapping his hand on the table.

"And mine will be alongside it," added Mencía.

Their plans were rapidly implemented. Mencía kept close to Luisa. Mateo was always watchful and traveled armed with arrows and knives. Guillermo would disappear in the evenings to keep watch on Don Gaspar's estate and not return until early in the morning.

The families attended mass that Sunday, which happened to be Advent Sunday, the first day of the Advent season. They saw Don Gaspar and his son at mass in their special box. He displayed all the appearances of a devout parishioner, praying and reflecting appropriately during the mass, but they noticed him stiffen when Mateo and Luisa's wedding was announced. After mass, he did not condescend to acknowledge their party and left right away without incident.

At night, Guillermo had been watching Don Gaspar's main house, sometimes from a stand of trees near the front and sometimes sneaking silently up close in back. Before long, he discovered a man making regular nightly visits to the house. He was able to get close enough in the dark to recognize him as one of Don Francisco's stablemen, a man named Jorge. The next day, he told Mencía and Mateo about him, and suggested that Mencía watch for a house servant making trips to the stable to pass information to him.

She thought she had seen a maid named Susana lurking around and acting suspicious. Still, a spy had no need to lurk, only to listen to all the chatter of the servants. But when she saw Susana walk furtively out to the stables several times, she followed her and saw her talking to the stableman Jorge. It confirmed what Mencía suspected, and she informed Guillermo and Mateo that the maid Susana was Don Gaspar's spy inside the house.

Guillermo did not notice any other suspicious activity at Don Gaspar's, besides the spying. Thinking it would still be easy for Don Gaspar to have his highwaymen friends ambush and kill Mateo, he recommended Pascual be sent for. As the days passed and the wedding day approached, they could not detect any discernable actions being taken by Don Gaspar.

The next Saturday at the mass for the Holy Day of Obligation, much the same happened as at the first Sunday mass. Don Gaspar paid no attention to them but stiffened more noticeably at the second announcement of the wedding. Dons Carlos and Francisco were not sure what to make of it.

The family attended Sunday mass the next day when the wedding announcement was made for the required third and final time. They all smiled at one another at hearing it. Don Gaspar seemed more irritated this time and glared at several parishioners who smiled at the announcement. He hastened away afterward without saying anything to them.

The families were delighted as they exited church and were greeted by the priest, who told Luisa, "It is done, my child, tomorrow you shall be wed."

That night, they kept a close watch on Don Gaspar's house, and Mencía kept close to Luisa. They saw no activity. Even so, Guillermo made several reports during the night to Mateo at Don Carlos' house.

When they awoke the next morning, the wedding day had finally arrived. Preparations in the morning were underway for a celebration dinner at Don Francisco's after the wedding ceremony in the afternoon. Their one meal-of-the-day on that day during Advent would be a big one, their wedding celebration dinner.

Being a special day, the families made plans to go together to morning mass to pray for a happy long marriage. But when they arrived at church, their wedding and celebration plans were suddenly turned upside down. Father Benito, looking sad and frustrated, came to them with the news that the wedding could not take place after all.

An hour earlier, a young woman had come to see Father Benito and shown him a Holy Sacrament of Matrimony document, saying she and Mateo had been married in a church in Seville two years earlier before he left on his voyage. The wedding could not take place until the matter was cleared up. An inquiry would be sent to the church in Seville to confirm or refute the document's authenticity. The wheels of the church move quite slowly in such matters, and it might take weeks or months to resolve.

"Where is this girl? Is she still here?" asked Mateo.

"No, she left without leaving a way to contact her."

"Surely you do not believe this document is real, Father Benito," said Don Francisco.

"No, I do not, but the matter must be resolved."

Everyone knew that Don Gaspar was behind it and gave no credence to the accusation. Still, the wedding had to be postponed and all were terribly upset and disappointed.

While most went inside to mass, Mateo, Don Francisco, and others remained outside and talked before going in.

"Don Francisco, I cannot imagine that your priest, Father Benito, has any part in this," speculated Mateo.

"No, Mateo. I am quite sure. He has received this false document and must verify or reject its authenticity per church doctrine. Father Benito has been our parish priest for many years. I am sure he is greatly disappointed by this accusation and wishes to clear it up as soon as possible. Luisa has been a favorite of his since a little girl. He would do anything for her."

"If that is the case, I would like to talk with him," replied Mateo deep in thought.

After the morning mass, Mateo, Luisa, and her father met with Father Benito. His first words were to Luisa.

"Luisa, my child," he said, taking her hands in his, "I looked forward so to performing this wedding. It saddens me greatly that it must be delayed."

"I know it is not your fault, Father," she said, patting his hands and melting his heart.

"Father Benito," began Mateo, "I know this document cannot be ignored, although I swear no such wedding took place. You said earlier that it may take weeks or months of correspondence with the church in Seville to resolve this question, but I wonder if there might not be a faster way to resolve it."

"What do you mean, my son?"

"Father, this document is an official church wedding certificate meaning the officiating priest verified all requirements beforehand, just as you recently did for us, is that true?"

"Yes, it is the same certificate I was preparing for your wedding this afternoon when the young woman brought hers."

"If my religious documents were required here for you, then they must have also been required for this supposed wedding. I know no such thing happened. If my parish priest, Father Giraldo, can confirm to you that my religious documents or copies of them have never left my parish during the time of the supposed wedding, then this document cannot be valid."

"Yes, that is true."

"Father Benito, we have a great favor to ask. Luisa and I ask if you will go without delay to my parish, where you can meet with Father Giraldo to verify that fact and confirm no such wedding ever took place. It is indeed a great deal to ask, a day and a half traveling by carriage there and back during Advent season when you are busy."

The elderly priest thought for a moment and looked from one hopeful face to another. Finally with his eyes resting on Luisa, he said, "For you, child, I will do it."

"Thank you so much, Father," she said, kissing his hands and beginning to cry.

"Child, your warm tears are falling on my hands. There is no need for it. Whenever I try to visualize an angel in heaven, your image always comes to mind. I am happy to do it."

Looking at the others who were smiling happily, he continued, "I have a visiting priest here now. He can take over for me for a while. We can leave tomorrow morning if you wish. It will be a nice break for me, now that I think of it."

Back at Don Francisco's, the news created a whirlwind of activity and excitement. The families would be leaving tomorrow with Father Benito to resolve the issue quickly. The staff worked busily to pack trunks and ready carriages for the trip. All the staff including the stablemen knew of the preparations for and intent of the trip. Guillermo had been watching the stableman Jorge, suspecting he would try to slip away at the earliest opportunity to report the news to Don Gaspar. So far, the overseer had been keeping him and the other stablemen busy with preparations for the trip.

As the families talked and thought more about it, they further decided that when the matter of the false document was cleared up at Mateo's parish, the wedding should take place there without delay. This decision added great significance to the trip. When the maid Susana heard, she rushed without her normal caution to the stables to tell the stableman Jorge.

From a window inside the house, Mencía saw her and called out to the others in a nearby room, "Mateo! Guillermo! The maid just ran out to the stables. She must have heard about the wedding plans and is telling the stableman!"

As the three of them dashed out to the stables, Mateo told them with exasperation, "We have been careless! Our families should not have talked so openly about it. We must keep that news from Don Gaspar if we can!"

But the stableman was already gone. When he heard the news from the maid, he had dropped all pretext of working for Don Francisco and jumped on the nearest saddled horse. As he galloped away, the others yelled, "Jorge! Jorge! Where are you going?"

When Guillermo found he was too late to stop him, he told the stablemen to get his horse ready and then went to get his archery gear. He was soon back and galloped off without delay.

Guillermo rode to Don Gaspar's estate and approached the house quietly tying his horse a distance off and stealthily making his way to the nearby stand of trees and tall grass, a location from where he had watched the house during the last several days and nights. He found Sebastian and another of Pascual's men hidden there and watching. Eyeing the house, he spotted a horse tied up in front.

"What have you seen, Sebastian?"

"A man rode up in a great rush and ran into the house. He has been inside about ten minutes."

"He is Don Francisco's stableman who is a spy for Don Gaspar. He just heard that we plan to travel north tomorrow to clear things up and conduct the wedding there. We tried to prevent him from reporting his news but failed. If he had not been so quick, we would have held him a day or two, and then dismissed him. But thanks to this cowardly spy and horse thief, Don Gaspar now knows."

"So what do you think this Don Gaspar will do?"

"He will try to prevent our travel, and bloodshed may result. This man's report has endangered our families, and he may soon regret his treachery and quickness."

"What do you want us to do?" asked Sebastian.

"We will watch for now. Has there been any other activity?"

"No, there have been no preparations of any kind. We heard a bit of laughing and celebrating earlier. Wait! Here he comes from the house. Yes, that is the same man."

Scrutinizing him carefully, Guillermo said, "Yes, that is Jorge, the lowly spy."

Pulling an arrow from his quiver, he told the others, "Get your bows ready. I may stir up a little activity."

The stableman was standing by his horse momentarily as Guillermo stood up and judged the distance to be seventy yards, a long shot. Taking a step forward from the trees, he took aim and let fly with an arrow that whistled through the air and struck the stableman square in the thigh. The man screamed and fell to the ground, writhing in pain.

With a resolute look, Guillermo stepped back to the trees and lay down in the tall grass out of sight.

Ch.12 Wrath of God

THE STABLEMAN, who he paid to spy on Don Francisco, had just left his study, and now Don Gaspar paced back and forth thinking to himself.

"Damnation! I thought that false wedding certificate would buy me much more time! At least a couple months to deal with this Mateo. Now they leave tomorrow for his parish where they will surely be married. I spent a great deal of money to have that document made so quickly. These curates who work for bishops are worse bandits than El Greco! And for what! It has gained me little or nothing! There is little time now. I must think!"

Just then, he heard a scream outside. He stopped and listened intently. He now heard more cries of pain and men shouting. He rushed to the door of his den and flung it open.

"What was that! What is happening?" he shouted.

"I do not know, Don Gaspar. I heard a scream from out front!" said one of his woman servants, pointing and shaking with fright.

Coming out the front door, he saw the stableman lying on the ground rocking back and forth in pain, grasping at his leg which had an arrow in it. The head of the arrow had passed through his thigh and stuck six inches out the back.

"What is this!" yelled Don Gaspar with rage as he looked about angrily, seeing no one.

"How is someone able to do this!" he shouted.

"You, Jorge! Who did this!" he demanded of the wounded man.

"I saw no one, Don Gaspar. I suspect it was the one named Guillermo from Don Francisco's. He is capable of it," said Jorge through gritted teeth.

"Guillermo?" said Don Gaspar with unease, looking about again.

Then looking down, he noticed scratches on the arrow and saw the words "Wrath of God" scratched onto the shaft.

"This Guillermo or someone sends me messages and threatens me at my own house on my own estate!"

By now, several men were gathered around, looking with amazement at the arrow through the man's leg.

"Do not stand there gaping. Carry him away and find a barber or someone to treat him!" he yelled.

Then pointing at one, he commanded, "Juan, ride to the camp of El Greco and tell him I want to see him immediately!"

"Yes, Don Gaspar," he replied, and off he ran.

Don Gaspar had no intention of reporting the matter and facing the possible embarrassment of having spies in Don Francisco's household. He would seek revenge himself.

El Greco, the head of a local band of highwaymen, was called whenever Don Gaspar needed his roughest work performed. An hour later, he was admitted into Don Gaspar's study.

"El Greco, did you hear what happened?"

"Yes, Don Gaspar."

"This Mateo de Cordoba first tries to steal away my son's bride and now this! They plan to leave in the morning. I want some mischief done tonight. If necessary, kill him! He will not marry Luisa. I have chosen her for my son!"

After a pause to consider the request, El Greco replied, "This Mateo and his father are great friends with a man named Pascual, who I have heard of before. Pascual and his men are here unseen. He visited me at my camp two nights ago and has told me that I do not want to get involved."

Don Gaspar slammed his fist down on his desk in anger, gritting his teeth.

"Pascual and his men are a force to be reckoned with, and I have no need to start a quarrel with him. Besides, Don Gaspar, you still have not paid us for our last work for you."

"Get out!" shouted Don Gaspar, standing up in rage.

"As you wish," El Greco said calmly and left.

For a half hour, Don Gaspar paced the floor fuming, trying to think of what he should do next. He poured himself a glass of sherry and guzzled it down in his frustration. Tomorrow, the families would be traveling to their parish, and he must somehow prevent it. El Greco would not help, so he must rely upon his own men. Perhaps, they might pose as men sent by the town's constable to arrest Mateo. They would carry him off, only to have him mysteriously disappear afterward for good. He racked his brain for a better plan, but it was all he could think of. He did not know if his men would be up to the task, yet no other options were left on such short notice.

"Mother of God!" he fumed in frustration, slamming his fist on his desk. "I must get moving. They must be stopped and there is much to prepare."

There was a knock on the door and a servant peered in to say, "Don Gaspar, a maid from Don Francisco's is here and wants to see you."

"Well, what does she want of me!" he shouted.

Pushing her way past, the maid Susana said, "Don Gaspar. I was caught, and they have dismissed me!"

"Well, you clumsy fool! What do you want of me? Get out!" The servant dragged her out as she protested, and the door was closed.

To himself, he vowed, "These people are clever, but I will get my revenge."

He then heard another knock, and his son entered.

"Father, why do you trouble yourself so about this girl? You know I do not wish to marry her."

Looking upward, Don Gaspar exclaimed in exasperation, "God in Heaven, why do you torment me so?"

"Father, I do not wish to marry her! They may go wherever they please to get married. It means nothing to me."

"Upon my cursed soul! Why can you not be half the man as this Mateo! Get out!" screamed Don Gaspar.

The son angrily turned and left the room.

After watching for two hours at Don Gaspar's house, Guillermo returned to update Mateo and the others.

"The stableman beat me there. So Don Gaspar knows all and will probably try to prevent our trip tomorrow. He called for El Greco, but thanks to our friend Pascual, El Greco declined to get involved. El Greco told Pascual that Don Gaspar wanted you killed tonight."

"Hmm, he seems to be fully aroused and determined. We can surely expect something tomorrow," said Mateo.

"Mencía questioned the maid who confessed to being a spy. She was dismissed," Mateo informed him.

"Yes, I saw her there and doubt if she got any sympathy from the good Don."

"The stableman never came back," continued Mateo. "Don Francisco thinks he was paid by Don Gaspar, and that he has left town and will not be coming back."

Guillermo casually replied, "Don Francisco may be correct that he will not be coming back. As to whether Don Gaspar paid him or not, I do not know. I only know that he received my pay."

The next morning, the families were gathered at Don Francisco's and preparing for the trip. Fearing the trip might involve some danger, their two boys were to stay behind with Don Carlos for the time being. Most of the party would ride horses, so they could better respond to any danger encountered. Even Dons Lorenzo and Francisco were armed with pistols in their belts.

After much hustle and bustle, the caravan of three carriages was loaded with baggage and food. When the Doñas and Luisa were helped into the carriages, all was ready. With a wave to the boys and the others, they started out.

The day before, Don Francisco had asked about bringing extra men. Don Lorenzo was listening and was surprised when Mateo replied that an escort had already been arranged.

As they departed the estate, six men rode up to join them. Recognizing them, Don Lorenzo rode to them and said,

"Pascual, my friend. I am glad to see you. So you have come to help protect us. You and your compadres are faithful friends."

"You honor me and my men with your friendship, Don Lorenzo."

After some quick greetings and introductions, they were off again. The caravan arrived in town and quickly picked up Father Benito. With Pascual and his men as well as Guillermo and Mencía in the lead, the caravan rolled out of town.

They had not gone far before they came to a place where the road crossed a wooded creek. As they turned a corner and the crossing came into view, they saw seven men wearing steel helmets and cutlasses. Several held pikes, two held crossbows at the ready, and two others carried pistols stuffed in their belts. They stood in the road with their horses nearby. One looked to be a constable holding up a paper in one hand and his other arm raised demanding they halt.

When these men saw the large contingency of armed men approaching and how many of them suddenly whipped out bows and were already pulling arrows from their quivers, they looked startled. Urgent thoughts began to race through the minds of these men in the road.

"Wait a minute! No one said we would actually have to use these weapons. Don Gaspar said the sight of us in our soldier gear brandishing these weapons would be enough. I have no skills with these things. For God's sake! I am just a farmhand! This is more than I bargained for or signed up to do!"

The constable nervously continued to demand that they stop. But when several arrows landed at their feet, he and his armed assistants threw down their pikes, crossbows, and paper. They rushed to their horses with pistols still in belts and frantically mounted their nervous horses and rode off.

When the caravan pulled up at the creek crossing, Pascual looked around at the others, laughing. One of his men picked up the paper and gave it to him. He looked at it and laughed.

"It appears to be some kind of proclamation," said Pascual, passing it to Guillermo.

Reading it quickly, Guillermo waved it in the air and said laughing, "Mateo! It is a warrant for your arrest! But they seemed to have lost their nerve to serve it. I am guessing they were imposters like this warrant, a game of our friend Don Gaspar. And not very well played either!"

Stopping suddenly to listen, Guillermo rode up next to Mateo on his horse. Handing him the warrant, he said, "Mateo, keep going. We will catch up with you."

He motioned to Sebastian and Mencía to stay, and the three of them watched as the caravan rolled away. Then they abruptly reined their horses around and raced into the woods along the creek. There they found Don Gaspar with two frightened men who dropped their crossbows and ran off, abandoning him.

They leaped from their horses, and Guillermo approached Don Gaspar. A large man, he stood erect and defiant.

"Who do you think you are, Youngster! Do you know who I am!"

"Yes, you are Don Gaspar. I was hoping to run into you for I have a message for you."

"How dare you! I am not interested in any message from you! Whoever you are!"

Guillermo leaped forward clouting Don Gaspar in the face several times and knocking him down. Looming over him angrily, Guillermo pressed his knife close under his chin.

"My name is Guillermo, and my message is this! If you ever bother the families of Don Francisco and Don Carlos again or set even one toe on their estates, I will put an arrow in you! Just like that cowardly spy of yours! Only yours will be in the chest!"

He jabbed the knife firmly against his throat drawing blood and causing Don Gaspar to jerk back wide-eyed in pain.

"You can believe it," warned Guillermo, getting up.

And with that, he, Mencía, and Sebastian jumped back on their horses and rode off. Spitting blood from his mouth and feeling his bloody neck, Don Gaspar sat up, heaved a great sigh, and resignedly eyed them as they left.

No further problems were encountered on their trip. After many hours of travel the first day, they stopped at an inn to spend the night. Being cold at night this time of the year, they found rooms inside for everyone. Spirits were high as they all supped together on the best food and drink the inn could offer. Considering the danger from Don Gaspar over, Pascual planned to leave early the next morning with his men. Don Lorenzo hugged him in thanks.

Father Benito felt more than a little jostled after a day of bouncing along in the carriage on the sometimes-rough roads. However, he was in good spirits the next morning, having been revived by a meal, wine, and some sleep. When they awoke, Pascual and his men were already gone. The caravan set out without delay and arrived at Don Lorenzo's estate at midday.

After some refreshments and a short rest, Father Benito took the marriage document in question with him to meet with the local priest, Father Giraldo.

Two weeks earlier, Father Giraldo had rejoiced and given thanks to God when Mateo had requested his documents for the planned wedding. Knowing the importance of the marriage and how happy the family must be, he gladly made the prescribed announcements during the three church masses. The news had caused a great stir of happiness within the parish.

Now believing the wedding had already taken place, he was surprised when Father Benito arrived and informed him it had not. He read and scoffed at the wedding document in question which he knew to be false.

He knew the marriage could not be a legal marriage since he had never been asked for Mateo's baptism, communion or confirmation documents or verified copies of them. They were church documents kept at the parish. Records were annotated if the documents were temporarily removed or copied. He already knew no such thing had happened before, but for completeness, they both looked at his records that confirmed it. The marriage document was declared to be false, annotated to that effect, and the wedding of Mateo and Luisa was approved to take place.

When the families back at the estate got word that the marriage document was officially determined to be fraudulent, they celebrated and began discussing plans for an immediate wedding. All agreed on a wedding ceremony with full mass as were the wishes of the two mothers. Since the ceremony would take place in Father Giraldo's church, it made sense for him to perform it, and Father Benito would assist.

When they asked Father Giraldo to perform it, he replied, "I cannot tell you how many times I have prayed with Doña Antonia for this event. I have also prayed that I would live long enough to someday perform it. Yes, I will do it, of course."

With all documents checked and the required three announcements already made, the ceremony would take place the next day at three o'clock. Being a weekday during Advent, they would be fasting until the celebration dinner that evening after the wedding. Their one meal of the day would probably last late into the night. Doña Antonia rationalized their transgression by saying that if God had gone to so much trouble to make the wedding possible, then he would not begrudge them one big meal during Advent.

At the assigned time in the afternoon, all the participants were in their places. Mateo and Luisa stood before the altar facing Father Giraldo with Father Benito beside him. Guillermo and Mencía were also invited in thanks for their efforts. They stood over on the side ever watchful. The parents were in the first row of pews. All were in place, and the ceremony began.

Father Giraldo had not gotten far into it, when someone quietly entered the front door of the church, which was located at the back of the ceremony. Father Giraldo was reading aloud and did not notice, but Father Benito saw the newcomer, recognized him, and looked surprised.

Guillermo and Mencía noticed him too. They recognized him and faced around poised for action. He seemed to be alone and making no threatening moves. Scanning around, they did not see anyone else.

Father Giraldo looked up, saw the man, and stopped reading. The ceremony was now completely disrupted, and everyone turned to look. Seeing the young man, Don Francisco said with surprise, "Don Luis? What a surprise! What are you doing here?"

Don Luis, the son of Don Gaspar, replied, "Don Francisco, I am sorry to interrupt, but I came to wish you well. I am genuinely happy for Luisa and want you to know I had nothing to do with my father's years of scheming and bullying."

Don Francisco, his wife, and daughter all went to welcome their surprise well-wisher with Don Francisco saying, "Come in, Luis, my boy, and join us. I tell you honestly that we never suspected you of being behind it. It is good of you to come."

Meanwhile, Don Lorenzo and his family held back a moment, not sure what to make of it. But seeing the apparent sincerity of the youth, they walked back to greet him too.

Don Francisco and his family welcomed the young man happily, shaking hands, and hugging. Luisa gave him a kiss on the cheek, which made Luis blush.

She told him, "Luis, I am sorry I did not pay more attention to you. I never thought you bad, perhaps just shy."

"Luisa, I have always thought you were the most beautiful girl in the entire world, much too good for me. I was unworthy of such a prize as you. And besides, we would be Luis and Luisa, how ridiculous!"

At this, they laughed and hugged again. By now, Don Lorenzo and his family had come back and were welcoming him warmly as well. Guillermo and Mencía greeted him too and began to relax, believing no trick was intended.

After the happy introductions and greetings, Don Francisco said, "Let us all go back and start the ceremony again. Luis, you may sit with us."

Ch.13 Happiness

WHEN THE WEDDING PARTY emerged from the church, the light rain outside did little to dampen their spirits. They hurried out and bustled into the covered carriages which were waiting outside. Guillermo and Mencía stood by the church door sheltered from the rain and watched. Having ridden their horses, they would wait a few minutes to see if the rain would let up.

They were both smiling as Mencía said, "The estate is about to be a scene of great happiness and celebration."

"Even so, the real celebrating must await the end of Advent," replied Guillermo.

"This son of Don Gaspar seems a good sort after all. He is obviously not part of some new mischief. No villainous plotter blushes in embarrassment at a kiss on the cheek as he did."

"I agree," said Guillermo with a laugh. "He may be a good sort after all."

"When I saw him in back, he did not appear threatening. I thought him possibly a diversion, but it proved not to be the case. It is sad to think we felt a need to be on guard inside a church, a holy place," noted Mencía.

"Yes, but a holy place where someone takes a bribe and produces a false wedding document on short notice. I was thinking of it on the ride back."

"All has turned out well, Guillermo. There is no need to stew over that point. Every barrel has its bad apples."

Looking at the sky and holding her hand out beyond their shelter, she added, "The rain seems to be letting up. Let us get the horses and catch up with them."

Nodding his agreement, Guillermo pulled his coat up closer around his neck, and they hurried off.

When the weather cleared up in the afternoon, the families of the estate as well as neighbors and friends became a steady stream of visitors to the main house to wish the newly married couple well.

Luis had come from the church with them in the carriages. Walking about smiling and talking with others at Don Lorenzo's house, he appeared as happy as everyone else at the marriage of Luisa. Before, Luis had never been interested in or interesting to Luisa, but now, he seemed a new person. He told her of his interest in another young girl, better suited for him, and of his hopes that he may now pursue that interest.

He told how his father had returned from the creek after the incident much deflated. Luis had heard from the others what happened and found his father sitting in his chair in his study. For the first time in his life, he had shouted at his father.

"Father, I heard how you were put in your place at the creek. I am glad! You deserved every bit of it!"

His father had started to rise from his chair in anger, but Luis had shoved him back down shouting, "I am not finished! I told you all along I did not want to marry her. You would not listen and now look what it got you. From now on, do not meddle concerning my marriage. You have done quite enough! It is time you start letting me do things here on the estate too!"

Don Gaspar had sat staring at him and finally said, "Perhaps, Luis, perhaps. I am feeling suddenly old. Please let me be for a while. We can talk about it at dinner."

"I will not be at dinner tonight. I am going to visit friends and will be back in several days. We can talk about it then," Luis had told him.

Don Gaspar had stared at his son again and replied, "Very well, son. I will see you when you return."

Ending his story, Luis said, "I left and then came here to wish you well."

"Bravo, Luis!" said Mateo, "Your father respects strength. Keep it up. If he ever tries to bully you again, give it right back to him. He will respect you for it."

"Yes, well done, Luis!" agreed Guillermo.

"I have you all to thank," Luis told them. "You brought him down a peg to where I may be able to deal with him."

Then looking about, he said, "Perhaps I should start back. I look forward to returning home for a change."

"Will you not stay for dinner?" asked Luisa.

"No but thank you for inviting me. I have intruded enough and should be going."

Standing, they all shook hands and wished him well. He went to thank the parents for their kindness and let them know he must be leaving. They came outside with him to see him off. One of the stablemen had already retrieved his horse from town and had it there waiting for him. After many farewells and good wishes, they all watched as Luis mounted, waved, and rode away.

Mencía went home after dinner and returned the next afternoon with her parents and sisters to add their congratulations. Her parents laughed together with Mateo's parents at the now apparent absurdity of their failed attempt to match Mateo and Mencía.

Her parents had no idea what to make of their daughter but were happy to see Mateo had found a lovely bride for himself. They marveled and smiled with pride when they heard how Mencía had protected Luisa during the struggle with the hostile neighbor.

All that Sunday after mass, the main house was a continual scene of visitors. Even Pascual, his men from the recent trip, and their women came to wish them well. Don Lorenzo had sent him a beef cow the day before in thanks for their friendship and assistance. The house staff were continually busy preparing and serving snacks, pastries, and drinks to the many visitors that day. They had already decorated the house with flowers from the hothouse as well as a multitude of nativity scenes for Christmas.

Father Benito had been an honored guest at their estate since his arrival. All greatly appreciated his important role in making the wedding happen and showed him much attention. He was taken to the oak meadows to see the black pigs rooting around for acorns and was amused by Don Lorenzo's enthusiasm for them. He got along very well with Father Giraldo and assisted him at mass that Sunday. Father Giraldo had come to visit him several times that week, and they would visit for hours, sipping wine as they sat contentedly near a warm fire in Don Lorenzo's study.

Father Benito enjoyed his stay very much and would have gladly stayed longer, but he needed to return to his parish. By leaving on Monday, he would miss only one Sunday during Advent. Guillermo and Mencía would accompany his carriage back. On the return trip, they would bring back Luisa's brothers and Don Carlos and Doña Catalina.

As he readied to leave on Monday morning, everyone came out to thank him again and wish him a good journey back. He had never felt more gratified as when this beautiful little girl, now grown up, tearfully thanked him for all he had done. Much moved, he climbed into the carriage and waved to the crowd as he left.

In four days, Guillermo and Mencía returned with Don Carlos, Doña Catalina, and the boys. Now they were all together again in time for the customary family dinner on Christmas Eve, only four days away.

Christmas in Andalusia is a holy day of obligation, a time for prayer, not a time for festive celebration and gift giving. The only gift giving during this time is to children at Little Christmas, in early January, which is meant to replicate the three wise men arriving later at the stable and giving gifts to the baby Jesus. With no more little children of their own, Don Lorenzo and Doña Antonia gave gifts instead to the children of families on the estate, ones like Pedrito, the son of Pedro and Juana.

Christmas Eve marked the end of Advent Season, which by itself, was cause for thanks after weeks of fasting. It was a night to gather for a family dinner. A cured ham leg was the traditional highlight of the meal. The ham was, in fact, the entire leg, including the hoof, of one of their prized black pigs, which had cured for three years. For such a large gathering, several hams would be needed. Beforehand in the curing room, they had performed their little ceremony of taking a small sample of each with their bone tool to ensure the ham meat underneath the outside hide was good and not spoiled as sometimes happened.

This year, the Christmas Eve dinner would be special. Their cousins as well as the families of Luisa, Mencía, and Guillermo were attending. Father Giraldo, their neighbor Don Felipe, Don Tomás, and several other friends from town were also invited.

Father Giraldo led off the night with a solemn prayer before the meal. Next, the dinner courses began as everyone talked about the many recent events. Don Francisco told how one of his stablemen had spied for Don Gaspar. When he said the man was probably generously rewarded for his treachery and had gotten away unscathed, Guillermo and Mateo did not correct him.

After hours of wine drinking and various appetizer courses, it was time for the highlight of the meal. With great show and anticipation, the cured hams were brought out for carving. Don Lorenzo had the honor of carefully cutting the first thin slices of the delectable meat from the leg. The cured but uncooked meat was cut transparently thin, so it melted in the mouth. Everyone raved about the ham this year as usual. With all the wine served and the recent wedding, the evening was more festive than usual. The other families on the estate were at the same time having their own family dinners as well with hams cured in their own attics.

Mencía's sister Margarita had brought her guiterna, which they asked her to bring out after dinner. Everyone came to look at its intricate carvings and four double pairs of strings. They all stood back in great anticipation as she readied her quill to begin playing. With her sister Cristina beside her, she played a short pretty tune to the hushed crowd. Then nodding to Cristina, they began to sing together as she played. Their audience was astonished with their beautiful rendition of two Christmas carols of the day. Their mother and father beamed with pride as they watched. When they finished and curtsied, everyone rushed forward gushing with compliments. They had never heard anything so beautiful. They swore they had heard angels in heaven. Father Giraldo was overwhelmed by their performance and asked if they might perform during their parish's holy week celebrations in the spring. Even Don Lorenzo called it the highlight of the dinner, more so than his cured ham, which was much for him to concede.

The next day, everyone attended Christmas mass. With much to be thankful for, many prayers of thanks were offered.

The wedding celebration for the estate's families as well as neighbors and friends took place two days after Christmas. The day was sunny although a little cool, but no one noticed. The celebration lasted from early afternoon late into the evening. Mateo and Luisa made a point of greeting and talking with all the attendees, thanking them for attending and for the well wishes. Seeing the handsome couple, attendees commented amongst themselves how beautiful their children will be and speculated when a new heir might arrive.

Mencía's sisters played and sang at the celebration. Their performance was a most uncommonly beautiful thing to hear for the simple, hardworking religious people of the estate and caused quite a sensation. Juana and other women began to cry as they listened, thinking they had been granted a rare glimpse of heaven. They went to the girls afterward and kissed their hands as if they were holy objects.

The day after the wedding celebration, Luisa's parents thought that after their two-week stay, the time had arrived for their return home. But before leaving, Don Lorenzo had to take Don Francisco and Don Carlos out for a last visit to the black pigs eating acorns under the oaks. As they walked out to a nearby meadow, Don Francisco commented on the large acreage of the estate and how fine the grounds looked.

Don Lorenzo replied, "Yes, it is a fine piece of land. It looks best this time of the year when everything is green from the rains. We are indeed fortunate. King Ferdinand III granted the estate to my family several years after the reconquest of Cordoba, about 350 years ago. Back then, a knight named Gonzalvo was one of the besiegers in front of the city walls of Cordoba which the Moors were defending. Gonzalvo was one of the knights who scaled a tower during a rainstorm, leading soldiers inside the walls and capturing a large part of the city. Their rapid success surprised the king who came quickly. He was able to celebrate the successful reconquest of the entire city only a few months later.

"Two years afterward, as I said, the king granted land to those prominent in the battle in appreciation of their services, including the knight Gonzalvo, who is my great, great, great, et cetera, et cetera, grandfather. When taking possession of the land, Gonzalvo changed his last name to 'de Cordoba' to reflect his new roots in this province of Cordoba. We owe it all to him. His descendants have been serving the king ever since and many generations of my family were born, lived, and died on this land."

"What a fine family history. Most remarkable, Lorenzo. You have a right to be proud of it."

"Yes, I suppose so. My family has quite a long history on this land," mused Don Lorenzo.

Don Carlos chimed in, "So you can imagine how concerned Lorenzo and Antonia are for the continuation of that history."

"Yes, I can see it," agreed Don Francisco.

"When Mateo came back safely from his voyage and stopped to see us," said Don Carlos, "my poor Catalina feared that he might not be as fortunate on a next voyage."

He added thoughtfully, "While in the Indies, he had looked for our sons without success. God only knows where they are or if they are still alive. My Catalina was determined to have Mateo married, so that the family line here might continue, sparing Lorenzo and Antonia from the uncertainty we feel."

"It was most kind of her to be so concerned. We can only pray that God shall someday return your sons," said Don Lorenzo with sympathy.

"As to the continuation of things here, there is new hope, Francisco, thanks to your lovely daughter marrying my son," he said, putting a hand on his shoulder.

Then looking up with excitement, Don Lorenzo pointed and exclaimed, "I see a group of pigs, there under those oaks."

They walked up to them and stood watching as the pigs ate and ignored them. Don Lorenzo was greatly pleased and smiling as he watched the pigs rooting around through the grass and chomping on the acorns.

"Look at how they feed," he said happily. "We are enjoying an excellent crop of acorns this year with all the rains. You would not believe how much fatter they will become before February when the acorn season ends. Then it becomes time to harvest a select number of the young fat ones during the Matanza, the slaughter. It is regrettable that you will not be here to see it. It is quite an event with much tradition involved. I am sure it differs in the various areas of Spain."

"Your hills here with your oaks and pigs are quite different from our valley," mused Don Francisco, "where we grow grains, which our rains support."

"Francisco, I am amazed each and every time I think about it," said Don Lorenzo mystified. "Wheat has been raised on your land for thirteen or fourteen centuries, from back when the Romans ruled here, and the Guadalquivir valley was an important breadbasket for Rome."

"Quite true, Lorenzo. It is hard to imagine that my soil has been producing wheat continuously for well over a thousand years, watered only by our rains."

"Even so," interjected Don Carlos, "remnants of the irrigation system built centuries ago by the Moors are still usable in our area, so Francisco and I are fortunate to also have a supply of irrigation water as well. The water from the ditches supports some measure of irrigated crops or orchards. Upon my irrigated land, I will attempt next spring to grow the peppers and other new plants from the Indies."

"I grow various garden crops as well as fruits and citrus from trees on my irrigated land," said Don Francisco.

"I remember your tasty orange juice, Francisco. If things work out, you shall have some seeds from the Indies as well."

"I will be watching Carlos' efforts with interest," replied Don Francisco.

"But, alas, you will soon be returning home and will regrettably miss our Matanza."

"Yes, but I have seen the Matanza before when visiting friends in the hills above the valley. I found it quite interesting."

"Quite so," began Don Lorenzo. "The Matanza is a time-honored event involving much work for the entire estate. Each of our families gets one of the hams to keep and cure for their Christmas dinner.

"A large wooden table is the traditional place for the butchering. The fattened pig is hoisted up and laid on his side on it. This, of course, gets the pig much excited, which is bad for the flavor of the meat. So the men gently stroke, massage, and say soothing things to it until it is calm again. Then they make a quick cut on his throat with a very sharp knife as they continue their soothing massage. The pig hardly notices the cut. In less than a minute, it calmly dies as the blood drains from it and is collected.

"As I tell you this, it suddenly occurs to me that we, here in Spain, treat our pigs far better than we treat our bulls. But that is an aside. Once the pig is dead, the important hams are set aside for curing, but every part of the pig is saved and used in some way. The sausage-making from the intestines, meat, and blood involves a great deal of work for our women.

"And of course, such an event would not be one of our traditions without being blessed by our church. We take the first carcass into town where it is blessed by our priest and given to the townspeople."

"The Matanza is done similarly in our nearby mountains," replied Don Francisco. "These pigs are important to us Spaniards.

It is good that such traditions show respect for them. They are important not only to our dinner tables but also to our religion."

"How true," said Don Carlos. "If our Moorish and Jewish converts refuse to eat pork, then they reveal themselves not to be true converts to Christianity, which can turn out very badly for them with our inquisition officials."

"I have no great interest for such things," said Don Lorenzo, shaking his head. "My interest lies in the delicious, sweet taste of the hams and the money to be made from them. Such is my interest. We butcher a sizable number of the pigs each year and sell many of the hams to merchants who come to buy them. It is quite lucrative."

Pointing out across the oak meadows, he continued, "Over generations, we have enclosed and divided our property with stone fences to keep in our pigs and cattle. We maintain the trees, but the animals maintain the meadows themselves by eating new oak trees, brush, and other vegetation under the established trees. It really is a beneficial arrangement and a good life they provide for us here."

"Yes, I see it is so," said Don Francisco, looking out across the oak meadows.

With emotion, he added, "And now my Luisa as well as all the future generations of their children have become part of that good life. I am incredibly happy for us, my dear friend Lorenzo."

The next day after heartfelt and emotional "goodbyes," Don Francisco, Don Carlos, and their families climbed into their carriages and left to return home. When bidding them farewell, Luisa and Mateo promised to visit them soon.

Over the next weeks, Mateo and Luisa got themselves situated in one wing of the main house, which became their own. Guillermo and Mencía visited them often as they became accustomed to their new married life. The three true friends continued to practice weapons skills and Luisa joined them in archery practice but only watched them in amazement when they practiced their knife throwing.

One day while talking in a sitting room, Luisa saw the hat on a chair and asked, "Mencía, I have meant to ask you about your hat. I noticed it the very first time I saw you and have not seen another like it. It looks wonderful on you. Where did you get it?"

"Try it on, Luisa. We will see how it fits you," said Mencía, handing it to her.

Luisa took the hat and paused a moment to admire the smooth black felt material and the lighter black hat band. She tried it on, and Mencía handed her a small hand mirror.

"I think it looks very charming on you, Luisa. We seem to be the same size. I will have another one made for you."

"Mencía, you have no need to do that, but I do admire it very much. You still have not told me where you got it."

"In my area, field hands wear a straw hat with a wide round stiff brim. I wanted a riding hat in that style, so I took one of the straw hats to a hat maker in Cordoba and asked him to make one like it, only in smooth black felt. He was very intrigued with the idea and was so happy with the resulting hat that he did not charge me for it. He kept saying how fashionable it was and how wonderful it looked on me. He planned to make one for display in his window and was certain it would become popular."

"I agree."

"It is very suitable for riding with the leather strings tightened snugly under the chin to keep it on. The wide stiff brim protects from the sun. If shade is not needed, I let it fall onto my back, and the strings around my neck hold it on. I will get one for you as your wedding gift."

"Let us surprise Mateo and Guillermo with ones too. They could use new hats, and I suspect they might look quite dashing in them."

When beginning a new life with new family on a new estate, one expects that adjustments will be necessary. Luisa did not expect to have difficulties in doing so, but she was surprised to find that she was instantly the most precious and adored person on the estate. The Don and Doña treasured Luisa because she made their son so happy and for being the future mother of all their hopes, dreams, and prayers. All the families on the estate also showed her their undying love for similar reasons. They enjoyed a good life on the estate as their parents before them had. Luisa represented the continuation of that good life for themselves, their children, and their children's children. She had to jokingly tell them to please stop treating her like a queen.

As January passed, Don Lorenzo happily watched the pigs continuing to feed and fatten in the meadows. All looked well for a good harvest of pigs in mid-to late-February. But beforehand would come Miguel's favorite time of the year.

At the end of January, little pink buds began to form on the almond trees. They soon puffed into blossoms with white petals showing just a tinge of pink. Miguel gazed with great satisfaction upon the trees covered with pretty blossoms. Luisa liked to walk about and admire them as well. She told Miguel how much she enjoyed them, which pleased him a great deal.

He was gratified to see a great many honeybees buzzing from blossom to blossom. A scattering of one variety of the almond trees was planted for pollinating the other main variety. Miguel was always amazed how the honeybees seemed to appear from nowhere every year during blossom time to pollinate the trees. He could only attribute it to God and said prayers of thanks.

After two weeks, blossom time was over, and a thin layer of the white blossom petals covered the ground. With his favorite time of the year over, Miguel told himself that the blossoms had been pretty while they lasted and would be back next year. The many blossoms and the pleasant weather for the bees boded well for a bountiful crop of almonds in the fall.

Miguel now shifted his attention elsewhere. The time had come to prepare in earnest for the Matanza, the slaughtering of the pigs. Don Lorenzo was getting excited about it when an unexpected announcement suddenly diverted his attention, at least temporarily.

Luisa announced she was with child, which caused a huge outpouring of happiness and good wishes from everyone. Her monthly time was several weeks overdue, and she was sure of the reason. The Don, Doña, and Mateo were ecstatic. Everyone was talking about it and saying prayers for it to be true.

Although mid-February was not the best time for traveling, Luisa desired to see her parents and share the good news with them. Doña Antonia was concerned about her riding horses, so Mateo and Luisa would instead travel in a carriage, leaving in a day or two.

Once there, Luisa's parents would want to throw a large wedding celebration for their friends and neighbors, one which normally would have taken place right after the wedding, but due to events, had to be postponed until the newlyweds came to visit. Mateo's parents also planned to attend but must travel separately later. Don Lorenzo was a key participant in their Matanza ceremonies and could not possibly leave beforehand.

Don Lorenzo told Luisa, "I fully understand you wanting to go right away to share your wonderful news, my dear. It is just a shame you will miss our traditional slaughtering of the pigs."

Hearing this and waving for him to go, his wife told him, "Lorenzo, *please.* If you must stroke your pigs, please go do it, and do not bother us with it!"

Luisa and Mateo had to stifle a laugh at this exchange, and then Mateo called to his abused father, "Father, I will come with you. We will check preparations together. It seems that Mother does not appreciate our time-honored traditions."

"I should say not. It seems that she esteems my pigs only after curing for three years, and not a moment before!" he said with a peeved look in his wife's direction.

Then they both marched out.

Ch.14 Curate

GUILLERMO WOULD ordinarily have offered at once to accompany Mateo on his trip, but he knew the time spent there at Luisa's parents would be wedding celebrations and much attention to the couple. He did not want to distract Mateo from those activities and duties. However, as he thought more about it, he increasingly felt as if he had unfinished business there. Guillermo wondered if he should tell Mateo that something has been bothering him for the last two months. He had not mentioned it to him before, but now the subject was starting to annoy him.

"Mateo, I wonder if Mencía and I might accompany you and Luisa. I want to look into something there."

"Uh-oh, Guillermo, what are you thinking? I know you. I hope you do not have more plans for Don Gaspar. Someone dropped a letter off last week from Luisa's parents and they had no complaints about him. In fact, they have not heard a peep from him. He seems to have received your message and requires no further punishment."

"No, I was not thinking of him, but something from that whole episode has been bothering me. It is that false wedding document."

"What?"

"The false wedding document that was thrown in your face the morning of your planned wedding. A church official with access to such a document must have produced it. Some supposed holy man is not as holy as he ought to be. I have an urge to find this fraud and teach him a lesson, put the fear of God back into him, so to speak."

"I hope you do not mean an arrow in the chest, Guillermo. God will punish this dishonest church official in the end, but there is no need to hasten his end."

"I do not go with that intent, but this document has been nagging at me. What did Luis know about it?"

"He said he heard his father fuming several times about paying a lot of money to a curate of the bishop."

"Did he hear a name?"

"No, but Don Gaspar was able to get the document quickly, so it must have been the bishop of Cordoba. Seville is too far away. The dishonest curate either must be with the bishop in Cordoba or assigned by the bishop to a nearby parish. There might be a number of curates so assigned."

"I desire to go there and nose around a little to see if I can find this wayward curate. Mencía can come along to help too. I think we should not bother Luis or his father anymore about it. Would you mind a little company on your trip?"

"No, join us, by all means, but I do not think I can be of any help in your efforts. Whether I wish it or not, Luisa and I will be the center of attention there and occupied with family activities."

"As you should be, Mateo. As I said, Mencía and I will nose around and see what we can find."

"We leave tomorrow early," said Mateo.

"We will be ready."

Two days later, Mateo pulled their carriage to a stop in front of the house of Luisa's parents. The housekeeper opened the door, saw them, and rushed back inside with excitement. Luisa's father, mother, and brothers soon rushed out happily to welcome them.

"What an unexpected, wonderful surprise! My sweet girl and handsome son, it is so good to see you both again," exclaimed her father jubilantly.

Then in jest, he declared, "What? Are they tired of you there already? Good! You must live here with us!"

As Luisa climbed from the carriage, Doña Isabel hugged her happily and said, "We did not expect you so soon but are so happy you have come. Luisa, dear, you look wonderful. You glow."

Then she suddenly gasped at her sudden realization.

"Isabel? What is it?" asked Don Francisco in confusion.

Luisa smiling, nodded to her mother, who then hugged her as she wept with happiness.

"What is it? What am I missing?" asked Don Francisco, looking about in confusion.

"We came to tell you the good news that Luisa is with child," Mateo told him.

Instantly beaming with happiness, he hugged Mateo saying, "Wonderful news, yes, wonderful news!" Then hugging his daughter and, looking over at his wife, he added, "These women! How can they always sense these things?"

Guillermo and Mencía were holding their horses on the other side of the carriage, watching and not wanting to interfere. Don Francisco happily welcomed them as well, then saying they all should go inside.

A short time later, Mateo's uncle and aunt arrived. Mateo and Luisa's happy news was almost more than Doña Catalina could bear. She swelled with pride at the thought that all this joy had resulted from her invitation and attempt to match Mateo to the girl Inés.

The news of Luisa's return spread quickly on the estate, and its families began coming in to congratulate her on her marriage. With the news that she was also with child, they were doubly happy for her.

Doña Isabel began making plans at once for the local wedding celebration and rapidly fixed its date on an upcoming Saturday in ten days. Luisa being with child was happy news to be shared but not the cause for celebration. It was too soon and perhaps bad luck to celebrate a baby not yet born.

Amid the hubbub, Don Francisco told Guillermo and Mencía how pleased he was to see them again. He insisted they stay with them.

"Thank you, Don Francisco. That is very kind of you."

"Nonsense, Guillermo. We owe you and Mencía much. You may stay here anytime for as long as you desire."

"You do not owe us anything, but I do have a favor to ask," replied Guillermo. "Would you mind greatly, Don Francisco, if Mencía and I did not take part in the wedding celebration and festivities for Mateo and Luisa? They have already received our best wishes a hundred times over, and we have some business we would like to pursue here."

"Of course not. This wedding celebration is principally for the benefit of our local friends and neighbors, so they can express their happiness for our Luisa who they have known since childhood. No, I do not mind but am curious to hear what business you have here?"

"Nothing serious. I wish to look up a friend, a curate who I think is assigned somewhere in the area."

"Our own parish has no assigned curate," said Don Francisco. "However, I know of two in neighboring parishes and will get you the parish names."

Then thinking aloud, he added, "These curates, they are representatives of the bishop supposedly sent to a parish to help with some problem. I am of the opinion, possibly an unfair one, that a curate is sent to a parish perhaps just to find a place that can pay his salary. I am uncertain what they actually do at a parish, meaning no disrespect to your friend."

"No, none taken. I am also curious to learn what he actually does."

The next morning, Guillermo was itching to start his investigation. He and Mencía rode to the parishes to check out the two curates. They first paid a visit to the parish church itself to find out the curate's names and then asked about them in the surrounding area. They found these two holy men were well regarded by the locals and considered assets to the parishes. Guillermo could only conclude that neither was the culprit, so they visited the neighboring parishes and found two others with curates. One of them was like the last two, well thought of by parishioners, but the fourth curate proved to be of interest.

Father Esteban was the curate unlike the others. He had been assigned to the parish less than a year. The people considered him somewhat arrogant, indifferent to them, and a burden rather than a benefit to their parish. Someone had heard he had been moved here from another parish due to some unexplained problem. One woman whispered she heard he has a mistress. All fingers pointed to Father Esteban as being the culprit, and he became the focus of their investigation.

Learning that he lived in a good sized second floor apartment near the church and ate well at restaurants, only heightened their interest in him. They decided that they would watch his apartment that night.

"Someone is leaving," said Mencía in a loud whisper.

From their place in an alcove down the street, they strained to see the dark figure that emerged from the curate's apartment.

"That must be him," she added. "No one else has entered it. He does not wear his cassock or priestly attire. He wears normal clothes with a big hat."

"Big hat down and collar up. It seems the curate does not wish to be recognized. There he goes. Let us follow him."

They trailed him at a distance as he skulked along narrow streets of white stucco houses with tile roofs, finally after a time coming to an iron gate on a stairway up to an apartment. He looked around before unlocking the gate and disappearing up the stairs. Guillermo and Mencía looked at each other and nodded.

"The apartment of his rumored mistress, perhaps?" suggested Mencía.

"It would seem so. You watch from here while I get the wraps from the saddlebags for some added warmth."

That chilly night, they sat on nearby steps, intending to take shifts watching for him to come out again. However, only an hour after going up, the same dark figure reappeared and left, cautiously walking up the street in the other direction. After following him and watching as he reentered his apartment, they got their horses and rode back to the estate to warm up.

The next morning, they were again on the nearby steps and watched a young woman come down from the apartment the curate had visited.

"She is pretty young," commented Guillermo.

"Priests do not have daughters," said Mencía. "Let us see where she goes."

They followed her to an open-air market where she purchased various foods. When she walked away from one woman vendor, they asked the vendor who the young woman was.

"Señorita María. She flirts with men here sometimes, so they know her name. Imagine such a strumpet having the holy name of María! She comes here every day at this time to buy food."

"How long has she been coming here?"

"Less than a year."

"What do you know about her?"

"Not much. She says little and likes to wear expensive jewelry. Lately, she has new jewelry that she likes to show off as she reaches for something. That is all I know."

"Thank you," Guillermo told her, and then to Mencía, "I have an idea. Let us go."

The next day, an enclosed carriage was parked along the street as the mistress María walked by on her way to the market. Guillermo sat in the open front looking frequently at a nearby doorway as if waiting for someone. The young girl eyed him, and he tipped his hat to her. She gave him a nice smile in return and continued to walk, looking back once or twice.

"Yes, she is the one," said Father Benito from the darkness inside the carriage. "She dressed and looked plainer before, but she is the young woman who brought me the false wedding document. How did you find her?"

Guillermo told Father Benito he could not say yet but thanked him for confirming she was the one. After returning him to his parish, they drove back to Don Francisco's estate.

Now they had no doubt that Father Esteban was the corrupt holy man. He had used his mistress to pose as Mateo's supposed wife. It would do no good to inform the church and let them take care of it. Apparently, it had happened before, and he had been quietly transferred to another parish. So Guillermo decided that he, himself, would take on the task of reforming this wayward priest. From Father Esteban's many expenses, Guillermo and Mencía guessed that he had a good deal of ill-gained money, probably hidden in his apartment.

Back at the estate, they found Mateo with Luisa and family receiving visiting family friends. Guillermo caught his eye and discretely motioned with a slight twitch of his head. Mateo excused himself and came out to them. Taking him aside, Guillermo quietly informed him that they had found the curate and the woman who delivered the document and claimed to be his wife. Mateo was astounded at the news and asked him what he intended to do now. Guillermo could only say he had not decided.

Afterward, Guillermo and Mencía went out to the stables. As Mencía brushed her horse, Guillermo sat on a nearby bench deep in thought. Don Francisco's overseer named Nicolas rode up and gave his horse to a stableman to put away.

Walking over, he said, "Guillermo, you look so serious. Is something troubling you?"

"Yes, Señor Nicolas, something has troubled me for some time. Now I must decide what to do about it."

"Perhaps you need a little diversion to lift your spirits." Turning around, he called, "Lucas! Marcos! We need some amusement. Do your monkey dance!"

The two stable hands dropped their things and scurried out in the open, smiling widely. They began capering around, scratching themselves, and walking on all fours as Guillermo watched intently. Next, they sat on their haunches and looked around making faces. One scampered over to Mencía and pawed at her arm. When she brushed his hand away laughing, he quickly scampered backward and sat down several steps away on his haunches, innocently gazing at her.

With a laugh, the overseer said, "Lucas and Marcos are brothers from Gibraltar where they have monkeys. They do their imitation so convincingly that we wonder if we got monkeys or men from Gibraltar. They enjoy putting on their show too."

Guillermo was also smiling at their antics. Each of the brothers was small and wiry with a broad somewhat ugly face. Guillermo had seen monkeys before in a traveling show and thought the brothers were talented at imitating them.

"All right, a fine performance, Lucas, Marcos, now back to work," the overseer told them.

The brothers smiled broadly as they stood up, took a bow, and went back to work.

Guillermo stood up and said, "Thank you, Señor Nicolas, I feel better now, and you may have given me an idea."

He walked over to the brothers and said, "Lucas, Marcos, most impressive! You are gifted performers."

"Thank you, Guillermo, we are glad you liked it," said Lucas.

Mencía and the overseer came over to listen as Guillermo asked the brothers, "And how are you at playing demons?"

"Oh, we love it. It is our favorite!" said Marcos enthusiastically as the two brothers began slinking around and making horrible faces.

With a knowing smile, Mencía said, "Guillermo, I can tell what you are thinking. And I like it."

The overseer asked, "What is this all about, Guillermo?"

The brothers stopped their slinking and listened too as Guillermo explained, "You remember the false wedding document with which Don Gaspar delayed Luisa's wedding?"

Nicolas and the brothers nodded.

"Well, Mencía and I have found the corrupt curate who Don Gaspar paid a good deal of money to produce that false document on short notice."

"Really!" said the overseer.

"He has a mistress…" began Guillermo.

"What?" interrupted Marcos.

"Yes, a mistress, who he used to pose as Mateo's supposed wife and deliver the document to Father Benito. This curate is not the holy man he should be, but instead, he is a wayward priest who has forgotten his vows of service and his fear of God. I believe a visit from two demons might be just the thing to remind him of it."

"Do you know for a fact these things are true?" asked the overseer.

"We do," said Mencía. "We ourselves watched him sneak off to visit his mistress' apartment at night. We brought Father Benito to see her, and he confirmed that she was the woman who gave him the false document. We know that Don Gaspar complained of having to pay a great deal of money to a curate for the false document, and this curate spends much money. He may not be above stealing money from the parish as well, but we do not know that."

"Such a priest is a stain on our holy church and should be reported to the bishop and disciplined," said the overseer.

"He is rumored to have been transferred to this parish after a problem at a previous one, so that may have already happened without any reform to his misbehavior. I am proposing our own effort at reforming this wayward priest, which the church seems incapable of doing," replied Guillermo.

"I see," said the overseer considering this.

"A corrupt curate with a mistress. Such a fraud deserves a lesson, I believe! God must want it too, to have revealed it to you," said the overseer with resolve.

After only a quick glimpse between the brothers, Lucas said smiling, "We are for it!"

Another man popped his head up from behind a stall and said, "I want to help too. Such a thing is an outrage. An unchaste priest deserves chastisement!"

"Good, Sancho, we need you to make sounds for us," said Marcos.

"Very good, Sancho, you too but no more," cautioned Guillermo. "We must keep this quiet. The Don and Doña may not agree that it is our place to reform this priest, so I think it best not to bother them with it. Do not tell anyone else."

He looked around at all their faces, and they all nodded their ascent.

"If you want, we can do it at our house," offered Marcos. "It is back away from other houses. We will need some red ochre."

"We have none on the estate," said the overseer. "In town is a small theater group. They must know where to get such things."

"Mencía can visit them today, while I watch this priest to learn his habits," said Guillermo.

"If we snatch him up at night when he sneaks out to see his mistress," added Guillermo, thinking aloud, "then we will have him for the night and can return him before dawn,"

"A good plan, Guillermo."

"We can work out all the details. If his habits are predictable, we can possibly do it as early as tomorrow night. Agreed?"

"Agreed," they all said in unison.

In town later, Guillermo found the curate eating a late lunch and enjoying wine at a table by himself. After he finished his meal and left, Guillermo went inside the restaurant and asked about him. The owner said he was an infrequent customer but lately had come regularly and was eating quite well.

"Something does not seem right to me when I see a priest spending money as he does," the owner told him.

Guillermo thanked him and left to continue his surveillance of Father Esteban. He caught up with him shortly before he entered the church, where he was again fulfilling his holy duties. Guillermo considered the things he had heard, more spending lately, new jewelry for the mistress. It sounded as if he had recently come into money, possibly more than just money for false documents, possibly money stolen from the parish.

Looking inside the church, Guillermo saw on an information board that now was a time for the parish priest to take confessions, which gave him an idea. As he approached the confessional booth, a devout old woman in black emerged. As she slowly shuffled past muttering prayers to herself, Guillermo wondered what great sins she could possibly have confessed.

Then, going to the confessional booth, he opened its door, climbed inside, and sat down. The priest on the other side of the partition said a prayer, which ended with him saying he was ready to receive his confession.

Guillermo told the priest through the screen, "Bless me Father, for I have sinned. It was I who stole your money."

"What?" exclaimed the priest with surprise. "Who are you and why did you do it? The money is much needed for roof repairs. You have indeed sinned, but God will forgive you. Tell me, my son, why would you do such a thing?"

Guillermo had his answer and now wanted to be on his way.

He began again, "Bless me Father, for I have sinned. I have just been untruthful with you. I did not steal your money, but I have a good idea where it is and will get it back for you. Excuse me, Father, but I must leave now," he said as he opened the confessional door and walked away briskly.

"Wait!" called the priest coming out of the confessional. "How did you know? I have told no one."

By then, Guillermo was starting to leave out a side door. Suddenly stopping and turning back to the priest, Guillermo told him, "Father, tell no one about this, no one at all. As I said before, I will get the stolen money back for you, but you must tell no one about this."

He then exited the church, leaving the priest standing with a bewildered look. Outside the church, Guillermo scanned around at the central plaza of the town and sauntered over to a nearby side street where he would continue to watch for Father Esteban leaving.

Mencía found Guillermo there later and smiled as she showed him a bag of red ochre powder as well as some black skin paints and clay. The theater group had been most helpful.

He told her what he had learned about the theft of the church's roof repair money.

"So, while he is learning to fear God, we will come back to his apartment and get it back," she guessed.

"Exactly."

Guillermo and Mencía took turns watching the priest for the rest of the evening and into the night. He again went after dark at about the same time to the apartment of his mistress. They concluded that he, in all likelihood, would make the same visit the next night, so the plan was set.

The next day, they checked on Father Esteban several times and found nothing to cause them to postpone their plans to reform him that night. Back at their house, the stablemen were being creative in their preparations. Lucas and Marcos had gathered candles and colored glass to make eerie lighting in the room. They had placed little hand mirrors and other shiny objects in pairs around the room to reflect light and appear like eyes. Sancho had made a crude drum and put beads in a small earthen pot to make a crude rattle. After practicing their dancing and sounds, they were satisfied that it should make a marked impression on the wayward curate, along with the marked impression made by sharp sewing needles, which they had borrowed from several wives.

Ch.15 Reform

LATE THAT NIGHT, Guillermo and Mencía were ready and hidden in a doorway by which the curate would pass. Sancho was unseen around the corner with a horse drawn wagon.

The street was dark, lit only by the light of a half-moon. The unsuspecting curate came walking up the street as expected. As he passed, he was forcibly pulled back into the doorway with a hand cupped over his mouth. Before he knew what was happening or thought to cry out for help, a sack was thrust over his head and a gag tied across his mouth. He was then speedily bound, put into the wagon, and on his way to the stablemen's house on Don Francisco's estate. Mencía rode ahead to tell the brothers he was coming and to put on their red ochre makeup and costume.

When the wagon arrived, all was ready. They brought the bound curate inside and tied him securely in a chair. When his gag was removed, he was one moment pleading, the next condemning them to eternal damnation, and a moment later pleading again.

"What is it you want? I have money! Spare my life. I am a priest!" he wailed without receiving a response.

When Guillermo saw all was ready, he nodded for the lesson to begin. Seeing nothing through his mask, the priest heard a devilish cackling, an eerie rattling sound, and a little rhythmic drum. He screamed and jolted when he felt the sharp pain in his thigh. Then more devilish laughing, someone moaning, and more stabs of pain. The bottom of his mask was lifted up, and he was startled to find two red devils hovering over him and leering wild-eyed. They were red all over and naked but for a loin cloth. Blackness about their eyes and a frightening pattern of black stripes on their faces and chests added to their grotesque appearance. They had little horns.

Pairs of eyes stared at him from all directions, illuminated by eerie flickering lights. One of the demons alternated between smiling monstrously and making open-mouthed faces as he held the curate's head in place forcing him to watch the other red demon slither about making grotesque shadows on the walls. Then he felt more stabs of pain in his back and sides. He screamed as the rattling, moaning, and rhythmic drumming continued. When the demon put his mask back down in place, the curate felt more pain and cried out, "What is happening?"

The rattle and drumming noises grew to a crescendo and then all was silent except for the sobs and pleadings of the curate.

After several minutes of silence, the curate began to hope it might be over. But then, the eerie rattle started up again and the curate screamed, "Nooooo!"

The drumming, moaning, rattling, dancing, and pain began again. As the demons performed, the curate begged and pleaded, but they said nothing.

At this point, the lesson seemed to be going well, so Guillermo motioned silently to the others that he and Mencía were leaving. The noise inside was more than enough cover for Guillermo and Mencía to slip out without notice.

Outside, the overseer had been standing guard should anyone on the estate happen by. The horses were tied up a short distance away. Silently, they waved to the overseer and walked to their horses. They were shortly on their way to the curate's apartment in town, carrying with them the curate's key from his coat pocket.

On arrival, they stopped short of his apartment to look and listen. They saw that all was quiet and went to his door. Using the key, they gained entry to his apartment. A candle on a table near the top of the stairs was lit. Thinking that the mistress might have come looking for him, they listened and heard nothing. They cautiously climbed the stairs and, peering inside, saw no one was there. They lit the candles they brought and began to quietly search his apartment. After an exhaustive search, they finally found a good-sized sack of coins and other valuables in the false bottom of a bureau drawer. They took it and left.

When they got back to the house, they silently crept inside and watched. The demons were still at it, much the same as when they had left two hours before. Guillermo took one of the needles and stabbed the curate in the leg himself. He was now only semi-conscious with his head slumped forward. He barely flinched when stuck and only whimpered. Guillermo motioned to the others that it was time to end it.

With the sack over his head and a gag again over his mouth, they untied him from the chair and carried him out to the wagon. With their reformed curate lying and moaning in the back of the wagon, still bound hand and foot, they hurriedly drove to town in order to return him to his apartment before daybreak when the townspeople would begin to stir.

They stopped with the wagon at his doorstep. Guillermo lifted the curate out and set him down on his front steps. Although still gagged with a sack over his head, the curate was mumbling and whining so pathetically that they actually felt sorry for him. Guillermo waved to Sancho to leave with the wagon. He carried the curate up the stairs to his apartment where he and Mencía laid him out on his bed and covered him with his coat. Quickly removing his gag and sack on his head and placing his hat over his face, they stood considering him for a moment. He was still weakly and pathetically muttering and praying. Seeing that he was not seriously harmed, they silently went back downstairs and closed the door behind them.

They got their horses and rode the short distance to the church. Guillermo pulled the curate's sack of coins and jewelry from his saddlebag and went inside the church while Mencía stayed with the horses.

Guillermo found a locked, metal contribution box mounted on the wall inside the entrance. After a minute or two, he was able to empty the contents of the sack into the wide slot of the box. When done, he looked down inside and saw the box was over half full. With a satisfied smile, he left the church.

"All done," he said to Mencía outside in the dark as he remounted. "Let us be on our way."

They caught up with Sancho driving the wagon back and continued together to the house, arriving with the sky in the east just starting to lighten. All the players were there in high spirits cleaning up from their night of activity. Lucas and Marcos were tired after all their dancing and grimacing. They were vigorously scrubbing out back at a tub of soap and water to get the red ochre and black paint off.

It would take two more days of scrubbing to finally get the redness off, during which time they avoided being seen. The overseer assigned another man to help in the stable in their absence, telling others that Lucas and Marcos were sick and should not be visited.

The parish priest was exceedingly surprised to find the money and valuables in the contribution box later that morning. He thanked God a hundred times and took pains to safeguard the money afterward. He was surprised to count more than double the amount that had been stolen. At the next Sunday mass, he announced a miracle had occurred. God had sent them enough money to complete the repairs on the church's roof.

It took Father Esteban several days to recover from the pain and shock of his ordeal. His mistress wondered what had become of him, not having seen him for several days. Needing money, she went to his apartment, something which he had told her never to do.

She found him still recovering, saying prayers, and subsisting on bread given him by a neighbor. When the curate saw her, he told her to go away. But she wanted money and was persistent. He told her that he had no money, which was true although she did not believe it. The curate now found himself confronted by an even more fearsome demon who screamed and slapped him about for some time before she finally tired of it, gave up, and left, cursing him as she slammed the door.

"God, I deserve all this punishment you send," said the curate looking heavenward. Hearing the door slam, he returned to his fervent prayers. Time would tell if the curate would truly change his ways, but he had, at least, received a degree of punishment for his misdeeds and was repentant for a time.

With their curate reform efforts completed so quickly, Guillermo and Mencía were pleased to find that they would be able to attend Luisa and Mateo's wedding celebration. Mateo, Luisa, and her parents were delighted to hear it. Actually, Luisa's mother had been getting concerned about them being gone together so much both night and day. She was greatly relieved to see them now joining in the family meals and activities.

Since their arrival, Mateo, Luisa, and her parents had been busy making plans for the wedding celebration and receiving a steady stream of guests and well-wishers. Even so, Mateo managed to break away for a time to visit his Uncle Carlos and see the preparations for growing the new plants. His gardener had just completed an initial planting of potato seeds and had a large area prepared for growing the other plants later in the spring. All seemed in readiness for their experiment at growing the new plants in this river valley location.

Mateo, Guillermo, and Mencía even found time to practice their archery and knife throwing, which drew a great deal of interest, especially from Luisa's excited younger brothers.

There was great disappointment when a few days before the planned celebration, a rider arrived with a letter from Don Lorenzo saying that Doña Antonia was sick in bed with a bad cold, and they regrettably would miss it.

Luis visited Mateo and Luisa the day beforehand to wish them well and inform them that he and his father would not be attending. His father was not yet ready for such public exposure given recent events. Luis also thought their presence might divert too much attention from the happy couple, where it belonged. They told Luis that they understood, considered him a good friend, and hoped he would stay in touch.

The wedding celebration was an enormous success attended by many people. Having looked forward to this event for years, the Don and Doña were ecstatically happy and relished every moment of it. Mateo and Luisa happily made rounds to visit with all the attendees. Many of the women attendees cried with happiness for the sweet little girl they had watched grow up and who now was so favorably married to such a fine young man.

Father Benito led the benediction and other prayers at the event. When Guillermo and Mencía paid their respects to him later, he started to ask them about the young woman and thought better of it.

He did ask with a sly look, "I have heard of a recent miracle in the parish where you took me, something about God depositing money in their contribution box for a new roof. Would you know anything about that, my son. Or you, my daughter?"

Turning to Mencía with an innocent look, Guillermo said, "I know nothing about miracles, do you, Mencía?"

"No, nothing about miracles," she replied.

"Even so," said Father Benito with a wry smile, "those who assist God in such miracles earn stars in their crowns in heaven and richly deserve earthly thanks as well."

Fortunately, the recent demons Lucas and Marcos were able to get their red ochre scrubbed off sufficiently to participate in the festivities, although several friends commented that they looked sunburned. Amid the celebration, the group of curate reformers reassembled for a happy moment of comradery and a cryptic toast to the success of the unnamed recent event.

At one point during the festivities, two attractive young women had captured Guillermo and were enthusiastically talking with him. He was a little flattered by their attention and engaged in their conversation. Don Carlos and Mencía had been chatting and noticed. Smiling and looking back at Mencía, he thought he saw a momentary frown on her face.

"Perhaps I should extricate poor Guillermo from the clutches of those two young ladies," said Don Carlos.

He started toward Guillermo, but his rescue effort proved to be unnecessary. The duenna of the young girls suddenly moved in and broke it up, taking them back to their parents. Guillermo politely said goodbye to them and found Don Carlos and Mencía.

With a wry smile, Mencía said, "You seem to have admirers."

Guillermo looked at her and said, "Mencía, do I detect a note of jealousy in that remark?"

"No, but after seeing those excitable young ladies, I better understand the need for duennas."

"It must have been my charm," said Guillermo with a debonair pose and then grin.

Luisa had spent two weeks in taxing activity leading up to the wedding event while suffering at times from bouts of morning sickness. With the celebration now over, Luisa was exhausted and spent the next four days resting. Feeling stronger afterward, Mateo asked her if she felt strong enough for the journey back. Her morning sickness had not been bad during recent days, so she thought that she could make the trip. Preparations then began for them to leave on the following morning.

On the morning of their departure, they said their goodbyes and thanks in front of the house. Mateo climbed into the carriage with Luisa. Guillermo and Mencía had just mounted their horses when Don Francisco remembered something.

"Say, Guillermo. With all the hubbub about the wedding celebration, I completely forgot to ask you if you and Mencía ever found your friend, the curate?"

With a smile, Guillermo replied, "Yes, we did. We had a very pleasant visit together."

Ch 16. Garden

THE TRIP BACK turned out to be difficult for Luisa, although she tried not to complain. The constant jostling of the carriage was not helpful for her morning sickness. She had a hard time keeping food down, and they needed to stop frequently to rest along the way. It took two full days to make the trip.

When they arrived in front of the main house, Don Lorenzo and Doña Antonia went out to welcome them back. Doña Antonia was greatly distressed at the sight of Luisa. Ignoring all the others, she went to Luisa and walked her back into the house.

"My child, you have overdone it. You look thin. We must get you to bed for some rest. You must be hungry too, poor child," she told her.

"Rosa! Let us get her a basin of warm water in her room so she can clean up and get to bed. And soup and wine," the Doña called to the housekeeper.

"Yes, Doña, right away," replied Rosa, rushing back into the house and also concerned at the sight of Luisa. Soon the house and its staff were a bustle of activity getting Luisa cleaned up, fed, and into bed.

"Do not worry, Doña Luisa. A few days of rest and you will feel much better," Rosa told her.

Only after Luisa was settled in and asleep, did Doña Antonia come out and even acknowledged the presence of the others. She gave Mateo one of her withering looks, which she usually reserved for her husband.

"I am sorry, Mother," he said. "We did not know she would suffer so much from her stomach sickness on the trip back."

"You must be more careful with her, Mateo," she scolded. "She looks weak. A few days of rest should help, and the morning sickness will hopefully not last much longer. No more traveling! She needs to stay here where we women can watch over her."

"Yes, Mother."

In a few days, Luisa was up and about again, doing better. Her bouts of nausea seemed to be lessening, so she was eating more and starting to get her glow back. Mateo wanted to be by her side, but his mother felt the need to shoo him away at times so Luisa could get more rest. On one such occasion, Mateo went with Miguel to visit Pedro and see how preparations for the new garden were progressing.

Last summer, Pedro had talked with Don Lorenzo and Miguel about the need for a new irrigated piece of ground for growing the peppers. They had decided upon a location inside an existing stonewall-enclosed area, a place close to their small creek where a short ditch could bring water to it.

Don Lorenzo and Miguel went into town to consult with stone masons about the construction of a stone dam across their small creek. Although unusual, the request to build a dam had aroused the interest of the masons, and they were at the estate the next day walking about in the creek bed and pacing off distances.

Never having built a dam before, they traveled an hour to visit an old dam built by the Moors centuries before. After inspecting its construction, they decided that they could complete their own version. A narrow spillway would allow water to overflow when full, and on one side, they would build a structure to release water into a ditch.

Don Lorenzo and Miguel were satisfied with their plans and commissioned the masons to build it. Soon wagons full of cut stone began lumbering up the drive. The masons finished the dam that summer during the almond harvest before the fall rains arrived.

During the fall and winter, Pedro and others had worked to prepare the new garden area itself. They dug the ditch, repaired the enclosing stone walls, and removed one large tree to add sunshine. Now in early March, Mateo and Miguel found Pedro and his young son Pedrito scattering dry manure over the newly tilled ground. After looking about, they were satisfied that the new garden was ready for planting time in a month.

Next, Pedro took them to his old garden where they watched as he performed the third planting of potatoes. Mateo had been told that the potato plants were a cooler weather plant, so a winter crop in warm climates. To find out the best time for planting in their climate, Pedro planted a small number of seeds each month. With the new garden area not yet ready, he had started planting them in January in his old garden. These monthly plantings looked to be growing well, without needing irrigation. The January plantings were expected to produce bulbs in early May.

The guidance for Pedro on growing potatoes was to plant the seeds deep in loose soil in full sun, keep the bulbs that form covered by soil while growing, and harvest the bulbs when the above-ground plant withers and dies, about four months later.

Months before in January, Father Giraldo had visited the estate to bless the new plants.

Looking at the potato seeds, he had asked, "Mateo, what is this new plant? You say it makes edible bulbs under the ground, and you want me to bless these new onions?"

"No, Father, I have seen and tasted one. They are quite different from onions. We ask for your blessing and God's help for these plants to grow successfully here like they do in the southern mountains of the Indies. With God's help, we will have some for you to taste in four months."

"God provides us with many vegetables already. Is there a need for more from the Indies?"

"If God wishes it," replied Mateo.

"Well said, my son," he said patting Mateo on the arm.

Mateo nodded to Pedro, who placed tiny seeds in each of the four places in the soft soil. After covering the seeds with soil and watering them, they all stood back as Father Giraldo said a blessing over the newly planted seeds.

April was an important month on the estate, being the time of Lent and Holy Week, the weeklong Spanish celebration of Easter. April was also the important time for spring planting. With the new garden ready for the planting of the seeds of the new plants from the Indies, Father Giraldo was called out to bless the new dam and garden.

The entire family and much of the extended family of the estate came to watch. Winter rains had filled the dam and water flowed over its spillway. They watched as he performed a ceremony to bless the new dam. A stack of wooden boards held in a slot of the ditch's stonework prevented water from flowing into the ditch. As a demonstration, the top board was removed, and a torrent of water poured over the other boards and down the ditch. Everyone clapped, cheered, and marveled at the new irrigation system.

Afterward, Father Giraldo led the gathering to the nearby new garden. At the garden, the onlookers found a dozen pepper and tomato seedlings in little containers on an oak tree stump. Pedro had been growing the little plants in a hot house for a month. Some bean and maize seeds were also there in cups. Everyone examined the seedlings and seeds with curiosity. Father Giraldo asked about the curious brown and white mottled beans.

"They grow in pods similar to peas only they are different," Mateo told him. "These little beans, such as they are, are poisonous. They must be cooked first and then they are very tasty and no longer poisonous."

"Quite curious," said Father Giraldo. "God works in mysterious ways. And I am to bless these poisonous seeds?"

"Yes, Father, if you would. You can judge their worth better after trying some cooked beans later."

"As you wish," he said and then proceeded to bless the beans and all the other seedlings and seeds. Pedro next carefully planted the seedlings and a dozen of each of the bean and maize seeds in their rows. He then carefully ladled water on them from a bucket as everyone watched. As part of his experimenting, he would plant more of each in two weeks. All seemed well with the new plants. Don Lorenzo and Miguel were pleased and hopeful.

The ceremony being over, the Don and Doña invited Father Giraldo inside for a glass of wine but no food, since it was already Lent and a day of fasting.

Holy week was the biggest event of the Spanish religious calendar. Elaborate masses were held daily from Palm Sunday to Easter Sunday as well as events such as religious processions and the custom of kissing the hand of a Holy Mother statue. The events and ceremonies of Holy Week were conducted in the same manner for hundreds of years and were deeply ingrained in the Spanish culture. This year, the arriving parishioners were also treated to the angelic voices of Mencía's sisters, playing and singing Easter carols before mass.

In the large cities, the Holy Week celebrations and processions were all day everyday spectacles. Even in their small town, religious processions were held several times during Holy Week. These processions would exit the church in the late afternoon, progress slowly along a route called the path of the cross and last well into the night. They featured elaborately decorated wooden floats, some with figures of Jesus and others with figures of a weeping Holy Mother. The local religious fraternity members carried these floats with a solemn rhythmic motion through the narrow streets. In front, walked fraternity members dressed in dark hooded robes carrying long candles. Behind, walked members in hooded robes acting as penitents carrying wooden crosses. As the procession slowly passed, the crowds solemnly watched, pointed at the figures on the floats, and said prayers.

Everyone on the estate and town attended the masses and ceremonies. Don Lorenzo, Doña Antonia, and the others said many prayers for Luisa and the coming baby. They had much for which to be thankful and much for which to worry and pray. A mother dying in childbirth was not uncommon.

By this time, Luisa was nearly four months pregnant. She was not suffering as much from nausea and was able to attend masses. Doña Antonia thought the hours of standing during the processions through the streets would be too tiring for her, so Luisa would only stay for the beginning of a procession.

The end of Holy Week was marked by a large gathering of family and friends for Easter Sunday dinner. Afterward, daily life on the estate would return to normal. The days of one meal per day fasting during Lent were over, and abstinence from meat was again only on Fridays.

In early May, the first potatoes from the plants sown in January were ready to be harvested and tasted for the first time. With great anticipation, Don Lorenzo, Miguel, Mateo, and Guillermo gathered at Pedro's garden to watch Pedro pull up the potato plants. Miguel's wife María and Pedro's wife Juana were also watching. The tough above-ground stems of the potato plants lay withered and lifeless on the ground.

"All right, Pedro. Let us see what we have," said Don Lorenzo as they excitedly watched. Not sure how to proceed, Pedro carefully scratched dirt away from around the plant on one side, uncovering several light-colored bulbs.

"Look! I see them!" said Don Lorenzo.

Pedro carefully scraped away dirt from them with his hands and pulled two fist sized potatoes loose from the dirt. He held them up smiling and handed them to Don Lorenzo. They all crowded around to look at them as Pedro tugged on the plant's dead stem. The attached roots pulled from the ground revealing several more potatoes. Pedro picked them from the dirt, set them aside, and dug through the loose dirt finding more.

"Look how many there are! Under just one plant!" he said, smiling.

Meanwhile Mateo had washed the dirt from the first two in a water bucket. With a slight smile, he cut a wedge from one and handed it to his father, who examined the white milky solid and took a bite.

He chewed momentarily, frowned, and spit out the piece.

"It does not taste good to me, Mateo!" he exclaimed in surprise. "You say they eat these in the Indies? It strikes me as very unpleasant to eat. I think we may have wasted much time and effort with these."

The others had been intently watching as he sampled the new vegetable for the first time and were disappointed to hear this, except for Mateo who still smiled slightly. Miguel took a bite of a second wedge, chewed a moment, and then spit it out.

"I agree. It is not very appealing," said Miguel, looking at Mateo questioningly.

"I am sorry, Father, Miguel, but I could not resist. Do you remember telling me when I was a little boy how good the olives on the trees tasted. So I tasted one and had to spit it out because of the horrible taste. It is an old trick and now I finally got to play it."

"Shame on you, Mateo," said Guillermo, laughing. "It is permissible for fathers to play such tricks on sons but not the other way around."

"I am sorry. I could not resist," said Mateo, laughing. "These potatoes do not taste good raw. They must be cooked before eating."

Don Lorenzo smacked his son on the chest with mock annoyance as the others laughed.

Turning to her, Mateo said, "Juana, please cut these up and boil them until they soften? Then salt them a little and bring them out for us to taste?"

"Yes, Don Mateo. I have the water boiling already as you asked and will be back shortly," she replied, smiling. Then she and María hurried off to the house.

This caused Guillermo to laugh again, and Don Lorenzo to smack Mateo again on the chest.

Meanwhile, Pedro began pulling up the three remaining withered plants and picking more potatoes from the soil. After satisfying himself that he had collected all of them, he had amassed four small piles of potatoes from the four plants.

"Look at all these," said Pedro, pointing. "One plant has only eight bulbs, but the others have many."

"January appears to be a good time for planting," said Miguel. "We must keep track of the numbers and see if February and March plantings do as well."

"Yes, Señor," said Pedro, dusting himself off. "Let me see how my Juana is doing." He headed to the nearby house as the others picked up several potatoes and examined them.

"I believe the next thing to do is simply to dust them off and store them in a dry cool place," said Mateo.

"And how long can they be stored?" asked Miguel.

"A month or two, I believe."

"Well, we shall see," commented Don Lorenzo. "I am less than enthused with these potatoes of yours, Mateo. Let us hope that they taste better cooked than they do raw."

When Pedro returned with a bowl of boiled potato slices, everyone reached in and picked out a piece. Each of them examined it closely and took a bite.

"Hmm, they seem much better now, but lack flavor," said Don Lorenzo.

"They have substance. The texture is fine, not slimy or unpleasant, and the taste is not bad," said Miguel. "Possibly something to go well with meats and fats."

"I, myself, am not convinced about these odd-looking bulbs from the soil. Fortunately, the peppers are our main interest. By the way, all this talk of food has made me hungry. How about if you all come and have some lunch at the house with me?" said Don Lorenzo, no longer interested in the potatoes.

"Thank you, Don Lorenzo. I want to try another taste and will be just a moment," Miguel told him.

Miguel and Mateo took more pieces from the bowl, tasting them again and rolling the flavor around in their mouths.

"It looks like your potatoes are not a big hit, Mateo," said Guillermo, consoling his friend.

"My little joke was a bad idea. I see that now, but I think these potatoes may yet prove themselves valuable," mused

Mateo. "Pedro, have Juana cut two more up and fry them in fat this time. Tell me what you think. We will be up at the house."

"Yes, Don Mateo. I too think it may help their flavor. We shall see shortly."

"Well then, let us go," said Don Lorenzo, turning to leave. Mateo handed the bowl to Pedro, then followed Don Lorenzo out the garden gate.

Pedro heard Don Lorenzo say as he left, "So you still hold that old olive trick against me after all these years, eh, Mateo?"

An hour later, they were sitting at their lunch table talking about the peppers when Pedro and his wife Juana came rushing into the house with a bowl.

"Don Lorenzo, Mateo, everyone, try this! It is delicious! You will not believe it!"

"What is it, Pedro?" asked Don Lorenzo with surprise.

"The potatoes fried with fat and some pork!"

They hurriedly passed the bowl around and put some on their plates. They tried it and their eyebrows rose in pleasant surprise.

"You are right, Pedro. It is incredibly good! It tastes delicious with the pork."

They all concurred after a taste. Then Luisa and Doña Antonia wanted to try it.

"Umm," said Luisa.

"It is good, Pedro. Was it hard to grow?"

"No, not at all, Doña Antonia."

Guillermo took several bites and swallowed, then commented, "The cooked bulb has much substance and is filling. It goes well with the other flavors. I think you may be on to something, Mateo."

Pedro excitedly said, "Yes, it is a vegetable almost like bread, but much easier to grow. No large field of wheat or mill to grind the wheat is needed. Any family with a garden can grow them."

Don Lorenzo had been listening carefully and the value of these bulbs was finally sinking in.

"By God, Pedro! You are right. These bulbs could be a valuable inexpensive food for many people." Then addressing Mateo, "And you are sure there is no risk in eating them?"

"No, none at all, Father. As I have said, the natives in the southern Indies have eaten them for centuries. I believe that other Spaniards have also brought back the seeds and are growing them. With time, I imagine their use will spread to other countries here too."

Shaking his head in disbelief, Don Lorenzo said, "It is all too much to comprehend. Only God can."

He spooned the remaining potatoes on his plate into his mouth. He chewed them with a satisfied look and said, "They really are quite enjoyable."

With a slap of his hand on the table, he announced, "I think a toast is called for. Get some wine for Pedro and Juana. Everyone fill your glasses."

When ready, they all raised their glasses and Don Lorenzo proclaimed, "To Pedro and his potatoes, this new gold from the Indies. God bless them."

Glancing about, he sighed and added, "And to Mateo too, I suppose, for bringing them to us, even if he likes to play underhanded tricks on his devoted father."

Ch.17 Dying Brother

A WEEK LATER, the estate was still abuzz with talk about the new vegetable that was like bread, when a man galloped up to the main house. He was carrying a message for Don Lorenzo from his brother Diego who lived northeast of Seville near the Guadalquivir River. The distance between them of over a hundred miles or four days travel time by carriage had prevented them from regularly seeing one another over the years. The message said his brother Diego was ill and feared he was dying. His brother asked Don Lorenzo to please come see him, adding "perhaps it is time."

"Perhaps it is time, hmm," Don Lorenzo said to himself. He walked back and forth in his study several times considering this. Going to the window and gazing out deep in thought, he repeated the phrase over in his mind. "Perhaps it is time." It seemed such a simple phrase, yet it held great meaning. With a sigh, he turned and walked to the door. Stepping outside the study, he asked Rosa the housekeeper if she would send someone to ask Miguel to see him.

A brief time later, Miguel arrived at his study and Don Lorenzo closed the door.

"Miguel, I hope you will forgive me for having to bring up this topic. It has been something we have avoided discussing for many years. I bring it up now only because I must."

Very few topics in his world could be so described, and Miguel had an idea what was coming.

"Yes, Don Lorenzo, please continue."

"When I brought you a baby boy years ago, you took him in without a single question."

"It is not difficult to explain. When my María and I had no children after several years of marriage, we said many, many prayers asking God to bring us a child. When later you brought us this beautiful baby boy, we saw it as from God. He had heard our prayers and provided the baby to us in answer to them, nothing else. There was no need for questions."

"Miguel, have you ever told Guillermo he is not your natural child?"

"No, as I said, he was from God. His means of delivery did not matter to us."

"Have you ever considered it might come up someday?"

"No, but now I fear it has," he said sadly.

"Yes, I am afraid so, my friend. I alone here have kept the secret of Guillermo's birth all these years. But unhappily, I have just received a message from my brother Diego telling me he is dying."

Miguel looked thoughtfully at Don Lorenzo for a long moment. After a sigh, he sadly said, "Ah, so that is the secret. It explains much. You have done so much for Guillermo over the years for which we are very grateful. You have indeed been a good uncle to him."

Staring vacantly, Miguel continued, "He has been our gift from God for many years, but now a dying father wishes to see his son before he dies. It is only right that he should. Guillermo has been a blessing to us, but now we must lose him."

"No, Miguel, you need not think such a thing, my friend. I believe you will still have a son afterward."

An hour later, Don Lorenzo announced he had received a message and must travel quickly on horseback to see his dying brother. Traveling with a carriage for his wife would be too slow, so she would stay. His son needed to stay with his expectant wife, so he would take Guillermo along to accompany him. They would leave first thing in the morning.

Miguel had already told Guillermo that he would be needed to accompany Don Lorenzo on the trip, without telling him more. Guillermo had readily accepted. Unfortunately, Mencía was out of town with her family visiting relatives. Mateo offered to go, but Don Lorenzo said he should stay with Luisa. He and Guillermo would come back as soon as they could.

The next morning when they were leaving, Guillermo's father hugged him longer than normal and said goodbye with teary eyes. Guillermo noticed and told him that he need not worry so. He would be back.

"I hope so, my son. God be with you."

Then they were off as Miguel and his wife María waved to them. He had not yet told her for fear that she would make an emotional scene when they departed.

After saying only a hurried hello to his friend Pascual on the way, they traveled first to Cordoba. From there, they made their way along the Guadalquivir River, traveling at a steady pace and stopping overnight at inns. His cousin and Luisa's family lived along the way, but they did not stop because of their hurry and to avoid the rudeness of only visiting briefly.

Don Lorenzo considered telling Guillermo on the way but thought better of it. It was something for his brother to tell.

Midmorning on the third day, they arrived at the entrance of his brother's estate against the hills near the river. Looking around as they rode to the main house, Guillermo was not impressed with the state of the grounds and fields. They looked neglected, with some fields reverting to weeds from lack of use.

At their knock, a longtime servant opened the door and recognized him.

"Don Lorenzo, please come in. Your brother is still alive. I will take you to see him in his bed."

Then looking at Guillermo beside him, she blinked her eyes in surprise. As they walked through the house, the servants they passed also looked with surprise at Guillermo. Noticing a portrait on the wall, Guillermo stopped to look. Don Lorenzo stopped too when he saw Guillermo staring at it.

"Who is that?" asked Guillermo.

"My brother Diego when he was younger."

The servant showed them into his brother's bedroom where they saw him lying in bed, pale and weak. At seeing his brother approaching, his spirits lifted, and he raised his hand in welcome.

Don Lorenzo took his hand and affectionately said, "Hello, Diego, my dear brother. I received your message and have come as soon as I could."

"At long last, it is so good to see you again, Lorenzo. I have missed you greatly and knew you would come."

"I have missed you too, Diego. And I have brought with me a young man whom I wish you to meet."

Then stepping aside, Don Lorenzo motioned for Guillermo to come forward.

"Guillermo, this is my brother, el Señor Don Diego de Cordoba."

His brother put out his hand to shake. Guillermo took it but was speechless as he looked down at him.

"At last, we meet," said Don Diego weakly.

Guillermo looked over to Don Lorenzo who nodded, saying, "Yes, it is true. We have much to tell you, things my brother has wanted to tell you for some time."

"But it is a long tale and will take some time to tell," said Don Diego. "You must be patient with me and not think too ill of me before you have heard it. First, let us get you some food and something to drink. You must be tired from your ride."

They called for a servant who brought in a basin for washing, then food and wine. After cleaning up and getting a glass, they return to Don Diego's bedside. Sitting beside his brother, Don Lorenzo looked him over with concern.

"Diego, you look so pale. What is it that ails you?"

"God only knows, Lorenzo, some kind of pox upon me, some kind of ague. The physicians that have been called in, they treat me daily with their cures, but I seem to weaken instead of improve. Before long, I think I will be together again with my beloved Teresa."

"You are not so old, my brother. Death should not loom over you so. I will say prayers for your recovery."

All three looked up at the knock on the door which then opened, and two well-dressed men carrying a bag entered.

"Ah, it is time for my treatment. Guillermo, I must ask you to be patient. I promise to tell all, but it must wait until after these physicians of mine have finished."

Guillermo looked at his pale weak father in bed and then more closely at the bandages on his arms. He watched as the doctors set their bag on a table and pulled out a scalpel and a basin. When they started toward Don Diego, he stepped in front of them.

"What are you up to?" he demanded.

"Young man, step aside. We are here to give him his daily bleeding," they answered with annoyance.

"What is this bleeding?"

"A proven medical procedure, the result of years of advanced medical learning and knowledge, if you must know! His sickness is caused by excessive internal pressure. We drain blood from his veins to relieve that pressure and make him better. Now step aside, young man. Our time is valuable and should not be wasted on such questions!"

Guillermo did not move aside. He stood thinking with a determined look on his face.

The physicians looked at him with annoyance when he did not step aside, then started to push his way past, saying, "Young man, we are busy men, so please step aside."

Finally, Guillermo came to a conclusion, saying, "He is already pale and weak from loss of blood! Anyone can see that!"

"It is plain to me too, Guillermo," said Don Lorenzo, standing.

"Nonsense! He is pale from his sickness. The bleeding helps him recover. It is a known medical fact, now step aside!"

"I beg to differ! You are killing him not curing him!" declared Guillermo.

He grabbed the scalpel from the physician's hand and put it quickly to his throat, "Now get out and take your things with you! Before I bleed you and give you a dose of your own medicine!"

The physicians looked shocked and backed away in fear. Taking their bag from the table, they retreated toward the door as Guillermo tossed their scalpel after them.

"And do not return!" he told them as they hurried out the door and closed it.

Don Diego had watched in admiration and now beamed with happiness after seeing his son's strength of character and concern for his wellbeing. It uplifted and rejuvenated him.

"Guillermo, *you* are the medicine I needed. I feel better already!"

To the frightened nurse standing in a corner, he said, "Nurse! Bring something to refresh these dressings on my arms!"

"Guillermo, you have grown to be quite a man. Again, do not think too ill of me. I will tell you all. I want to embrace you at last, but I need these wounds from their scalpels to heal a bit first. God, I feel so much better. Thank you, Lorenzo, for bringing him to me."

After the nurse dressed the cuts on his arms, they asked her to wait outside and told her they did not want to be disturbed.

Don Lorenzo and Guillermo raised Don Diego up and put pillows behind him to prop him up. They gave him a glass of wine and he said, "Ahhh, this medicine is more to my liking."

He sipped some down and nibbled on some bread as he began to tell his story.

"Years ago, I was happily married to my dear wife, Teresa, God rest her beautiful soul, she died two years ago from the ague."

"I was sorry to hear it, Diego. She was a lovely woman," interrupted Don Lorenzo.

"Yes, she was. Thank you, Lorenzo."

"As I was saying, I was happily married and had no desire or inclination to consort with other women. But I became enamored with a beautiful young woman and could not help myself. She was a dancer in a local flamenco dance group. They would perform at local events, and I would see her. Flamenco is meant to stir the blood for romance, and it succeeded in my case. I found I was in love with this girl, whose name was Floriana.

"I approached her after a performance and confessed my love for her, but she repulsed my advance, knowing I was already married. I heard she was in love with and hoped to marry a young man off on soldier duty. But I could not help myself. I continued to make advances to her and was always repulsed. When she later heard her young man had been killed, she was devastated, and in her weakness at the time, she gave in to me.

Later, when she discovered she was with child, I sent her to a nunnery to have the baby in secret. It would have broken my Teresa's heart to find out, so I concealed the truth from her.

I wanted the baby brought up well, but in our society, the child of an unwed mother would have no chance of it. When Floriana said there was no man who she wanted to marry to fill the role of father, we decided the best thing to do was to find a good home for the baby far away from prying eyes and wagging tongues.

I consulted my brother Lorenzo, whose judgment I have long trusted. After considering my dilemma, he told me he knew the answer. His overseer and his wife could not have children even though they badly wanted them. He was a good man, and Lorenzo was sure they would give the baby a fine upbringing. Lorenzo would be there to help.

I thought the idea was splendid, because I also could visit my brother periodically and see how the child was doing without arousing suspicions. Lorenzo asked his overseer about it, and they very much wanted the child.

With much heartache and many tears, Floriana reluctantly gave up the baby boy after its birth. My dear brother Lorenzo had supplied the solution. You became the son of Miguel and María."

Here Don Lorenzo interjected, "Guillermo, I must add that your parents had been childless and had prayed many years to have a child. They saw their beautiful new baby boy as a gift from God, which is what they told anyone who asked from where you came. They neither cared nor asked about the identity of the parents. I kept the secret of your birth to myself all these years. Only the day I received the letter from my brother and told Miguel that a dying father needed to see his son, did he become aware of the secret."

"That explains his tears when I left. My father thought he was losing me," said Guillermo thoughtfully.

"I meant to cause no pain, Guillermo, to them or you. It was only the unexplainable need of a father to see his son before dying. But alas, I should continue with my story.

"As I was saying, my dear brother Lorenzo had supplied the solution. As I had hoped, I was able to see you at one and two years of age during annual trips with my Teresa to visit my brother. But as you can see yourself, you look very much like me. At two years of age, the resemblance was already becoming noticeable, so much so, that I feared my Teresa or Lorenzo's Antonia or anyone else there on the estate would realize the secret. I regrettably was forced to stop my visits. But seeing you were well situated, had loving parents, and were growing up under the watchful eye of my good brother, I reconciled myself to the fact that I would no longer be able to see you.

Over the years, my brother wrote me cryptic notes in his letters to let me know you were faring well. In one such letter, he told me two years ago that you would be going with Mateo to deliver almonds to the merchant in Cordoba. I wanted to go there and see you and Mateo together, but I was so heartsick from the recent death of my dear wife that I was unable to go. My brother said in his letters that you and Mateo were good friends, and it warms my heart to think it."

"We are true friends, Mateo and I. Now I find that we are cousins as well," said Guillermo thoughtfully. "Perhaps we knew it all along."

"And what became of my mother?" asked Guillermo, with a serious look at Don Diego.

"She again took up her flamenco dancing, at which she was very talented, a star of her dance troupe. We remained friends, and I would see her perform at various events. I took pains to see that she lived comfortably. She always asked about you and, after several years, expressed to me a fervent desire to see her baby boy for herself."

Don Lorenzo took over, "I arranged for her dance troupe to perform at our estate one time when you were four years old. I had a difficult time explaining to my wife the need for a dance troupe from so far away. I told her the troupe was touring.

Your mother came and performed at the estate. Many people including you, Guillermo, came to see. She finally got to see you and was so happy. Without being too obvious, she was able to hug and kiss you, put you on her lap, and talk with you."

"I remember her!" said Guillermo with a start. "I thought she was so beautiful. She gave me a St. Christopher medal which I still have!"

He turned away for a moment and said with emotion, "I can still see her."

After an emotional minute deep in thought, Guillermo turned back around and asked, "And where is she now?"

"Several years after seeing you, she married one of the men in her dance troupe. She and the troupe had become so well known that they moved to Seville. They no longer performed in our area, and I lost touch with her."

He added with sadness, "Several years later, I am deeply sorry to say that I heard she had died. I never heard from what. She was a lovely woman, God rest her soul, and I was incredibly sad to hear it. She was still a great love for me, though a love from afar as they say. I am sorry, Guillermo, I wish I could tell you she is still alive.

"When my Teresa, God rest her soul, died two years ago, I thought of going to see you and telling you all, but could not quite do it. I thought what a stir it would cause there. How unfair it would be to your parents, Miguel and María, for me to show up suddenly with such news. So it was perhaps best that I got sick and now you are here."

After a pause, he continued with emotion, "It must have been my dear Teresa up in heaven. She has forgiven me and has sent you here."

This caused Don Diego to begin to cry and look away. Don Lorenzo and Guillermo sat in thought for a moment, quietly sipping their wine.

Their silence was disturbed by a knock on the door, and Don Diego's son, Agustin, poked in his head.

"Father, we understand you have visitors and do not want to be disturbed, but it has been an eternity. Andrés and I have tried to be patient, but we have heard such curious things out here and greatly desire to meet your visitors."

Then noticing his father sitting up and showing much more color, he added with surprise, "Father! What has happened? You are up and look much recovered!"

Laughing, Don Diego replied, "I do feel better, Agustin. I am sorry to have neglected you and Andrés. Come in and close the door. I have someone for you to meet."

The door opened, and the two brothers came in, closing it behind them. They were well dressed, thin, and bookish in appearance.

Don Lorenzo went to them saying, "My goodness, Andrés, Agustin, I have not seen you for many years. You are now grown and scholars."

"My sons, do you remember your Uncle Lorenzo?" asked Don Diego.

"Barely, Father. At last, we meet again, Uncle Lorenzo," said Agustin, coming to shake his hand.

"Father speaks so highly of you, Uncle," added Andrés, also coming to shake his hand, "but never takes us to visit you. It has been an unanswered mystery of our …"

"Goodness, Andrés, look!" interrupted Agustin, in surprise when he saw Guillermo. They looked from him to their father and back again.

"What we heard outside is true then," said Andrés. "Your other visitor looks remarkably like you, Father."

"Yes, quite true and for a good reason, my sons. Come here to meet your brother Guillermo. And Guillermo, these are your brothers Agustin and Andrés. I should say more accurately that you are half-brothers."

They came together and exchanged greetings.

"Agustin, Andrés, I will fully explain later. But for now, let me say that I think you will find Guillermo a most remarkable young man, someone possibly for your poetry."

Looking at Guillermo, Don Diego explained, "Guillermo, you take after me, which is plain to see. Your brothers, on the other hand, take after their mother. They are scholars and poets who have studied at the university in Salamanca. Here in Spain, we seem to either be men-at-arms or poets and scholars. They are the latter. Although unlike me, I am still immensely proud of them. Someday, they may be famous for their plays and poetry."

Guillermo shook their hands, saying, "It is an honor to meet such learned brothers. You should meet our cousin Mateo. He is an admirer of such things as *Amadis of Gaul* and could appreciate you more."

"Oh, those volumes are dreadfully overrated," said Agustin, shaking his head. "There are so many finer examples of heraldic literature."

With a laugh, Guillermo said, "I have told him that such stories are so much silliness, but he has proven me wrong. He himself has rescued a beautiful girl from the clutches of an ogre and made her his wife. She is more divine than any distressed damsel in any castle tower."

After a moment of dumbstruck awe, Andrés said, "Oh! Guillermo, you absolutely must tell us more. Oh! If we could but meet this divine creature. What an inspiration she might be! Think of it, Agustin. What verse we might compose!"

Ch.18 Neglected Estate

IN TWO DAYS, Don Diego was recovered enough to leave the bedroom and walk tentatively about in the house. For the first time in weeks or even months, he dined that night at the dinner table with the others. His housekeeper had ordered his favorite meal be prepared to celebrate the event. He was enjoying his meal and wine immensely as they talked.

Although not wanting to upset the delicate state of his brother, Don Lorenzo felt compelled to say something about what had been bothering both he and Guillermo.

"Diego, I am sorry to bring this up, but from the moment we arrived, I noted that your estate is not what it once was. Guillermo and I walked around today. The fields, buildings, and trees have looked far better in the past."

"Sadly, I must agree, Lorenzo. In my despondency over my dear Teresa's death and my poor health, I have neglected it badly. Now with conditions here worse than ever, I wonder if it is worth the difficulties."

"But you have an overseer! His job is to keep it up!"

"He tells me our neighbor has cut off our shared water for our irrigated fields in the summer, so they wither. The oaks, wheat, and olives only require rain. But with few cattle anymore, the oaks are of little use. The wheat yield is low. Only the olives now provide a modest income. It seems such a mountain of difficulties with which to deal."

"Why do you tolerate this!" said Don Lorenzo hotly.

Don Diego looked at the servants who stood watching and listening, and said, "Perhaps we should reserve such topics for later in my study. Right now, let us enjoy this excellent meal, which my staff has taken great trouble to prepare."

He acknowledged the housekeeper standing nearby with a tip of his glass. They turned and looked as she said, "We are all pleased and thank God you are so much better, Don Diego."

"Thank you, Francisca." Then turning back to his brother, he said lightheartedly, "Lorenzo, let us talk about something pleasant. Tell me about your son Mateo and his divine wife, this rescued damsel of his."

After dinner, Guillermo took Don Lorenzo aside and told him, "Before going into the study with your brother, we should talk ourselves about this overseer of his. I saw him briefly today and he was most uncooperative and surly. I wanted to throttle him but restrained my urges. I suspected he was a bad apple when we arrived and saw the state of things. Now I am sure of it. I took the liberty of watching his house last night and saw him lead his horse quietly away a distance and then ride off. I suspect he rode to see the neighbor, with whom he is most likely in league. He ought to be discharged, if not worse."

"But my brother cannot do without an overseer or someone to run the place."

He paused, eyeing Guillermo, who understood his look.

"No, I see what you are thinking, but I do not believe it is my place to take over here. Perhaps someday, I do not know, but this is all too new. For now, I wish to continue at your estate if you will allow me. I want to continue to be with my parents and friends there."

"Nothing would bring me greater pleasure."

"But first, I want to set things right here for your brother," said Guillermo with a determined look. "I am confident I can straighten out his neighbor, but what to do about a new overseer?"

"I believe I have the answer. Our neighbor Don Felipe recently lamented to me that he feared he would be losing a capable man on his estate. He believes the man may be unwilling to wait the unknown number of years until his current overseer might retire."

"Exactly the man we need! We should talk with your brother. If he agrees, I can ride in the morning to bring back this new man as well as bring other help. I could be back in less than a week, and then we can act."

"That is the third time you have said 'your brother' instead of 'my father.' Are you troubled by all this, Guillermo?"

"No. I do not think so. It is just too new. The words do not flow off my tongue easily. Perhaps with time."

In the study later, Don Diego took up again with Don Lorenzo and Guillermo the unhappy topic of his neglected estate.

"I mentioned before at dinner about my neighbor and our shared irrigation water. For many years, my close friend Don Hernando and I have lived amiably together here in our small valley. But in my despondency these last couple years, our friendship has suffered, and I lost touch with him. Now we have this dispute over water. I suppose I should tell of it from the beginning.

"Centuries ago, the Moors built a small dam across the creek in our valley with ditches to supply irrigation water for the two properties. When the Moors were conquered, the new Christian owners continued to use their irrigation system, but a flood destroyed the dam not long afterward. Their priest called it a message from God not to use the wicked works of the unchristian Moors, so they abandoned their irrigation system and their irrigated crops.

"But forty years ago, the two landowners, Hernando's father and a relative of my wife Teresa, wanted to grow irrigated crops again, so together they rebuilt the dam and cleared the ditches. Eventually, the estates were passed to Hernando and my Teresa. For the last twenty-five years, Hernando and I have been good friends and shared the water harmoniously until recently.

"I have not seen much of my neighbor lately. My overseer tells me he has claimed primary rights to the water since the dam was built on his property. He releases little water to us, so the overseer says he has been forced to cut back our irrigated crops accordingly.

"In my grief and sickness, I have been too preoccupied to address it, and my sons have no interest or talent for such things. Perhaps it would be better for us to move to Seville where my sons can blossom in their craft.

"The neighbor has seen my distracted state, is possibly aware of such thoughts in my head, and tries to encourage them. He may hope to acquire my estate at a bargain price. I suspect my overseer collaborates with him in this plot and is doing his part in the encouragement. Perhaps they are right. I should move to the city."

Guillermo had listened to this without speaking but now said, "You are correct that the overseer is in league with the neighbor. I watched last night and saw the villain quietly leave, probably to report to the neighbor. If you will permit me, I have a plan to right your situation here. Don Lorenzo has a candidate to replace your overseer, and I have friends to help bring your neighbor around. If you agree, I will leave tomorrow and be back in less than a week. Say nothing to anyone about it until I return."

Don Diego looked at him in surprise and then at his brother. Don Lorenzo said with a laugh, "My brother Diego, your son is a force to be reckoned with. You have no idea. I have heard he is called the 'Wrath of God' for good reasons."

Don Diego looked even more surprised. Finally shaking his head in wonder, he said, "No, Lorenzo, I do have an idea of his strength of character and so do my physicians. Very well, my son, go tomorrow. I bow to your knowledge and skills in such matters. Your assistance is most welcome and greatly appreciated."

"Good, when I arrive back home, I will first meet with Don Felipe."

"Don Felipe is my neighbor and best friend," said Don Lorenzo. "He has a capable man for the position, and I know Felipe will help. I will write a letter for Guillermo to take to him."

"If this man accepts the position, I will bring him and others back with me. Keep a close eye on your overseer while I am gone. I hope to be back without delay, and then we can begin to set things right here."

The next morning, Guillermo got his own horse ready and brought it out front. The staff was told he had forgotten an important engagement back home and needed to leave abruptly. His father, uncle, and brothers were there to see him off as he stuffed some food in his saddlebag for his trip. Then with a resolute look, he mounted his horse, gave a wave, and rode off. The overseer watched from a distance, suspecting nothing.

Over the next week, Don Diego observed his overseer more closely than he had for some time. While not doing anything suspicious, he noted that the overseer walked about, acting busy but actually accomplishing no work. Don Diego regretted having paid so little attention before.

Don Diego was rapidly recovering his health and feeling much better. He and his brother enjoyed their time together after being separated for so many years. They reminisced about old times and their parents. Their time together was a memorable and enjoyable one for them, even though the upcoming fight to right things was not far from their minds.

Thinking that Agustin and Andrés should not be involved in the upcoming danger, he did not tell them of Guillermo's plan and hustled the two poets off to Seville the day before Guillermo's expected return.

Guillermo arrived back in a week with the new overseer as well as Mencía, Sebastian, and José, another of Pascual's men.

Halting the group at the entrance to Don Diego's estate, Guillermo glanced over at the new overseer, who was looking around at the neglected fields, buildings, and trees.

"You see it now, Rodrigo. Before we continue, I must ask. Do you still want the job?"

"Yes. Absolutely! I see much potential here."

"Good! I knew I liked you, Rodrigo."

With that, they rode in and stopped to refresh and eat at the main house.

Guillermo soon after went by himself to see the overseer who sat in his chair in front of his house and watched as Guillermo approached. He did not get up and said nothing.

Guillermo stopped in front of him and said, "Salvador, do you remember me? I talked with you briefly last week."

Salvador said with a sneer, "Yes, I remember you. You are the Don's bastard son, I believe."

"I prefer the term 'long lost' son. I have come to tell you to pack your things and leave. You are dismissed and have one hour to be gone. Otherwise, I will take immense pleasure in personally throwing you off."

"Who are you to tell me what to do! I will take no orders from you!" he shouted as he started to get up to show Guillermo what a big man he was.

Before he was able to stand fully upright to show off his height, Guillermo lit into him, pummeling him mercilessly with blow after blow of his fists, knocking him from one end of his porch to the other several times. Finally, Salvador collapsed to the ground, bloody faced and wondering what happened. As he lay there half-dazed looking up, Guillermo smashed the chair on his head as finishing punctuation to his message.

With the ex-overseer lying unconscious in the debris of the chair, Guillermo looked around and spotted a pitcher of water. He poured its contents on Salvador's face, and he began to stir.

"Wake up, my friend," said Guillermo, giving him a hard slap across the face.

With the overseer now awake, Guillermo hauled him to his feet and shoved him into the house.

"You have one hour to be gone! I did not use my knife this time. Next time I will! One hour!" he threatened and left.

Not being an enormous success in life, the ex-overseer owned few possessions. Within ten minutes, he dragged himself up onto a horse and painfully rode away.

Going back into the main house, Guillermo saw that the new overseer and Don Diego seemed to be getting on well. The Don was giving him a brief description of the state of affairs, and Rodrigo seemed eager to get to work. Right away, he was off to see who still worked on the estate and to let them know a new man was in charge.

The next task was getting the estate's irrigation water back. That night, Guillermo, Mencía, Sebastian, and José went unseen to the neighbor's estate to acquaint themselves with the situation there. After watching the activity at the outbuildings and stables for a time, they guessed they might face eight, maybe ten men, which they thought was a number that could be handled.

They inspected the location where the ditch from the dam branched into two ditches. Don Diego's ditch was blocked by a stack of wooden boards held in a slot of the ditch's stonework, not unlike the gate installed in Don Lorenzo's new dam. A similar structure in the neighbor's ditch had all its boards removed.

Only a small amount of water was flowing in the ditch, but tomorrow, they would make their point that the water was to be shared, even this trickle. Satisfied that they had learned what they needed, they returned to Don Diego's and got some sleep.

The next morning, they told Don Diego what they learned and of their intention to tear the boards out that morning to send his neighbor a message. When Don Hernando came down to complain or threaten, they would be ready for him.

"I plan to remove the boards by myself as a message and show of force," said Guillermo.

"No," interrupted Rodrigo. "It is my place to remove the boards. They must learn respect for me if I am to be overseer here!"

"Rodrigo, I knew I liked you!" said Guillermo with admiration. "You are right, but I will be there to support you, and we can have the others hidden nearby to assist if needed."

With this plan in mind, they set out mid-morning for Don Hernando's estate. The others stayed concealed in nearby brush as Rodrigo and Guillermo went forward to the place where the boards blocked the ditch. A couple field hands saw them coming and hurried off wide-eyed. When they got there, Rodrigo began prying the boards out. A good deal of silt was accumulated against them, and he had brought a shovel to clear it away. When he removed the last board and threw it into the nearby tall weeds, the small amount of water began working its way down Don Diego's ditch. Rodrigo looked over at Guillermo and smiled.

Just then two men raced up on horses and yelled, "Hey, what do you think you are doing! Get away from there!"

Rodrigo stood with his shovel and yelled back, "I am here with a message for Don Hernando. He is not to interfere with Don Diego's water anymore.

"And who are you!"

"My name is Rodrigo. I am Don Diego's new overseer, so give that message to your Don!"

"And who is this!" he demanded, pointing at Guillermo.

"I am Guillermo. Salvador may have told you about me."

"Yes, you are the bastard son. Ha!"

Then with a sneer, he shouted, "So we are to give a message to Don Hernando, are we? I think instead we may just give *you* a message, written on your hides with our whips!"

He grabbed his nine-foot-long bullwhip coiled on his saddle. Spurring his horse forward, he began to snap it at Rodrigo. The second rider was starting to do the same at Guillermo when Rodrigo threw his shovel at the first horse's head, spooking it. It reared up and threw its rider to the ground.

In the confusion, Guillermo had raced forward and leaped up to drag the other rider from his horse. After smashing him several times in the face with his fists, he now had him subdued on the ground with a knife at his throat.

He looked over at Rodrigo, standing over the other man, who was lying in the dirt and holding his bloody head. Rodrigo had picked up his shovel again after throwing it. When the man was getting up from his fall, Rodrigo had bashed him on the head with it. The two men offered no more resistance. Their knives were taken from their belts and tossed in the weeds.

Guillermo stood them up together and said, "I also have a message for Don Hernando. Are you listening?"

Seeing a defiant sneer on the first man's face, Guillermo punched him hard in the stomach, doubling the man over in pain. Hauling him upright roughly by the collar of his shirt as the man gasped and coughed, Guillermo then repeated himself.

"I *said*, I also have a message for Don Hernando. Are you listening?"

They both looked at him dejectedly and nodded.

"My name is Guillermo. I have been called the 'Wrath of God' before. I like it. It suits me, and I mean to earn the title in full if your Don does not live up to his agreement to share water."

Then putting the point of his knife close under the chin of the first man, he said with venom, "By the way, I prefer the term 'long lost' son. The next person who calls me by the other term is going to lose a few fingers. Tell your friends that. Now, get out of here, before I take a few of yours! Start walking!"

Both men staggered away sullenly without speaking. Guillermo turned to Rodrigo and said, "I knew I liked you, Rodrigo! You wield a shovel quite well. Let us go back and see what our friends thought of our performance."

As they walked down, their friends appeared from their cover into view, laughing and smiling.

"Well done! I believe your message was clear enough," said Mencía.

"Rodrigo is going to do very well here," said Guillermo, clapping him on the back. "Let us get back. We may have visitors soon."

Ch.19 Setting It Right

THAT AFTERNOON, Don Hernando rode up to the front of Don Diego's main house with eight of his men. They were mostly armed with machetes and knives. Two wore cutlasses in their belts. On each side of Don Hernando were two men with a pistol in their belts. They stayed in their saddles as Don Diego came out his front door. Along with him came Don Lorenzo, Guillermo, Mencía, and Rodrigo who carried a loaded crossbow which Don Diego had only given him minutes before.

Guillermo stood facing the men on one side of Don Hernando. Mencía stood facing the men on his other side. With their throwing knives out and ready, their attention was focused on the men carrying the pistols. They had their bows and quivers resting nearby against chairs.

Don Hernando spent a moment looking at Don Diego and the others with him and said, "Diego, we have been friends and neighbors a good while, and now you attack my men."

"I desire to be friends still, Hernando, but not with one who does not honor his agreements. It is a reasonable demand."

"You make demands when you are weak and disinterested? I have claimed rights to the water for a time without opposition from you. Why should I think you have the strength to oppose me now?"

"I am interested again, and you should not underestimate our strength, Hernando. Tell your men to take their pistols and machetes and go. You can stay, and we will talk. We were once good friends and can be again."

Don Hernando looked at Don Diego and seemed to be considering it when one of the men beside him yelled, "They do not frighten us!"

He reached for the pistol in his belt. The other men excitedly followed suit reaching for their pistols. The first man was on Guillermo's side, and he screamed in pain as Guillermo's knife buried itself deep in his shoulder. Two other cries of pain came from the other side of Don Hernando, who looked about in dismay.

"Sebastian! José!" shouted Guillermo, and they quickly appeared on each side of them with arrows strung and pointed threateningly at the men.

The fourth man had been slow in reaching for his pistol and still had his hand on it. Seeing that the game was up, he prudently released his grip on the pistol and slowly moved his hand away.

"Drop your weapons!" commanded Guillermo. Mencía had also snatched up her bow and had an arrow pointed at them. The horses of the men nervously paced and turned about with their riders not sure what to do.

"Drop your weapons, he said!" shouted Sebastian ferociously, pulling even harder on his bow string.

"Now!" shouted José.

With so many weapons aimed at them, they reluctantly submitted. They all gingerly reached for their weapons and dropped them to the dirt. Don Hernando meanwhile sat silently on his horse with a troubled look.

Rodrigo had his crossbow also trained on them. Mencía had been so fast with her knives that he had not discharged it. Putting it down, he went forward and retrieved the knives from the shoulders of the three men, each wincing in pain as he did so.

With the situation defused, Don Diego said, "Hernando, tell your men to go home and please come inside so we can have some wine and talk."

Nodding sadly, he turned each way and motioned for them to leave. They reined their horses about without speaking and slowly left down the drive. Don Hernando climbed down from his horse and went inside with Don Diego and his brother.

Seeing no further threat, the bows were lowered, and the defenders came together on the front porch, shaking hands, smiling, and slapping one another on the back. Guillermo praised them for their bravery and a job well done.

They all laughed when Rodrigo asked Mencía in amazement how she had done it. He had started to aim his crossbow at a man reaching for his pistol when knives suddenly appeared in the shoulders of both men, and they screamed dropping their pistols. He had looked over at her in surprise and saw her with a third knife already in her hand, still intently focused on the men.

Wine was brought out, and they happily toasted to their success. Guillermo then excused himself, motioned to Rodrigo, and went inside with him to join the meeting in the study.

When Guillermo and Rodrigo entered the study, they saw Don Hernando looking remorseful without any display of defiance as the three of them sat in comfortable chairs, sipping wine. Don Diego had been telling him how it was a shame that things had come to this.

"Yes, it is a true shame," he said. "We have been good friends and worked so well together in the past. Hernando, I believe it is my fault. I have been listless and distracted since my Teresa left me. I have badly neglected my estate and our friendship."

Don Hernando had listened and seemed to be struggling with what to say. Pointing at Guillermo, he finally said, "Diego, earlier today I was threatened with the Wrath of God, this young man here. But now, I fear the Wrath of God even beyond his. The incident outside has made me think that I deserved such treatment. I attend mass every Sunday and think I am devout. But I am not the neighbor and devout man I perceived myself to be."

"Hernando, all is settled. We can share water again and be good neighbors. I can forgive you for your error if you can forgive me for my folly. We can then pray that God will forgive us both."

"I do not know what possessed me," pondered Don Hernando. "A devil whispered in my ear, and instead of shunning him, I listened. He told me you were weak, tired, and downhearted. If I were to make things difficult for you here, you would retreat to the city, and I could get your land at little cost."

"Who was this devil?" asked Don Diego, keenly interested.

"Salvador, your overseer."

"Oh, the villain!" exclaimed Guillermo. "I wish I had thrashed him more!"

"I suppose he thought he would reap some benefit from it," pondered Don Hernando.

"And where is this devil now?" asked Guillermo.

"I believe he is out in my stables, recovering from your beating and probably brooding now with his two wounded friends."

"What do you mean, Hernando?" asked Don Diego.

"The man who first reached for his pistol and one of the others you wounded are Salvador's friends."

"The first one was also the one I bashed in the head with the shovel this morning. He does not learn well," said Rodrigo.

"I confess that, against the advice of my overseer, these two troublemakers goaded me into coming to confront you. I have been weak in this regard also. My overseer was right, and I should have listened to him. He does not like these two but is old and probably fears them."

"I recommend you go back at once and tell these two troublemakers and that villain Salvador to leave. They cannot be a good influence on the rest of the men. I will happily come along. If the fools try something, my knives will find something more vital this time," Guillermo told him, fuming.

"I can come too, if you like," offered Rodrigo.

"No, I will go alone," replied Don Hernando. "I would not deserve the respect of anyone there if I did not order them to leave myself."

With that, he begged to be excused, said a pleasant goodbye, and started for the door. As he passed Rodrigo, he stopped to look him over and shook his hand.

"So you are Rodrigo, the new overseer. You must come with Don Diego for a visit soon, so you can meet my overseer, Bastía. I think you will get on well," he said.

Rodrigo nodded, and Don Hernando left the study.

The others, still out in front relaxing after the excitement, stopped talking and watched as Don Hernando came out, mounted his horse, and rode slowly away.

Guillermo came out and gazed at Don Hernando riding down the drive.

He told the others, "Don Hernando is repentant and plans to dismiss some troublemakers from his ranks. He may need our support, so gather your weapons. We will stay concealed in the trees that we saw last night near his main house."

Laughing and pointing, Sebastian said, "They should not be much trouble. Their weapons are all in a pile there."

"Quite true," said Guillermo with a laugh, "but still I want no harm to come to Don Hernando. I believe he would have reconciled with Don Diego if that troublemaker had not started the incident."

A short time later, they were creeping forward unseen to the trees near the main house of Don Hernando. Rodrigo had left the cumbersome crossbow behind and brought along a cutlass and pistol.

From the trees, they spotted the two troublemakers with white dressings on their shoulder wounds, sitting at the stables with Salvador. Guillermo estimated they were about fifty yards away, not a hard shot, and there was little wind.

They watched as Don Hernando came from the house out to the stables. They could hear and see him sternly telling the threesome to pack up their things and leave, pointing to the road. When done, he turned and started to walk back toward the house. Other men were nearby watching. His two troublemakers chased after Don Hernando and grasped him by the shoulder to turn him around. Salvador had now joined them as they argued threateningly with Don Hernando.

Guillermo, Mencía, and Sebastian were already up with arrows back and taking aim, when the other men there with Don Hernando intervened on his behalf. They pushed the three troublemakers away and, whipping out clubs, they beat on them until the three collapsed onto the ground pleading for mercy.

But they got none. Instead, they got kicks and more blows from the clubs. Soon, their saddled horses were brought out, and the three battered men were then roughly hoisted up onto them. The men gave a slap on the rump to the horses, which then trotted away with their riders bouncing in the saddles and slumped over in obvious pain. The previously white dressings on two of them were now bright red.

Guillermo, Mencía, and Sebastian were still standing but now leaning on their bows. They looked at one another, then at Rodrigo and José.

"It seems our services were not required, my friends. Let us walk over to congratulate Don Hernando," said Guillermo.

They casually walked together toward the stables where Don Hernando was talking with and thanking the men. When his men noticed Guillermo's armed group coming across the open area toward them, they pointed at them with alarm.

Don Hernando turning and seeing them, called out happily, "Guillermo, you came after all. Welcome. Did you see? I am very proud of these men."

"Yes, we saw the whole thing. They are to be commended," called Guillermo. When he was closer, he added, "My only regret is that I was about to put an arrow in the villain Salvador and their fine efforts made it unnecessary."

"But, yes, they are indeed to be commended. They handled those troublemakers most appropriately," said Guillermo, looking them over and smiling.

Don Hernando's men were looking at Guillermo's group with much respect and awe. Some had been at the earlier incident and the others had all heard about it. One of them asked excitedly, "Is this the girl? The one who threw the knives?"

"Yes, it was her," said another.

Laughing, Guillermo said, "Mencía, my friend, your reputation precedes you. Perhaps a demonstration is warranted."

"Mencía," several men repeated her name in awe.

Smiling at him and shaking her head, she glanced around casually as she put her bow and quiver on the ground. Standing upright again, she turned and quickly threw two knives that landed thunk, thunk, inside a horseshoe, which was nailed on the wooden planking of a stable wall. It caused quite a sensation in the onlookers, which required some time to die down.

Wine was brought out, introductions were made, and a celebration of the happy outcome began. Don Hernando introduced Rodrigo as Don Diego's new overseer, telling all that he had already earned his own respect and deserved theirs too. Rodrigo met the Don's overseer, Bastía, who had craftily orchestrated, on his own, the drubbing and expulsion to the troublemakers. A rider was sent, and soon, Dons Diego and Lorenzo rode up and joined in the celebration. The results of the day could not have been better.

During the high spirits that afternoon, one curious conversation took place. Mencía was humbly approached by Martín who was the third man who received a knife in the shoulder and now sported a dressing wrap on his wound.

"Señorita Mencía," he told her with profound respect, "I wanted you to know that I harbor no ill will against you. In fact, quite the opposite, I owe you my life. Not only did you not put your knife in my throat as you easily could have done, but your quickness saved me from a bolt from the crossbow. So I owe you my life and am at your disposal. If you ever need assistance of any kind in the future, all you need do is ask."

"It is quite unnecessary, Martín. You have no need to owe me your life."

"Still, if you ever need assistance in any way, please ask."

"Thank you, Martín, I will remember."

The next day, Don Hernando held a dinner to celebrate a renewed friendship, which Guillermo and the rest attended. The future looked bright for the neighbors. Rodrigo was now established there and expected in a few short years to have the estate returned to its old prosperous ways. It marked a new beginning for the fortunes of his father.

The departure of Don Lorenzo, Guillermo, and the others a few days later was a scene of great emotion and thanks. The visit proved to be much better than Don Lorenzo could ever have imagined. Guillermo hugged his father and brothers and said a heartfelt farewell before climbing on his horse. He promised to visit regularly.

Don Diego waved with tears in his eyes as he watched them all go. His sons Andrés and Agustin were also there smiling and waving farewell. They had returned the day before from Seville to find things on the estate much altered. When informed of events, they told their father that had they known, they would have stayed and tried to help. But seeing the happy outcome and the resulting happiness of their father, they made no issue of it. They suspected, in any case, that their presence would not have lent substantial value to the efforts, so being in Seville may have been for the best.

Putting an arm around the shoulder of his nearest son, he said, "Agustin, Andrés, my sons, we must all go to visit them soon. Just think of all the new material for your poetry."

"Most assuredly!" said Agustin. "From what you tell us, Father, our new brother seems to be a spirit warrior, capable of slaying evildoers, left and right."

"Quite true, but, Father, you absolutely must tell us more about Mencía!" joined in Andrés excitedly. "She is most extraordinary! I just cannot imagine what fantastic inspiration she might provide. Oh, I wish we had come home sooner."

Ch.20 New Crop

"THESE GREEN BULBS continue to swell. I wonder how much bigger they get?" asked Miguel as he bent down and felt a tomato on one of the plants.

"We will see," replied Pedro. "Mateo says the bulbs will turn red and soften when they ripen."

Looking up, Miguel saw Manuelito, one of the other children of the estate, running toward them. Seeing his gaze, Pedro turned to look too.

"Señor Miguel! Señor Miguel! They are back! Don Lorenzo and Guillermo and Mencía!" the boy called as he approached.

Smiling at the news, Miguel called back, "Thank you, Manuelito! I am coming!"

"Pedro, I must go. I think you may expect Don Lorenzo to be out soon to see the garden," said Miguel with a laugh as he walked away along a line of plants toward the gate.

"Yes, no doubt," said Pedro, smiling.

María was already there in front of the main house and hugging her son. Happily hurrying over to them, Miguel gave his son a hug and said, "Welcome back, Guillermo. We have missed you."

"I have missed you too, Father. And you Mother," he said turning to María.

"It is so good to hear you say so," María said beside him with her head on Guillermo's shoulder and wiping her teary eyes.

"I hope everything went well on your trip," inquired Miguel. "You were in such haste to return with the new overseer and your friends that we barely got to talk."

"Yes, we had remarkable success in straightening out the problems there. I will tell you all about it."

"And how is Don Diego's health?"

"His health is greatly improved. Our visit seemed to have been a terrific tonic for him. I am sure Don Lorenzo will tell you about it. Fixing his problems seemed to have lifted a great burden from him. And my presence did much to awaken his spirit."

"I am sure of it. I can imagine how proud he must have been to see what a fine young man you have become."

"Perhaps so. I am a different kind of son than he is accustomed to."

Their conversation was then interrupted by Don Lorenzo, who came out the front door and beckoned them all to come inside for refreshments. Mencía had been inside cleaning up and now came out to greet Miguel and María as they started to come in.

"Mencía, my dear, it is wonderful to see you too," María said hugging her. "You look so well and rested." Turning to her son, she added, "And Guillermo, the silly boy, thought there would be trouble."

A week earlier when Guillermo had returned to get the new overseer and the others, he had arrived in the evening and first gone to Don Felipe's estate. Guillermo had briefly described the purpose of his visit and gave Don Lorenzo's letter to him. Don Felipe had read it carefully and pondered for a few moments.

"Yes, I can recommend a man here named Rodrigo for the position. If we must lose him, I am glad it will be of help to my friend Don Lorenzo and his brother. I will send someone to get him."

"If I may suggest, Don Felipe. It will be much quicker if I go directly to see him. Do I have your permission?"

"Yes, certainly."

Five minutes later, Guillermo knocked on Rodrigo's door, and a solid young man answered, "Yes?"

"I am looking for Rodrigo Montoya."

"That is me. What can I do for you?"

"I have a proposal for you. Let us talk about it inside," and he started to push past him.

But Rodrigo blocked his way and said, "I did not invite you in. What is it you want?"

"As I just said, I have a proposal for you, now let me in!" Guillermo demanded and started to push his way past again.

Rodrigo blocked his way again and pushed Guillermo backward and away from his door.

"Perhaps you should take your proposal and go," he said firmly.

Guillermo smiled and, in a more cordial tone, said, "Rodrigo, my friend, I have just come from Don Felipe's house and have his permission to offer you an overseer position on another estate. My name is Guillermo from Don Lorenzo's estate. Here is the letter from him to Don Felipe seeking the overseer."

He handed the letter to Rodrigo who looked at him warily and began to read. After reading it, he brightened up a bit and Guillermo came forward smiling to shake hands. Rodrigo, also smiling, shook it and invited him in.

When inside, Guillermo told him, "I am sorry about that little episode, but the estate is in terrible shape and will require a good man to correct years of neglect. I think I have seen you in town before, but I do not know you. I wanted to see if you were as sturdy as you looked, to see if I liked you. And I do."

"I have heard of you, Guillermo. I hope I will merit your good opinion after two years and not just two minutes."

Smiling and shaking his head, Guillermo said, "Those would have been my exact sentiments were I in your place. Rodrigo, I knew I liked you! So now, about the position, the estate is northeast of Seville, about a three-day ride from here. An overseer is needed right away. Do you want the job?"

"Yes."

"I want to leave first thing in the morning from Don Lorenzo's. Can you do it?"

"Yes, I may need to leave some things behind for now, but I will be there."

"Excellent," said Guillermo, getting up and shaking his hand. "I have other people to see tonight, so I must leave now. Tomorrow morning, then?"

"I will be there."

Guillermo had already stopped at Pascual's camp on the way there and had seen Sebastian. Now he went to see Mencía. From Mencía's house, he rode back to the estate and saw Mateo to apprise him of what was happening.

"So you will be confronting this neighbor," said Mateo. "I will come with you."

"No, I do not believe there is a need for it. I am taking the new overseer, Mencía, and Sebastian as well as José from Pascual's camp. They should be more than enough. I believe your father would want you to stay."

"Well, I can be ready in the morning if you change your mind."

"Thank you, Mateo. Come see us off."

"I will."

As Guillermo was leaving, he said, "Mateo, we are still true friends, are we not?"

"Uh-oh, Guillermo, do you have another secret to share?"

"Yes," he said pausing, "but I think it can wait until I get back."

Next, Guillermo went to his parent's house to see them and get some sleep. When they heard the horse outside, Miguel and María came rushing out.

Crying and hugging him, María said, "Oh Guillermo, you have come back. I thought we might not see you again."

"Do not think such things, Mother. Nothing has changed for us."

Miguel was also beside him teary-eyed with his arm around Guillermo's shoulder.

"We feared we might have to give up our gift from God."

"Father, I have heard you and Mother call me that many times over the years and only now do I know how much you really meant it," said Guillermo with tears in his eyes.

"Do not worry. I am still your son. I must leave again tomorrow but only to help straighten out matters there. I will be back."

That conversation had taken place over a week ago, and now, Guillermo was back again as he had promised. When he was bringing his things from the trip into his parent's house, Miguel asked Guillermo if he thought he might be moving into the main house.

"No, Father. I am happy with the current state of things. I see no reason for change. I have no desire or need to be called Don Guillermo. On the return ride home, Don Lorenzo asked the others to keep the secret to ourselves for a time. I have not told Mateo yet. He will be surprised."

That evening, after some rest and food, Mencía was ready for her ride home. Mateo and Guillermo were there to see her off. Guillermo thanked her again for her help as she mounted her horse. With a big smile, she waved and galloped off.

They both watched with admiration as she rode away, and Guillermo asked, "How is it that we were so lucky to have found Mencía? I hope it does not make you jealous, Mateo, but I consider her a true friend like you."

Mateo laughed and asked, "And have you shared secrets with your new true friend?"

"No, not yet, perhaps someday."

"Speaking of sharing secrets, Guillermo, before you left a week ago your mentioned you had a secret. So, my true friend, what is the secret you wish to share?"

"You first, Mateo."

"But you are the one with the secret, Guillermo!"

"No, you first."

"All right, a secret I have never told anyone else is that I have lied to Luisa."

"What?"

"Yes, Luisa showed me her growing belly and worried I might think it unattractive. I thought she looked as if she had swallowed a cannonball, but I told her she looked beautiful."

After their laughter, Mateo was able to say, "So, Guillermo, what is your secret?"

"Oh, nothing really." He paused, then added nonchalantly, "only that I am the son of your uncle, and we are cousins."

Mateo's jaw dropped, and he stared at Guillermo speechless for a moment.

"So that is what this trip was about. Then, you just learned?" he finally said.

"Yes, your uncle Diego wanted to see his son before dying. My poor father and mother just learned also and were worried sick they had lost their son. I assured them they had not. I look just like your uncle Diego. There can be no doubt that he is my natural father."

"So that is the reason we never see him. He was afraid someone would notice."

"Yes, someone such as your mother. I wonder what her opinion of it will be."

"I imagine she will be fine with it, only angry at my father for not having shared the secret with her."

"Yes, I would say he is in big trouble on that count."

Putting his arm around Guillermo's shoulder, Mateo said, "It is funny. Perhaps we knew it all along."

"I said the same thing. I am still Guillermo, your true friend, which is much more meaningful than cousin."

"I agree, Guillermo, but welcome to the family anyway."

By June, Luisa was noticeably pregnant and managing much better, no more stomach sickness. Doña Antonia and Rosa were taking good care of her and happy with her progress. Luisa went for morning walks with Mateo and his mother without any difficulties or tiring. Luisa's growing baby was the most important thing to everyone on the family's estate.

The next most important growing things were the new plants in the garden. Pedro had grown more of the little tomato plants and replanted them two weeks and four weeks after the first planting. The three plantings displayed a progression of the life of the plants and resulted in three dozen tomato plants. With so many tomatoes formed on each of the plants, it looked as if a sizable number of tomatoes would be available for seed and sampling.

In late June, the tomatoes of the first planting had turned red, and Pedro would tug gently on them to see if they would separate from the plant. One morning, seven of them finally came off, and he brought them to the main house for everyone to see.

Four smaller ones, two medium-sized ones, and a large one were laid on the table. Everyone crowded around to watch as Don Lorenzo cut the two medium sized ones in half. The red flesh inside created much curiosity and talk as they passed them around and inspected them closely.

"Look how many seeds are inside!" marveled Pedro.

Don Lorenzo rapped his knuckles on the table to get everyone's attention and raised his hands to indicate he wanted to speak. They all looked and listened as he turned to Mateo.

"Now, my son," he said pointedly, "none of your tricks this time! Are these bulbs to be eaten raw or cooked?"

With an innocent smile, Mateo replied, "I cannot remember, Father. Cut a wedge and taste it."

"No! I shall not fall for that trick twice!"

María ran her finger across the flesh of one in her hand and put a juicy finger in her mouth.

"Umm," she said brightly, "It is very tasty and a little sweet."

A flurry of activity and talking ensued as the halves were cut into wedges, and everyone tried a piece. Soon those samples were consumed, and they cut the large one into many samples.

They all were impressed. Don Lorenzo asked Rosa to take the four small tomatoes to the kitchen, cut them in small pieces, and try cooking them. María and Juana went with Rosa to watch.

"Mateo, these red tomatoes of yours have an excellent taste. They are eaten there in the Indies without harm?"

"Yes, Father, the natives there have eaten all the new plants for centuries."

"These new vegetables from the Indies may be quite as valuable as the silver from it," he declared. Then remembering Mateo's gift, he added, "Not to diminish the wonderful silver spurs you brought me from there, Mateo, of course."

At this, Guillermo turned away and struggled to control his laughter while Mateo, trying to keep a calm straight face, said, "Yes, Father. I am sure you are right."

Glasses were filled, and they toasted Pedro and his tomatoes.

When Rosa, María, and Juana returned with a plate of cooked tomatoes, Rosa said excitedly, "Don Lorenzo, we cut them up and cooked them in olive oil with a little salt. They smell delicious."

He took the spoon on the plate and tasted a small spoonful.

"My God, they *are* delicious! I want more! But here, pass this around and taste some."

Everyone eagerly took a small taste as the plate made a quick round.

"Everyone on the estate shall get some of these marvelous seeds to grow tomatoes for their kitchens. Another toast!"

After a scurry to get glasses filled and raised, Don Lorenzo said, "To my son Mateo. God bless him for bringing them to us."

Mateo bowed in acknowledgement, and all heartily toasted him.

Don Lorenzo and Miguel soon huddled with Pedro concerning the now highly regarded tomatoes.

"These later plantings are growing well too?" asked Don Lorenzo with great interest.

"Yes, I believe so," replied Pedro.

"Does it make sense to try planting more now?" asked Miguel.

"I do not know. I have two little seedlings that I started last month out of curiosity. I can plant them."

"Yes, by all means," said Don Lorenzo. "We need to let most of the crop go to seed and save every precious one of the seeds. But I wish to have more for sampling too. I had no idea they would taste so good."

Mencía had been visiting and was present at the sampling. Afterward, she and Guillermo were sitting and talking out back on the outdoor patio of the main house.

"These new plants from the Indies are quite a find."

"Yes, and we still have peppers, maize and beans to sample."

"Guillermo, I noticed your struggle to control laughing when Don Lorenzo mentioned the silver spurs. What was so funny?"

"Oh, nothing. It is a private joke between Mateo and me."

"Then it is a secret."

"Yes."

"I have a secret too," said Mencía with mystery.

"I am sorry, Mencía. I would tell you, but it is not my secret to share. You must ask Mateo."

"Well, I will share my secret with you anyway."

"No, that would be unfair. There is no need."

"I do not mind."

"It sounds like you want to tell it. Now I am curious. What is this secret of yours?"

"My secret is," she paused as Guillermo leaned forward to listen, "Don Lorenzo knows that Mateo bought the spurs in Seville."

"What!" blurted out Guillermo, nearly falling off his chair.

"How do you know!" he finally said after recovering from his surprise.

"He recently confided it to me. I am not supposed to tell anyone, but I think he hopes it will get back to Mateo to ease his conscience."

"How did he find out?"

"He knew right away from the decorations on them. It is apparently a famous pattern of one silversmith in Seville."

"And he did not say anything?"

"No, he did not want to embarrass Mateo, so he acted as if they were a wonderful gift from the Indies."

"It seems that Mateo is not as clever as he thinks. Well, this uncle of mine, Don Lorenzo, is certainly full of surprises," he said, shaking his head in amazement.

"And how are you with being his nephew now?"

"I feel no different but know now that I owe him very much. He found good parents for me and kept the burden of the secret himself all these years. I have been most fortunate in my upbringing and see no reason to alter things now."

"Yes, I suppose you did not turn out so badly," said Mencía with a disinterested tone.

"Thanks!" he said, smacking her on the shoulder.

"My pleasure," she said with a grin.

Two days later, a carriage and horses arrived, bringing Luisa's parents and brothers for a visit. Don Francisco and Doña Isabel had been concerned for their daughter's wellbeing and were greatly relieved and pleased to find her in such fine health. The estate became a stir of happiness, meals, men talk, women talk, talk of babies, talk of the wedding celebration, news updates, tours of the gardens and oak meadows, and activities for the boys. Guillermo and Mencía took the boys out daily for archery practice, which delighted them as well as their father who occasionally would watch proudly.

Luisa's parents had greatly missed their daughter and spent as much time as they could with her. She took periodic rests, which enabled her to keep up with all the excitement, visiting, and activities without getting overly tired. Father Giraldo was invited out to take part in the happiness, which he had a part in making possible. Their neighbor Don Felipe also came to visit periodically and joined in the festivities.

Luisa's family had not yet tasted tomatoes. Back home, Don Carlos' gardener had not grown seedlings early in a hot house, so they were not yet ripe. A special dinner was therefore prepared one night so Don Francisco and his family could taste tomatoes. The cooks added them to a sausage and rice dish, and it caused quite a sensation.

One day, Mencía and Guillermo took Luisa's brothers on a horseback ride to visit and have lunch with Mencía's family. Her sisters played and sang for them. The two boys were fascinated by Margarita's guiterna. She showed them how to play and Domingo, the older of the two, was able to strum a few chords as she looked on giving encouragement. As Guillermo observed them, he was thinking that it would not be long before these two girls would need the dreaded duenna.

As a diversion, their cavalier friend, Don Tomás, was invited out one day for a session of saber and cutlass training. It had been some time since the last session, and he was excited to come. The boys watched as Mateo, Guillermo, and Mencía stepped through their training and practiced their moves. They soon had the boys taking part to their delight. The others watched and voiced their encouragement. Don Tomás still revered Mencía as a warrior princess and retold the story of their first training session often.

After two weeks, Luisa's parents thought they should be returning although the boys wanted to stay. Reluctantly, her parents said an emotional goodbye to Luisa. If she were to die in childbirth, this would be the last time they would see their daughter alive. They would be saying many prayers between now and late September when the baby was due. After hugs, handshakes, and farewells, they climbed into the carriage and mounted horses. With a nudge to the horses, they waved and reluctantly started off.

With tomatoes still coming in from the various plantings, the time for harvesting their maize had also arrived. With great interest, Don Lorenzo, Miguel, and Pedro had been watching as the maize seed packets grew on the tall straight stalks. Mateo's notes said when the tassels on top of the packets withered and darkened, they would be ready to pick.

When that happened in early July, Pedro cut one of the seed packets off and took it into the house for sampling. As everyone watched, Pedro pulled the husk off the packet revealing the neat rows and columns of yellowish seeds on the cylinder inside, which was a new sight for them. He pulled several seeds from the fibrous cylinder and Don Lorenzo cautiously tasted one. Not thinking much of the raw taste of the seeds, they cut the seeds from the cylinder and boiled them. When the cooked seeds were tasted, they did not generate the same enthusiasm experienced previously with the other plants.

Mateo told them the natives of the Indies dried and pounded the seeds into a meal from which they baked flat cakes. Since wheat and flour were unknown to the natives there, the maize meal was their equivalent of flour. Mateo knew the importance of maize to the natives of the Indies. Therefore, he thought that maize would surely become useful here, once they learned how to use the big yellowish seeds.

Miguel told the others that while they still may be learning to use the seeds, he knew what to do with the stalks. The cattle and pigs loved them.

Concerning the other new plants, Don Lorenzo was delighted to find the tomato plants were continuing to produce new tomatoes, although not in the amounts and sizes of the first offerings. The second planting of potatoes in February had produced well in June. The potato plants had grown well in the winter and spring, but not so well in the hot dry summer, so it made sense not to plant them again until October when the weather cools and the rains start.

Mateo had been getting together with Pedro to write down what they had learned about growing the new seeds. Thus far, they had good knowledge on potatoes, tomatoes, and maize. The intent was to supply their guidance to the family and friends who received seeds. Guillermo spent time in the evenings with Mateo writing copies of the guidance. After their harvesting, the guidance for peppers and beans could be completed as well.

Peppers, the original crop of interest, proved to be the most difficult to grow. Pedro had grown pepper seedlings and planted them like the tomato seedlings. While the tomato plants had blossomed and formed bulbs, they were not having the same success with the pepper plants. Not many blossoms had formed on the plants, and when they did form, some soon fell off. With Don Lorenzo getting concerned, Miguel and Mateo reviewed his notes without finding anything that may have been overlooked.

By the time the maize ripened, little green peppers shaped like fat peapods were finally forming from the blossoms that survived. Not until early August did the peppers on the first planting turn red and ripen. Then the peppers were brought in, carefully cut open, and the seeds removed.

They tasted the skins and found them to be spicy hot, exactly as they had hoped. They added a diced pepper skin to one of their normal recipes. After tasting the resulting dish, they rejoiced with happiness, getting up and hugging one another at the table. The new peppers had added a sweet spiciness to their food, an interesting flavor far better than the expensive black peppercorns from the East.

They had succeeded in growing their own pepper spice, although they were not satisfied with their skill at doing it. Pedro wanted to hear from the gardener at Don Carlos' to see if he had better luck. They began to harvest the peppers, cutting them open and saving the seeds. The skins were used in the kitchens on the estate and given to neighbors to sample.

As Mateo had seen in the Indies, they strung up a test sample of peppers in the sun to dry and preserve for later use in the kitchen. Mateo finished the guidance for growing peppers and made copies.

The last of the new plants, the bean plant with its pods, looked similar to pea plants. But unlike peas which are good to eat raw, Mateo had been warned that beans produced were poisonous when raw and needed to be boiled fifteen minutes to make them safe to eat. Don Lorenzo had questioned why they should grow these seeds if their beans are poisonous.

"Because they are very tasty and healthy when cooked. You must wait to see, Father."

When the pods on the plant dried and were ready to pick, Juana was to cook the beans first before bringing them to the house for tasting. Miguel was with Pedro as he picked the pods from the bean plant and brought a bowlful to Juana. They pulled the pods apart and examined the beans inside with curiosity. Juana put the beans in a pot of water and boiled them for a half hour.

Not wanting to risk poisoning the Don and his family, Pedro decided to eat a small bowlful himself. After noting their pleasant earthy taste, he went to sit down and wait. Miguel and Juana sat with him to observe and help him if needed.

After fifteen minutes, Miguel asked, "How do you feel, Pedro?"

"I feel fine, only my stomach seems to be rumbling a bit." Moving in his chair to ease the discomfort, he suddenly passed gas loudly.

"Pedro! What manners!" his wife scolded.

Miguel said with a laugh, "I suppose you feel better now."

With embarrassment, he replied, "Yes, much better. I feel fine, except for maybe a little gas."

"A little!" said Juana.

"Juana, I have been savoring the flavor of these beans while I sit," said Pedro. "I think a little onion and garlic flavor may add much to it. Let us go back into the kitchen."

Juana fried a little onion and garlic in olive oil and added it to the beans, which they boiled for another half hour. The beans and the remaining water in the pot were brown and gave off a rich earthy aroma. All three gathered around the pot sniffing and savoring. They decided they would all try a spoonful just to be sure. They passed around the spoon as each took a sample of the beans, which they all thought were quite tasty.

Juana removed the pot from the heat, and they went back into another room where they sat for ten minutes looking at one another.

"I feel fine," said Miguel finally.

"Me too," agreed Pedro and Juana.

"Let's take the pot to the main house and let them try it," Miguel suggested.

Don Lorenzo was hesitant to taste the beans, so Mateo tried them as the others watched with great interest.

"These are quite delicious, Juana," said Mateo. "Even better than I remember."

"We added a bit of onion and garlic."

Now more than curious, Don Lorenzo took the bowl and tried a spoonful.

"Quite delicious," said Don Lorenzo, passing the bowl to the others, who agreed, commenting on the wonderful flavor, good alone and probably in other dishes.

Before Pedro and Juana left to prepare more beans for further sampling at dinner, Don Lorenzo happily led a toast to them and the beans.

Miguel and Pedro did not think it appropriate to mention the new beans might produce gas. They thought it better to let the others make that discovery on their own.

Ch.21 Brothers

WITH THE SUCCESSFUL harvesting of beans, Mateo and Guillermo finished the guidance for growing the new plants and made necessary copies. It was the middle of August, the hottest time of the year and not the best time for travel, but the seeds and instructions needed to be delivered to the various family members. With Luisa nearly eight months pregnant, Mateo would not be going. So it would be up to Guillermo.

The trip to deliver them to Don Diego was also a chance for Guillermo to spend time with his father and take Rodrigo's remaining personal belongings to him. Guillermo told his father he would be back for the almond harvest in early September.

"No, there is no need for it. I can manage the almond harvest. You should spend time with your father and brothers. Just be back by late September when Doña Luisa is due."

"Thank you, Father. I will. Perhaps I should ask Mencía and Sebastian to join me. We could do some hunting while there as well."

"A fine idea, my son. I suspect that very little arm-twisting will be required to convince them to go," said Miguel, smiling.

Later when asked, both Mencía and Sebastian broke into big smiles, and the threesome began to prepare for the trip.

Their first deliveries would be to Dons Francisco and Carlos, west of Cordoba, but prior to that, Mencía wanted to stop in Cordoba to buy another hat. When she mentioned it to Guillermo, he gave her a puzzled look. Such frivolous things as shopping for hats normally did not interest Mencía.

"Why do you need another hat, Mencía? The one you have looks fine," he asked.

"Guillermo, I am a woman, you know," she said with mock seriousness.

"Yes, I am aware of that fact. And a quite handsome one, but is there a need to wear two hats at once?"

"Thank you for the compliment, I think," she said coyly. "I thought you liked my hat."

"I do, very much so."

"Well, if you must know, Luisa admires my hat very much too, and I want to buy one for her."

"Well, I feel better now, Mencía. You had me worried."

"Luisa also thinks it would look dashing on Mateo and wants to buy one for him as a surprise, so do not tell him. If you have the same hat size, we can use you as his model at the hat maker."

"Oh good, I will, at least, be of some use on this trip," said Guillermo drolly. "I believe we are the same size. I will check."

"That would be nice," said Mencía, smiling.

"Perhaps I shall get one for myself too. I am not averse to a dashing look," he announced as he left to find Mateo's hat.

Sebastian, who had been listening, said to Mencía with a laugh, "You two sound like some old married couple. And let me guess, you wanted all along for him to buy one of these hats, only you wanted him to believe it was his idea."

Mencía just smiled and said, "You give me too much credit, Sebastian."

"No, I do not think so."

The next day, they were ready. With an extra horse loaded with a large pack of Rodrigo's things and other supplies for the trip, they set out. They spent the night at Mencía's relations near Cordoba and then made the short trip to the hat shop in Cordoba the next morning.

Sebastian gladly offered to stay outside with the horses while Mencía took Guillermo inside the hat shop. Upon entering, the hatmaker greeted her with great enthusiasm.

"Señorita Mencía, my wonderful Mencía! Your hat has become quite popular! I have sold a great many, in two colors now, gray and black."

"I am so glad for you, Señor Muñiz. I need three more of them myself, for which I will pay you. There is no need for you to give me free hats."

"If you wish, Mencía, but I am indeed greatly indebted to you, my dear."

Putting her hand on Guillermo next to her, she said, "Señor Muñiz, this is my friend, Señor Guillermo Ramos. He is your model for two of them."

"An honor, Señor," said both men as they shook hands.

Then looking at Guillermo from side to side, the hat maker said, "Ah yes, he will indeed look handsome in one. I have already made a dozen for other men."

Pulling a cloth tape measure from his pocket, he said, "Señor Ramos, let us remove your hat for a moment to get a measurement. Yours is a fine hat, but I believe you will be pleased with the look of the new one. Yes, I believe it will suit you quite well."

Guillermo complied, and the hat maker reached up and put the tape measure around his head. With an uncomfortable look, Guillermo glanced over at Mencía, who smiled.

The next stop was at Luisa's parents where they were warmly received out front, especially by the boys who wanted to practice more archery. After taking their horses to the stables to say hello to their friends there, they came inside with the overseer where they visited with Luisa's family and delivered their seeds and instructions. Guillermo expressed his deep regret that they did not have more time to visit, but they must next be off to talk about plants with Don Carlos, spend the night, and then be off the next morning to deliver things to Don Diego.

After delivering letters from Luisa and others, giving them the seeds, and going over the guidance, Don Francisco suggested that they all go to their neighbor Don Carlos where they could continue to visit. It was agreed and they soon were on their way.

Don Carlos and Doña Antonia were delighted and surprised to see the travelers and friends coming in their drive and happily came out to greet them. They went inside to visit for a time, where Don Carlos told him of his gardener's success with the new plants.

"The pepper plants too?" asked Guillermo with astonishment.

"Yes, we just started picking them. A great many pepper pods are on the plants. You can see for yourself," said Don Carlos with enthusiasm.

"Really? That is extremely good news. We did not have good luck with them. My father and our gardener will be very interested to know what you did differently."

They all went straight out with Don Carlos to their garden. His overseer and gardener were there carefully cutting the pepper pods from the plants. Guillermo was surprised and laughed with delight at the sight of the large number of pepper pods on the plants. Then looking intently about, he noticed their pepper plants had been planted differently with more space between them. He looked at the soil and asked about their fertilizing. They had fertilized much less and experienced no trouble with blossoms forming. Pedro will be excited to learn this.

Their potatoes had not done as well in the heat of the valley and needed to be planted earlier. Now they would delay any further potato planting until the fall when winter rains started.

Their gardener also had good success with other new plants. They would read the instructions he had brought and have their own comments and observations written down by the time they returned.

Guillermo showed them how Mateo made a string of the peppers to hang in the sun to dry and told them about Pedro adding onion and garlic to the beans for added flavor. The cooking of the new vegetables was a topic of as much animated conversation as the planting and growing of them.

That night they enjoyed a dinner into which the home-grown peppers had been added. Everyone thought the peppers added an enjoyable spiciness to the meal. Don Carlos and his wife could not believe that they could now grow their own pepper seasoning. It was something they could not have imagined only a year before.

After a pleasing dinner, pleasant visit, and restful night, the threesome left the next morning as the Don and Doña waved farewell.

A day and a half later, they pulled to a stop in front of Don Diego's main house. As they climbed down from their horses, Don Diego hurried out and happily welcomed them.

"Mencía, Guillermo, Sebastian, it is wonderful to see you. I was not expecting you back so soon. What a pleasant surprise," he said as he embraced them and smiled.

"It is very good to see you again as well, Father," said Guillermo. "We have come to visit as well as bring you the seeds from the Indies."

"Ah, yes, Mateo's seeds. My brother Lorenzo was very excited and hopeful about them."

"We have just come from your cousin Carlos," added Guillermo. "He grew them this spring and summer and is also very excited."

Looking about, Guillermo asked, "Where are those two brothers of mine, Agustin and Andrés?"

"They are in Seville again. They go there regularly. We did not expect you, or they would have stayed to greet you."

"Well, I cannot visit without seeing them. We can travel to Seville if need be."

"No, there is no need for it. They do not stay there long and should be back any day. They will surely be pleased to see you as well. Oh, it gladdens my heart to see you again."

Rodrigo had seen them coming up the drive and now arrived with a stableman to take their horses.

Rodrigo, good to see you," said Guillermo, grasping his hand and clapping his shoulder. "You have made great progress already. We noticed immediately. But I knew you would."

"Thank you, Guillermo. Good day, Mencía, Sebastian."

After further exchanges of greetings, Guillermo pointed to the pack horse and said, "Rodrigo, the pack contents are mostly your belongings, the things you left behind. We also have brought the seeds for plants from the Indies."

"Ah, the seeds you talked about before."

"Yes, and also instructions on growing the plants."

"Very good."

"My goodness, the sun is quite hot today," said Don Diego, wiping his brow. "Come inside, my son, and we can talk more where it is cooler. You too, Mencía, Sebastian."

"Thank you, Don Diego, but I should help with the horses," said Sebastian respectfully.

"If you must, Sebastian, but both you and Rodrigo are invited to dinner tonight."

They both nodded and started toward the stables with the stableman and horses.

At dinner that night, Don Diego told what a splendid job Rodrigo was doing.

"He has revitalized the activities here. Much work has been accomplished. A number of our farmhands had grown unaccustomed to work and had to be dismissed. Fortunately, several of Don Hernando's men had relations and friends who needed work, and they are now here."

"We noticed, even as we rode in, that the fields, trees, grounds, and buildings all show much improvement in three months," agreed Guillermo.

"I hope to make some needed repairs to roof tiles on some of our buildings before it starts raining this fall," said Rodrigo.

"Speaking of the rains, when you are planting your winter wheat crop, you should also try planting the new vegetable called potato. I will go over the instructions with you tomorrow."

"These peppers from the Indies. My brother Lorenzo was so enthused about them," mused Don Diego. "It seems too good to be true. Is there really a chance of growing them here?"

Smiling, Guillermo reached in his pocket and pulled out a pepper, freshly picked from Don Carlos' garden.

"Yes, they do grow here. Smell this," he said, handing it to Don Diego.

With astonishment, he took the pepper and looked it over curiously, saying, "So this is what they look like."

Putting it to his nose, he drew back, saying, "Saints in heaven, it even smells spicy hot."

As Don Diego passed it to Rodrigo, Guillermo told his father, "Save the seeds inside, but have your cooks chop up the rest to use in their cooking tomorrow for dinner. They add a great deal of flavor to our normal foods. I think you will like it."

"Wonderful."

The next morning, Guillermo spent two hours with Don Diego and Rodrigo showing them the seeds and going over the guidance. Meanwhile, Mencía and Sebastian practiced archery and got gear ready for hunting. The neighbor Don Hernando would be joining them for dinner, and they would ask him if they could hunt on the back side of his property farther up in the hills above the valley.

In the afternoon, Guillermo and Mencía had joined Don Diego for a late lunch. He told them how he and Don Hernando were again close friends who visited each other regularly and went to church together.

Don Diego looked up when he thought he heard horses and a carriage pull up out front. Hearing it too, a servant left to see who had arrived.

Then they heard a sudden loud commotion as the front door burst open and Andrés frantically called, "Father! Father!"

Everyone at the table bolted up in alarm, wondering what was wrong. A breathless and distressed Andrés flew into the room and stopped in surprise at seeing Guillermo and Mencía.

"Guillermo, Mencía, you are here!"

"Andrés! What is the matter?" asked Don Diego anxiously.

"Father, Guillermo, we found her!"

"Who, Andrés? Who have you found?" asked Don Diego, greatly distressed.

"We found Floriana, Guillermo's mother!"

They gaped in stunned surprise as Andrés turned and rushed back out.

"Dear God! Can it be, be true?" stammered Don Diego as Guillermo and Mencía rushed out behind Andrés.

Outside they saw Agustin helping a thin and frail elderly woman down from the carriage as another woman in the carriage steadied her from behind. Now Andrés was supporting the elderly woman on one side and Agustin on the other as she collected herself. Guillermo and Mencía were there now too. As Andrés and Agustin started walking the elderly woman toward the front door, Guillermo helped the other thin woman down from the carriage.

It had been thirteen or more years since last seeing her, but Guillermo recognized his mother. She gave him a sweet look as she climbed down without speaking. She seemed a little unsteady too, so he held his arm out, and she took it as they walked inside. Mencía watched the touching scene for a moment and then gathered their things from the carriage to bring them in. Don Diego was at the door as Andrés and Agustin brought the elderly woman in. The housekeeper was directing them to one of the guest rooms. Don Diego stood half-stunned as Guillermo walked his mother past him through the door.

"Floriana, dear Floriana, I grieved so very much when I heard you died, but thanks be to God, it was untrue. You are alive."

"Yes, Diego, it is a long story, which I will tell you. Let me first take care of my dear mother and regain some strength, then I can do so."

She patted him on the arm as she passed and soon disappeared into the guest bedroom into which they had brought the elderly woman. Mencía followed them in with their things. In a minute, the brothers, Guillermo, and Mencía came back out, and the door was closed. The housekeeper called for other servants to help and for food and wine to be brought in. In a short while, the two new arrivals were cleaned up, fed, and resting in bed.

Meanwhile, back in the dining room, Don Diego was tearfully hugging and thanking his sons, hardly knowing what to say. Guillermo offered heartfelt thanks to them as well. They were tired, but calmer now. Seeing the food on the table, they remembered they were more than a little hungry as well.

They all sat back down at the table and had a thousand questions for the two brothers. After downing several glasses of sherry, the brothers looked to be finally able to offer some explanation.

Agustin started by saying, "She has been victimized and living in hiding, in desperate poverty. It took us all these months of trips to Seville to find her."

Guillermo's jaw tightened at hearing that his mother had been victimized.

"We have only heard bits and pieces of her story, so we will let her tell it."

"Tell us then, my sons, how you were able to find her?"

"And how did you think to even look for her?" asked Guillermo.

"Well," started Andrés, "when Father told us your story and that of your mother, he said he had heard Floriana died, but never heard how. It seemed a tragic, but unfinished play to us. After discussing it for several weeks between ourselves and our poet friends, Agustin and I concluded that Father and Guillermo deserved to know the final scene of this tragedy. We resolved to find it out if we could. We never imagined it would turn out as it has.

"Whenever we went to Seville for our theater activities, we would visit the flamenco shows and ask the performers if they had heard of Floriana. I mean, after all, it is an uncommon name. Even so, we got nowhere with these performers. They seemed tight-lipped. When we asked men in the audience, they remembered her and told us she had been with a dance troupe named *Romance de Seville.*"

"Her dance troupe must have changed their name when they went there," said Don Diego.

"We found the club where this dance troupe regularly performed every Friday and Saturday. After their show, we asked several dancers about her. They looked at us suspiciously and told us that she unfortunately died suddenly four years ago. We asked where she was buried, and they did not know. We asked about her husband and were told he was dead too, some unfortunate accident. One of them wanted to know why we asked about her. We told him our father was a great admirer of her dancing and wanted to find out. He told us that she was indeed to be admired and a tragic loss to them, but he could help us no further. Such was the extent of our success after two trips. Agustin, take over the telling while I have some food."

"Yes, Andrés, by all means," Agustin said, continuing their story, "On the next trip, we again visited the club of the dance troupe and inquired about her with other patrons. One woman on the second night remembered Floriana and her husband Alvaro. She had even been to their apartment, and she told us its address.

"We went there and asked the landlord if he remembered a woman who lived there four years ago named Floriana. Yes, Floriana López and her husband Alvaro. He remembered them but seemed to remember little about them. 'She died several weeks after her husband died, I think,' he told us. When asked if she died here in the apartment, he looked about and finally said yes. When asked if he was the one who discovered her body, he became irritated. He told us that we ask too many questions. He had nothing more to say and told us to leave."

"The interview was far less than satisfying," added Andrés

"We next went to the priest of that parish and asked about them," continued Agustin. "He showed us records of their deaths. The records confirmed that she died several weeks after her husband. No information was shown as to cause of death. The documents said they were both buried in the church cemetery in unmarked graves. We asked the priest where, and he could not remember. We looked about in their small cemetery not really expecting to find a trace of either of them. And we did not. Somewhere in the ground beneath our footsteps was the final resting place of Floriana."

"Agustin and I stood there gazing upon the small cemetery, feeling wretched," said Andrés. "We thought we had arrived at the sad end of our tragic play, still not knowing the final scene. We had seen a document of her death without finding her final resting place or learning how she died."

"Exactly so, Andrés," continued Agustin. "We were quite disheartened yet unwavering in our resolve to discover what happened. I suggested we go back to the landlord and pester him until he told us more. And Andres agreed. With new determination, we set out again.

But as we were leaving the church grounds, we were accosted by one of the men from the dance troupe. He demanded to know why we were asking about Floriana. And he did not want to hear any lame story about our father being an admirer! Well, we saw no way around it.

"We asked him, 'What if we told you that she has a son who wishes to find her?'

"He responded, 'Then I would say you are both crazy! She has no son!'

"We assured him, 'There you are wrong. She does.'

"At hearing this, he stared back and forth at us for a time and then abruptly left. This was on a Sunday and their next regular show was on Friday, so we went home, planning to return."

Now Agustin stopped to eat as Andrés continued, "We went back to the club the next Friday only to find another dance troupe was performing. The other dance troupe *Romance de Seville* would be gone for two weeks performing in Málaga.

Greatly disappointed, we resigned ourselves to the fact that we must wait for their return to see this man again.

"When the troupe finally returned, we went to their show and talked with him. He would tell us nothing but asked where we were staying. With a good deal of trepidation, we told him our address. Early the next evening, we heard a knock on our door. We opened it, and there he was. He asked if we had horses, and we told him yes. He said to meet him below when we got them, which we did.

"We rode on the main road south out of the city not far, perhaps four or five miles. He pulled up at a path leading back from the road into trees. Pointing, he told us the woman we seek lives in hiding with her mother-in-law in a house there back in the trees. He regretted to say that her living conditions were quite poor, which he had only just discovered. And with that, he rode off."

"Did he say why she must live in hiding?" asked Guillermo.

"No, he gave no explanation," answered Andrés.

"We walked our horses back into the trees," he began again, "and discovered a battered, broken-down house. When we knocked on the door, a woman's voice asked what we wanted. We said we were looking for Floriana López, and that her son and the father of her son wished to find her. She replied, 'If that be true, then you can tell me their names.'

"After we said the names, the door opened a bit and an elegant thin woman's face peered out at us. After looking us over, she asked who we were, and we told her Andrés and Agustin, two sons of Don Diego de Cordoba. At hearing this, she paused and considered us again. I suppose that we might have been heirs to an estate trying to eliminate evidence of other heirs. But she must have concluded we did not have the appearance or manner of such villains.

"With a distressed look, she told us that she and her mother were, in fact, in great need of assistance. They had little food and her mother's health was failing. She asked if they could stay for a time with us until she was better again. I told her that we most assuredly desired to help and would return shortly with a carriage. 'God bless you,' she said and closed the door.

"By the time we rented a carriage and came back for them, the night was already late, so we took them to our apartment where we gave them bread and wine and spent the night. In the morning, her mother, as she called her, seemed strong enough, so we put her in the carriage and brought them straight here."

"My dear sons, I am so proud of you and thankful to you. I truly believe your dear mother up in heaven was looking down upon you and guiding your efforts," he said emotionally.

"Yes, Andrés, Agustin, I thank you too. It would seem this play has more acts to follow," said Guillermo with determination. "I intend to bring the curtain down hard on any who have wronged my mother."

Ch.22 Her Story

FOR THE REMAINDER of the day and the morning of the following day, the two new arrivals stayed in their room. Don Diego did not want them disturbed except for the food and drink which the housekeeper brought in for them. She reported that Floriana was up and about, in better health, and taking care of her mother who was still in bed but appeared to be improving from her weak state.

In the afternoon, Floriana emerged from the room and came out to sit with the others who were anxious over her condition, as well as curious to hear her story.

She no longer possessed the youthful looks she once did, but she still cut a fine figure as she walked steadily to a comfortable chair in the living room and sat down. She patted Andrés and Agustin lightly on the shoulder thanking them as she passed. Don Diego, his three sons, and Mencía presently gathered near her, sitting and standing.

She drank a little from a glass of wine, which was offered, and looked about serenely.

"It is wonderful to see you looking better, Floriana. Can we get you some food?" asked Don Diego.

"No, I am fine. I thank you so much for your hospitality and care. And thank you, Andrés and Agustin, for rescuing us from our desperate situation. For quite some time, our only means of survival has been my mother begging for food and money on the roadside. When she became ill, we had no means, and our food ran out. But by the grace of God, you found us."

"And we truly thank God for it, I assure you," said Don Diego, patting her hand.

"Floriana, my dear, you have not been introduced to all here. You know my sons Andrés and Agustin. This handsome young woman is Mencía," he said, gesturing towards her.

They both nodded to each other.

"She is the close friend of the young man standing beside her, who I am sure you have surmised to be your son Guillermo."

Guillermo came forward, knelt beside his mother, kissed her hand, and said, "Hello Mother. I am Guillermo, your son."

"Yes, I recognize you, my son. I wanted so much to be your mother, but it was God's will that I should not. And you have grown to be a fine young man."

"Mother, I am extremely grieved to hear you were forced to live so miserably. I wish to bring punishment on whomever has victimized you and caused it."

"I appreciate your feelings, but blood precious to me has already been shed in an unsuccessful attempt at redress. I do not wish to add yours as well."

"Please, Mother. It sounds as if you have been grievously wronged, and someone should be punished for it. It will torment me terribly if not allowed to do so."

"Guillermo," interrupted Don Diego, "perhaps we should let your mother first tell us what happened. Floriana, are you up to it now or would you prefer to wait until you are stronger?"

"No, you deserve to hear how I have returned from the dead. It is not a pretty story, but I will tell it."

As she paused to take another drink, Don Diego motioned to Andrés, near the door. Andrés nodded and got up to shut it. After a deep breath, Floriana began.

"As you all probably know, I was a dancer in a flamenco dance troupe here in this area when I met your father. Guillermo was born and placed with those fine people at his brother's estate. I went there once when you were four years old to see you."

"I remember," said Guillermo.

"You looked so much like your father, even then. It was wonderful to finally see you and to see how well your parents treated you. Well, I am straying from my story and should return to it."

Glancing about, she continued, "After you were born, I went back to the only thing I knew, flamenco dancing. I rejoined the dance troupe, and after a time, we gained such fame that we moved to Seville where the best dance troupes perform.

"Several years later, I married one of the dancers in the troupe. Alvaro was a good man and treated me well. We made a good living for several years and lived in an apartment in town. But God in his infinite wisdom saw fit to turn our lives upside down one night.

"One of the men in the audience was a man, made wealthy by trade with the Indies. I paid attention to him during my dancing, thinking it might result in a large gratuity. After our show, he beckoned me unsuspecting to a backstage corridor. But instead of a gratuity, he and an accomplice abducted me. They carried me away before my Alvaro or the others knew, to an apartment where I was…"

Floriana hesitated before saying, "where I was 'shamed.' He laid some money on a table before he left, but I took none of it. Alvaro had been frantically searching for me all night. When I came back to the apartment, I told Alvaro what happened. He rushed out, found the man, and challenged him to a duel. But alas, this man was a skilled duelist, and my Alvaro was killed."

She paused for a moment in sad reflection.

"Afterward, I was afraid to leave my apartment. I went out only one time to see Alvaro's mother to tell her of her son's death. She lived not far south of the city and had visited us periodically over the years. My own parents died when I was young. I am fond of her and call her 'Mother.' She is the only mother I have known. My news of Alvaro's death caused great sadness for her.

"I returned to the apartment, not knowing what to do. I kept the door bolted and prayed for God's help. I watched outside and was frightened when I saw the same evil wealthy man ride by on the street looking up at my window. For two weeks, I hid inside the apartment, fearing to go out and be abducted by him again.

"The dancers of our dance troupe got up a collection for me and brought me some money and food. But they could do nothing for me otherwise. Not knowing what else to do, I slipped out and went to see our parish priest.

"I confessed to him what had happened. He was greatly disturbed by the egregious misdeeds of the man, saying God should have brought him into confession, not me. I told him I saw the man watching my apartment and feared he would attack me again. I told him I wanted to die, which was very distressing to him.

"After a long pause in thought and a heavy sigh, he said perhaps dying would be the best thing in my case, not actually dying, but supposedly dying. He offered to prepare a death record for me if I were to choose to be declared dead and go into hiding, so this predator would no longer stalk me. For him to do so, he said, was technically a sin, but it would be a small sin to help prevent larger, more terrible ones.

"I went back to talk with the landlord. He was a boyhood friend of Alvaro, and he agreed to cooperate in my supposed death. I thanked him and tried to pay him the rent owed, but he would not take it. I told him I would pack a few things, leave the rest for him, and go back to see the priest. My death would be dated tomorrow, and he could act accordingly.

"Another man named Matias in the dance troupe was also a boyhood friend of Alvaro and the landlord. He was the only other one who would know the truth and would later tell the other dancers that I had died alone in the apartment of heartbreak over Alvaro's death. I imagine that upon hearing this they were so troubled by it that they never wanted to talk of it.

"The landlord wished me well, and I slipped away. From the church, I went to see Alvaro's mother who insisted I stay with her. I had only a little money, and she received a little money monthly from her other son, much like what Alvaro and I had also done previously. That was four years ago."

"You have been in hiding for four years?" asked Don Diego with sympathy.

"Yes."

"I wish you would have thought of me for help, my poor Floriana," he said sadly.

"I did think of you, Diego, but I believed you to still be married and could not think of how to discreetly do it."

"At the time, I was married to my dear Teresa, God rest her soul. She died two years ago."

"I am sorry, Diego."

"I believe my dear Teresa, up in heaven, has forgiven me for my transgression. She has sent you here, so I may help you," he said with tears.

"Perhaps my Alvaro is there helping too," said Floriana with her own tears.

"Yes, perhaps. He sounds like a good man, an honorable man. He tried to avenge your honor, although he knew he would probably be killed."

She nodded sadly in agreement and said, "Now that God has taken him from us, I try to be good to his mother as he would have wanted. I have always treated her kindly, as she has done me. I did what I could for her while in hiding. For a year, we were able to subsist on the money from her son and the food grown in our garden. But then, the money from the son stopped. We later learned he had died of a fever.

"Our money soon ran out, and Mother was forced to beg for alms along the road. Thanks be to God, some of the muleteers and travelers on this main road south to Jerez were good souls and gave her money. I thought of dressing like a gypsy and dancing at a local inn. But it would only have invited more trouble, so I decided against it. I stayed in hiding and grew what food I could in the garden to help.

"We were able to scrape by for three years until Mother became ill and could no longer beg for alms on the roadside. Out of desperation, I began to beg by the roadside myself. Although I was fully covered up with barely my face showing, the stares I received from some of the passing muleteers frightened me, and I had to stop. We were near the end of our rope when Matias, the dancer from our troupe, found us.

"He was shocked to see our poverty and said he came to ask me if I had a son. When I confessed that I did, he was taken aback and deep in thought for a time.

"Finally, he said, 'Then they were not lying.' He told me about Andrés and Agustin, who he thought would help us. He then left to bring them back. The rest of the story you probably know."

"Yes, my dear, and I am so thankful they found you in time. I hope your mother is recovering. You and she are special guests here and welcome to stay for as long as you may wish," said Don Diego.

"Thank you, Diego. I believe she is doing better. I should check on her."

"Mother, it is gratifying to hear there were, at least, a few good players in your tragic tale. But I wish you would tell me the name of this evil man who so victimized you and your husband," asked Guillermo earnestly.

"No, my son, I will let God punish him."

Guillermo considered this for a moment, then looked up at his mother and patted her hands.

"Mother, perhaps you are right to rest easy in that thought. Perhaps these evil men will someday experience the Wrath of God," said Guillermo with a glance over to Mencía.

Ch.23 Trader

AFTER TELLING HER TALE, Floriana stood up and went back into the guest room to check on her mother.

Guillermo motioned for Mencía to join him outside where they quickly made their way out to the stables and found Sebastian. They walked a distance from the stable to talk privately and gave Sebastian a brief account of Floriana's story.

"What do you plan to do?" asked Sebastian.

"I do not know yet, but this wealthy trader and his accomplice will pay dearly. I am not certain if the three of us will be sufficient for the task. I do not intend to involve Rodrigo. He is too valuable here. It is a long trip back to Pascual's camp for added help."

"I know of a man here who will help," said Mencía.

"Who?"

"A man named Martín who works for Don Hernando."

"I remember him," said Sebastian. "He seems like a man who can be counted on."

"I believe I remember him too. You wounded him with your knife. Why will he want to help?" asked Guillermo.

"He believes he owes me his life for not killing him during our incident. He has told me if I ever need anything, just ask. I believe he is a Morisco, and these people take such things quite seriously."

"I agree," said Sebastian.

"Then we have four for our task. That may be sufficient until we find out more," said Guillermo. "We intended to talk to Don Hernando about hunting but now have more pressing matters. We should ride to his estate now so that we may talk to Martín and set things in motion."

All seemed to be settled, so they hurried back to the stables, got their horses saddled, and rode to see Don Hernando, who was pleased to see them. The day before, he had heard of Floriana's return and expressed his happiness for his friend. He then listened attentively as Guillermo told how she had been well enough to tell that she had hidden in poverty for years after being victimized and of his desire to go to Seville to seek justice for her. Don Hernando had no problem with Martín going and offered them the use of his pistols and anything else they needed.

Martín was delighted and honored that Mencía had remembered him. He accepted without hesitation and quickly gathered up his things, saddled his horse, and was ready to ride anywhere and face anything with them.

For now, they just rode back to Don Diego's where they sat and talked. First, they needed to identify the wealthy trader and his accomplice. Next, they would watch them and decide on a course of action.

Their first step seemed straightforward enough. Matias the dancer would be the starting point. An introduction through Andrés or Agustin would help since Matias already trusted them. The brothers' apartment there in Seville would also be a useful base of operations. While Sebastian and Martín started getting things ready, Guillermo and Mencía went in to solicit the assistance of his brothers.

When Guillermo asked his brothers for their help, Andrés answered with enthusiasm, "Oh Guillermo, how exciting! Of course, we will help."

"Yes, yes, I agree!" said Agustin. "But what is Father to tell your mother when she sees we have gone? Did she not say to seek no vengeance on this monster?"

"He can tell her that we left to return the carriage and get their things, I suppose. We will tell him the same, so he will not be lying."

Two hours later, they were gone without seeing Floriana who was in with her mother.

At the flamenco club, Matias noticed the two brothers in the audience sitting with the young man and woman. He had not expected to see them again so soon. After discovering the desperately poor circumstances of Floriana and her mother, it would ease his mind to know they had been rescued. The brothers perhaps wanted to inform him they had done so.

During a break in their performance, he went to their table, and they beckoned for him to sit down with them, which he did.

"Matias, Señor, we have taken Floriana and her mother away from their hiding place, and they are being well cared for," Andrés told him.

"So you know my name now. You must have heard the story from Floriana."

"Yes, we have. As we told you before, she has a son. He sits now before you."

Matias shifted his gaze to Guillermo as Andrés continued, "This is her son Guillermo and his friend Señorita Mencía."

Matias nodded cautiously, and they nodded back.

"If I may call you Matias," Guillermo said in a low friendly voice, "I want to say that I owe you a great debt of gratitude for your assistance in finding my mother. You cannot imagine how much it has meant to me."

"I only regret I did not discover sooner how miserable their conditions were. I would have tried to help them earlier."

"I place no blame on you. I only ask for one more bit of assistance, and then we will bother you no more."

"What is it you need?"

"Tell me the name of the wealthy trader who victimized my mother."

Matias looked at him for a moment, considering the request, and finally said, "His name is Bartolomé Gómez. He is a regular at these flamenco clubs and flaunts his money and reputation as a womanizer."

With a look of grim determination, Guillermo said, "Thank you, Matias. Are you certain that it was this man Gómez?"

"Yes. I know positively that Gómez attacked your mother and shot Alvaro. I was Alvaro's second at the duel, and I watched him do it."

"And yet this devil goes unpunished?"

"He has much influence here in Seville."

"And where do I find this trader Gómez?"

"It will not be difficult for you to find him, my young friend, but you must be calm when I tell you," said Matias, pausing.

Guillermo nodded and listened intently.

"He sits at the table across the dance floor. The one with the large dark eyebrows and mustache."

Everyone at the table froze in surprise and then took furtive glances across at the man.

"The one wearing the red bandana?" asked Guillermo, making sure.

"Yes, and the man beside him is his bodyguard, a dangerous man. He has been with Señor Gomez for many years and was his accomplice in the crime against your mother."

Guillermo stiffened as a moment of rage passed over him. Then he relaxed again and, reaching across the table, discreetly shook Matias' hand.

"Thank you, Matias. I shall not forget your assistance. Perhaps you should go now so we do not draw attention to you."

"Let me know if you need more. I, too, think he should pay for what he has done. Again, be careful of his bodyguard," he said as he got up and walked away to rejoin his troupe.

It was already dark when the foursome left the club not long afterward and walked down the street. Stopping in a doorway, Guillermo said he and Mencía would stay and watch for them coming out. The two brothers should go back to the apartment and have Sebastian and Martín come back. Guillermo did not expect trouble but wanted them to see the club and the area.

As they watched, people were coming and going from the club. A brief time later, Sebastian and Martín came. Martín said he used to work on the docks here, so he and Sebastian set out to see what could be learned about this trader Gómez.

Two hours later, Guillermo and Mencía saw the trader and his bodyguard emerge from the club and begin walking up the street. They followed well behind them for several blocks and saw them stop at a gated entrance in the high masonry wall of what looked to be a residential compound. A guard inside unlocked the massive, ornate iron gate and came outside as he swung it open for them. He wore a plumed hat, leather breast armor, and a pistol and cutlass in his belt. He stood respectfully as they came inside the gate. Then coming back inside himself, he swung the gate closed and relocked it.

Guillermo and Mencía watched with interest from a dark alcove. They considered what to do next and decided against nonchalantly walking by the gate to get a closer look. It was too risky since the bodyguard might be by the gate and recognize them from the club. So they stayed in the dark alcove for two hours before the trader and his bodyguard came out and began walking in their direction.

As the pair approached, Guillermo and Mencía had their knives ready. The trader smugly strolled along while the bodyguard was cautiously eyeing about. He eyed their alcove too but did not see them in its darkness. The two men continued past, walked to a square, and climbed in a carriage. No longer able to follow, Guillermo and Mencía went back to the apartment.

The next morning, they talked about what had been learned. Martín learned the trader had spent time in the Indies where he amassed a fortune probably through smuggling and exploitation. Ten years before, he had returned and set up a business trading goods with the Indies on ships of the annual treasure fleets. His warehouse on the docks currently housed a great deal of goods from the return of the fleet several months before. His money buys enormous influence with city and trade officials. He lived in an affluent section of Seville with a wife brought back from the Indies. He was described as ruthless, abusive, and not God-fearing.

"God is not the one he now needs to fear," said Guillermo with firmness after hearing this.

"I am not sure what to make of the place with the guard at the gate," said Guillermo, thinking of the day's activities. "How about if you two, Sebastian and Martín, watch it today and perhaps we can visit it tonight to learn more about what is inside. Mencía and Agustin, you watch the trader to learn his daily habits. I will ride down with Andrés to visit my mother's shack. We will be back in several hours and find you then."

A short time later, Guillermo got down from his horse and walked to the door of the dilapidated house. Opening it, he looked inside and saw no one. Going in, he was angered at seeing the wretched conditions under which his mother had been forced to live for years. He noticed a few personal things, which he thought she might want, and gathered them up.

"They lived under most destitute circumstances," said Andrés as he entered the house and saw the rickety furniture, empty shelves, and shabby clothes in a drawer.

"Not much looks to be worth saving," said Guillermo, glancing around sadly.

They went outside and looked about. There looked to be water in the well. He saw her meager garden. Looking around at the trees, he thought how they had helped hide and protect his mother all those years. He felt like he owed them a debt of gratitude. The place and its trees might still prove useful as a gathering or hiding place for their efforts.

With the small bag of things collected, they got on their horses and started back north to the city.

The trader left his residence late in the morning, paid a brief visit to his warehouse, spent a three-hour lunch with apparent business associates, visited the gated compound for two hours, had dinner with other men for another three hours, and went back to his residence late in the evening, always with his bodyguard close by.

From nearby flat rooftops, Sebastian and Martín watched as several deliveries were made to the gated compound. The guard would unlock and open the gate. The drivers would carry their goods inside the gate and set them down. A locked inner gate provided an added level of security. Once the goods were inside, the outer gate was locked, and the inner gate was unlocked. Another guard from the house brought out a dark servant who carried the goods into the house under the stern direction of the guards. When the trader visited the compound, the guard unlocked the inner gate as soon as he came inside the outer one. These guards change places every two to three hours.

"Are there any other entrances?" asked Guillermo.

"No," replied Sebastian. "There is a courtyard between the gated wall in front and the main house behind. The adjoining buildings on each side enclose the courtyard so the front gate is the only way in and out. The house has no windows on the ground floor. Both the front and back of the house have second and third floor windows with narrow balconies and iron railings. But the windows are bricked up except for narrow ventilation slits. The roofs of the adjoining buildings are flat, and we can travel from one to the next if we want. But they would probably hear us walking on their roof."

"The back wall of the main house faces an alley. I could climb up without noise to one of the second-floor window balconies to hear and maybe see inside. We can try it tonight," offered Martín.

"Very good. Sebastian can be below in the alley with you. Mencía and I will cover you from a rooftop. Andrés and Agustin, perhaps you should watch the street in front to warn us should the guards come out the front gate for any reason."

Late that night, Guillermo and Mencía watched from a nearby flat roof with their bows and arrows ready. Martín and Sebastian stood below in the alley behind the house. Looking up at the second story window balcony above him, Martín swung his rope around several times and quietly lassoed an ornamental point on the iron railing. He gave the rope a couple tugs and nodded to Sebastian. Silently, he pulled himself up and climbed over the low railing to stand on the narrow balcony. He stood for a moment listening, then put his ear to the bricked-up window.

As they watched, Martín listened intently for a time and then took a quick peek inside through one of the narrow slits, maybe only a thumb-width wide. Then Guillermo was surprised to see him tap lightly on the bricks, listen again, tap again, and then whisper something into the slit to someone inside. Then he listened for a time, whispered back, then more back and forth, before climbing silently back over the railing and down the rope. After flipping his lasso from the iron railing, he and Sebastian crept silently down the alley.

Guillermo and Mencía, eager to hear what happened, got down from the roof and joined them a distance away.

Martín told them when he first got onto the balcony and listened, he could hear someone inside crying unhappily. He peeked inside and saw a young girl lying on a bed sobbing. When he tapped lightly on the brick, her crying suddenly stopped, and he could hear her coming over. When he tapped again, she tapped in reply.

"Are you being held here against your will?"

"Yes, I was kidnapped and am part of a harem here."

"How many are held here?"

"Three other girls. Please save us."

"How many guards are here?"

"One at the gate and one inside as far as I know. There are moriscos slaves here too, one man and two women."

"Will they help the guards?"

"No, the guards abuse them. They will not resist you."

"Say nothing to anyone. We will make a plan for your rescue."

"God bless you."

Guillermo grew angry and more determined after hearing this.

"Yes, Martín, we certainly will. It seems the behavior of Señor Gómez has gotten even more deplorable. Let us get Andrés and Agustin, and head back to the apartment."

On the way back to the apartment, Guillermo was already formulating a plan in his mind. When back at the apartment, they huddled together to hear what he proposed.

"The front gate is the only access inside, so that is where we must attack to gain entry," began Guillermo. "It must be done at night under the cover of darkness, which means we attack when the trader and his bodyguard come after visiting the flamenco club. I noticed the high stucco wall with a wide opening across the street from the gate. We should have a closer look at it.

"When the guard opens the gate to let them in, we can burst out from there and, with our arrows, ambush the trader, his bodyguard, and the gate guard. There should be sufficient light from the lantern hung there by the gate. Then we unlock the inner gate quickly and dispatch the other guard when he comes out. None of these men deserve our sympathy. The element of surprise will be a great advantage for us."

The others nodded in agreement.

"The next time the trader goes to the flamenco show, we shall assume he is going afterward to visit his harem. We will not get such forewarning at any other time. We strike when the guard opens the gate for him. The flamenco shows are on Friday or Saturday, and this is Sunday morning, sufficient time for preparations. Andrés and Agustin will be standing by with two covered carriages for transporting the captive girls quickly away from the house and out of the city.

"As I think about it, it will be night and traveling all night to my father's estate is out of the question. That leaves my mother's shack, which is close, deserted, and secluded. We have time to set up a camp there behind the house. Perhaps we will only need the camp for the one night. The next day, we will take the girls in the carriages to their families and the rest of us will return to my father's estate."

"And what about the morisco slaves?" asked Martín.

"I was going to ask you about them, Martín. Do you think they will want to run away or come with us?"

"We can give them the choice and should bring them with us if they want. They are my kinsmen and victims of this man just as the young girls are," said Martín.

"And what do we do with them after bringing them away?" asked Mencía.

"Let them go freely on their way," offered Martín.

"Can we trust them?" Sebastian asked.

"We are freeing them. I think we can trust them to help us and keep quiet about it. It is to their benefit," said Martín.

"True enough, Martín. If they want, we will bring them with us, and they can spend the night at the camp. The next morning when we leave with the girls in the carriages, they can go their way from there."

"I will ask my friends on the docks for the name of a barber-surgeon who can attend to wounds, should we receive any," said Martín.

"Good thinking, Martín. Well, what do you all think?" They all agreed it was a good plan.

During the week, they would set up a camp at the shack, work out the details of the attack, and continue their surveillance and preparations, all the while taking pains to avoid creating suspicion. When Friday came, they were ready.

Ch.24 Rescue

ON FRIDAY EVENING, Guillermo and Mencía watched intently as the trader and his bodyguard appeared and entered the flamenco club.

"You stay here, Mencía. I will let the others know."

Two and a half hours later, the trader and his bodyguard left the club and walked up the street to the gated compound. When the guard saw them approaching, he unlocked the heavy iron gate and pushed it open. The gate guard stood in front of the gate and nodded to acknowledge his boss.

The bodyguard, a little behind the trader, noticed a movement across the street from the corner of his eye and quickly looked, but was immediately struck through the throat with an arrow. Clutching his throat as the blood spurted out, he could only make a gurgling sound.

At the same instant, the rich trader was haughtily eyeing the kowtowing guard by the gate when suddenly an arrow appeared in the guard's throat. The guard staggered in surprise, grasped at his neck, and then stared wide-eyed in shock at the blood on his hands. Staggering a step forward, he fell to the ground at the feet of the trader, who had watched him in stunned silence.

Turning in shock, the trader saw several dark figures running toward him. He saw something flash through the air and then felt a sudden sharp pain in his groin. Grimacing in pain and looking down, he saw an arrow deeply imbedded in his lower body.

Terror-stricken, he glanced around for help from his bodyguard, who he saw reeling about with an arrow in his neck and desperately clutching for the pistol inside his coat. A second arrow then struck the bodyguard in the chest, and he collapsed to the ground.

The trader felt intense pain and started to cry out but was struck hard in the face by one of the dark figures who were now upon him. He fell backward to the ground as they rushed past.

Martín now had the key ring from the outer gate and was hurriedly trying the other keys on the inner gate. He got it unlocked and pushed open, then raced forward to get beside the door of the house before the guard inside came out.

He was almost there when the door burst open and the guard inside aimed a pistol at him. Suddenly an arrow appeared in the guard's chest, and he dropped the gun and crumpled forward out the door and onto the ground. Martín quickly rolled the guard's body over and found a key ring. Shoving the body aside, he hurried inside with his pistol drawn. Mencía was close behind him.

Outside, Guillermo and Sebastian were busy, hastily dragging the dead men and the trader out of sight along the walls of the interior courtyard. After shutting and locking the outer gate, they quickly bound and gagged the trader who was still alive but losing blood. Within only a minute or two, they completed their work and raced inside the house.

Meanwhile inside, Martín had climbed the stairs and raced to the room where he had previously heard the girl crying. On the way, he and Mencía had passed by two of the morisco slaves who had shrunk away backward in a frightened, non-threatening manner. Mencía had motioned to them to be quiet and stay put.

At the girl's door, Martín saw that it was bolted closed with a lock on the bolt. Mencía was there beside him, keeping an eye out for more guards and poised for action. She held a candle for him as he tried a key in the lock.

"Hello inside! We are here to free you! Are you there?" Martín called out as he tried different keys.

"Yes, yes, was it you the other night?"

"Yes," he said as the key finally turned, and he unbolted and opened the door. The girl was crying with happiness as she came forward.

"You see. We have come. Quickly, show us where the others are!"

The girl came out the door and looked in wonder at the unfamiliar faces of her rescuers. Then hurrying past and pointing, she said, "Down here!"

Running to a door, she knocked excitedly and shouted, "Ana, people are here to free us! Are you there?"

"Dear God, yes, I am here, Beatriz. I am here."

Martín was trying keys in the door lock by the light of Mencía's candle when Sebastian arrived.

"Do you need any help here?" he asked.

"No, Sebastian. We are fine here. We should have the second girl free soon," said Mencía.

He nodded and hurried back down.

A key finally turned the lock and Martín opened the door. The young girl rushed from the room and hugged the first girl, crying.

"Quickly, where are the others?" Mencía asked them firmly.

"This way," they said hurrying down the hallway with Martín and Mencía close behind.

Downstairs, Sebastian found Guillermo talking to the three slaves, one man and two women. One of the women was ringing her hands and rocking back and forth in a religious fervor.

"Praise God! You are going to free us? No, we have nowhere to go and want to come with you," the man was telling him.

"Keep your voices down. We will take you with us and then let you go where you want. How many girls do you know of here?"

"He keeps four here now. I heard them talk that he wants more," the man told Guillermo.

"All right, gather up your things. We leave in several minutes."

"Thank you, thank you, thank you," said the man.

The second dark woman approached Guillermo and said, "I have something to show you."

"Please, we do not have much time!"

She walked down the hall carrying a lit candle and beckoned him to come. He followed her, and she whispered, "A money box is hidden in a room down here. I can show you where it is."

Guillermo looked at her in surprise, not sure if he should believe her. He heard Martín call down, "We have freed all four girls. They are getting their things together for leaving."

"Martín! Let me have the keys," he called.

Soon he had them in hand and was following the woman down the hallway. She pointed to a door, and he tried several keys until one turned the lock. Opening the door, he went inside, and the woman pointed to a large wooden cabinet.

"There is a shelf hidden in the wall behind that," she said. Guillermo moved the heavy cabinet away from the wall and pulled a heavy wooden box from a shelf there. He sat it on the floor with a thud.

"I found it one day when I was cleaning. It would be a shame to leave it."

Going to the door, Guillermo put his head out and called, "Sebastian, come quickly. I need your help with something."

Sebastian had been at the front door checking outside, where he saw all was quiet in the courtyard. Hearing Guillermo call for him, he rushed back and found Guillermo standing over the locked box.

"Sebastian, it is heavy. Grab a handle, and we will take it with us."

Guillermo and Sebastian each grabbed one of the two handles and carried the box into the hallway.

"It must weigh a hundredweight," Sebastian said. "What is in it?"

"I do not know. We will find out later," said Guillermo as they carried it from the house and put it down by the inner gate.

"Are we ready to go?" he asked, coming back inside.

After seeing the excited nods of everyone, he told them, "Wait here while we wave for the carriages. I will signal when to come out."

Sebastian was already out by the street, and Guillermo signaled him to have the carriages come. Looking down the street, Sebastian waved with an extended arm to come forward. In less than a minute the carriages were out front, and they had the box loaded in the first carriage beside Andrés.

"Take care of this box," Guillermo told him, handing him a pistol. Andrés took the pistol and put it beside him.

They signaled back to the house, and people began silently hastening from it. As they passed through the courtyard, they saw the villain who had been their captor. He was propped up against a side wall sitting in a pool of his own blood, gagged, and now moaning in pain from the arrow sticking from his bloody groin. Filing out through the gates, they climbed quietly into the carriages.

"Get started for the shack, Andrés. We will catch up with you shortly," Guillermo told him in a low voice. Andrés nodded and with a flick of the reins, the first carriage began to roll slowly away. The second carriage followed, and as Agustin slowly passed, Guillermo handed him a pistol. Agustin took it with a nod, and the carriages were away.

After closing the front door of the house, the four of them stood in the courtyard looking about. They quickly retrieved their arrows from the bodies of the dead guards and bodyguard. The wounded trader was moaning in pain as he sat, slumped against a side wall. Guillermo strode over and stood before him.

Looking down at him for a moment, he resolved, "I will not permit this man with the large dark eyebrows and mustache to kidnap and shame another woman or girl."

Guillermo slapped the man's face to get his attention, and he opened his eyes and weakly looked up at him.

"It is time, Señor Gómez, for you to suffer the Wrath of God for your sins," he said in a low voice.

Going back to the others ten yards away, he got out an arrow. As the trader watched with dull eyes, weakly shaking his head, Guillermo put the arrow on his bowstring and pulled back, taking aim with grim determination.

But before he let fly the arrow, the man went limp and slumped over to one side, apparently dead. Guillermo relaxed and lowered his bow, looking at the man. He went to him and felt his neck for a pulse, finding none.

"He is dead."

Walking back and motioning to the others, they hurried out the large inner gate. Guillermo closed and was about to lock it, when Martín said, "One second, Guillermo, there is something I must do."

Brushing past Guillermo quickly, he went back into the courtyard. A moment later, he returned, putting his knife back in its sheath on his belt.

"He was dead, but I made sure," he said.

They looked at one another momentarily before Guillermo finished locking the inner gate. Once outside, they swung the heavy iron outer gate closed. Reaching through from the outside, Guillermo locked the outer gate and tossed the key ring inside where it landed out of sight. The four of them then walked briskly to get their horses.

Ten minutes later, they caught up with the carriages and continued with them. Finding the side road in the dark, Guillermo waved the carriages in. They clattered onto the rough path, drove back into the trees to the house, pulled around the back out of sight, and stopped. Everyone climbed out and began happily hugging and saying prayers of thanks for their release. A prepared firewood pile was lit, and food and wine were brought out. The freed captives sat around the fire as they happily ate while being questioned to find out what arrangements would be needed in the morning.

Guillermo and Mencía questioned the girls to learn where their families were located. The first young girl was from a city on the coast by Cádiz. A year before, she had been kidnapped on her way to a friend's house. The second girl named Ana was from

Jerez. She had been kidnapped a year and a half earlier as she left the party of a friend. The third girl was from another city near Cádiz, another victim of kidnapping a year earlier.

The fourth girl named Beatriz was from Huelva. She had been training in flamenco dance in Seville and was kidnapped after one of the shows. She told them she could not go back to her parents. What happened to her would be too shameful for them to accept her back. Guillermo told her sympathetically that the evil trader had been the shameful one, not her. She asked if they could find work for her away from Seville, and Guillermo told her they would take her back to his father's estate for now.

The three freed slaves told Martín and then Guillermo that they had nowhere to go if they were to leave tomorrow from the camp. So it was decided that they would be taken back to his father's estate where they would have time to rest and better decide what to do.

The three young girls from Jerez and near Cádiz were from an area to the south. Only one carriage would be needed to take them back to their families. The second carriage could be used to take the others to the estate.

If money was in the box, it was fitting that the three girls should have some of it, so it needed to be opened. Sebastian and Guillermo carried the box into the house. With a hatchet Sebastian found, they broke the lock and opened it as Mencía and Martín watched. They gasped and stared in surprise at its contents.

"It is full of gold doubloons. It must be a fortune," said Martín in awe.

Picking one up and examining it, Guillermo said, "Not just doubloons, but doubloons of eight escudos, the largest kind, each one worth, let me see, 128 reales. Just ten or so of these are worth more than our entire almond crop this year.

Digging his hand down into the coins and examining the ones below, Sebastian said, "They all look to be the same, a whole box of them!"

"Well, again, it is only fair that each girl gets a share. Let us get started," said Guillermo.

They ripped three squares from an old blanket they found. Guillermo reached in with both hands and put a double handful of coins onto the first square, then repeating it for the other two. It barely made a dent in the pile of coins in the box. They tied the squares up into three sacks to take with them and secured the top of the box down again, using Sebastian's leather belt.

"We should do the same with the remaining girl and the slaves too. After all, it was the one slave woman who pointed it out to us. Each should get a double handful of the coins like the three girls.

"Mencía and I will leave at daybreak to take these girls back to their parents. Sebastian and Martín, you and Andrés and Agustin can take this box and the rest back to my father's estate in the other carriage. I do not see why you cannot leave tomorrow morning too. Just give Seville a wide berth, and we will see you at the estate, probably in a week."

"Are you sure you can trust us with all this gold?" asked Martín with a smile.

"I can," said Guillermo, clapping Martín on the back.

"I also should mention, my compadres, you all were magnificent back there at the house, truly magnificent," he said smiling broadly, then adding, "We will celebrate when we are back at the estate."

"By the way, who put the arrow in the guard at the door?" asked Martín.

With a laugh, they pointed at Mencía who smiled brightly.

Shaking his head, Martín said with exasperation, "I owe her my life again!"

Back out by the fire, they announced their plans, which pleased everyone. They would only be spending one night here at the camp. They all began to stretch out on blankets and saddles near the fire. The money box and coin bundles were kept under close watch within the camp. The freed captives were soon resting peacefully, more peacefully than they had in some time. The four compadres and the brothers would keep the fire going during the night and stand three-person watches to ensure their camp was not surprised by thieves.

At dawn, the carriages and horses were readied. The three young girls, carrying their small bags of belongings, climbed into the lead carriage. Food, wine, and the three sacks of coins were put beside them. Mencía tied Guillermo's horse to the back of the carriage and mounted hers. With Guillermo driving the carriage, they waved to the others and started off.

It would require a day and a half to reach Jerez, their first stop. They stayed at an inn on the way and kept close guard on the coin sacks. In the early afternoon of the next day, their carriage arrived at the home of the girl Ana. Her parents cried and cried at the miraculous return of their little girl. They grieved much when she told them what happened and were gratified to hear the perpetrator had been severely punished. Healing would take much time and many prayers. They did not know what to do with the money. It was a small fortune for them, but at the price of their daughter's misery and shame. They would put it away and perhaps someday would make use of it.

After an hour with the grateful family, Guillermo, Mencía, and the other two girls continued to the home of the next girl in El Puerto de Santa Maria where they arrived in the early evening. The scene here of overjoyed and grateful parents reacting to the miraculous return of their daughter was very similar in nature to the previous scene at Jerez. Guillermo, Mencía and the remaining girl spent the night here with the family and left early the next morning to take the last girl to her home in Puerto Real.

They arrived in the late morning to another emotional homecoming and grateful reception. The rescue of the girls was an unforeseen but gratifying outcome to their operation, which had also accomplished its original intent of finding and punishing Floriana's wrongdoers.

With much of the day left, Guillermo and Mencía began the trip back and made it beyond Jerez before stopping for the night at an inn.

After a long day of travel the next day, Guillermo and Mencía returned the carriage late in the evening to the stable in Seville. They found the city was astir over the news that one of its sterling citizens, a beloved, respected son of the city, had been egregiously murdered. Authorities could not explain his purpose at the building, which he apparently owned. But the magistrate was tirelessly working the case, and his constables would soon find the fiends who had perpetrated the ghastly murder of one of the pillars of their community and church.

Guillermo and Mencía slept that night in the separate bedrooms of his brother's apartment. While getting a bite to eat before leaving in the morning, they overheard someone at the next table say that the slain trader's wife had probably hired someone to kill him, since she hated him.

They had earlier found a news notice in the lobby of their apartment building that sang the praises of Señor Gómez. After reading it with a laugh, Guillermo shoved it in his pocket, thinking it might also prove to be amusing reading for the others.

Back at the stable, they climbed on their horses and started on their way. The news notice also told how this great man and three other men had been killed by arrows, such that no one had heard or seen a thing.

As he and Mencía rode through the streets of Seville on their way out, Guillermo was hoping that no one would take notice of the bows strapped to their saddles.

Ch.25 Compadres

THAT EVENING, Guillermo and Mencía rode quietly past the house and pulled up their horses at the stable on his father's estate. Guillermo climbed down and stretched his sore muscles. He patted his horse on the neck and took the saddlebags down from its back. Mencía next to him was doing the same. A stableman appeared and said, "Señor Guillermo, Señorita Mencía, welcome back. Let me take care of your horses."

"Thank you, Manuel. Is all here well?" asked Guillermo.

"Yes, Señor. But as we say in the stables, Don Diego has been chomping at the bit, awaiting your return," he said, grinning.

"Come, Mencía," said Guillermo, chuckling, "We must go inside before he wears down his teeth."

Coming into the house, his father and mother rose excitedly from their chairs at seeing them and hurried forward happily to greet them. Andrés and Agustin then appeared and joined in the hubbub of hugging, laughing, and questions. Beatriz, the girl they rescued, was also there and came to thank them. Floriana's mother sat in a chair looking well and smiling at the joyful scene. The housekeeper was already bringing out food and wine.

"Guillermo! Mencía! You are back!" they heard from behind over the uproar.

It was Sebastian and Martín. The four compadres came together happily as the hubbub continued around them.

"Sebastian, did everything go well?" asked Guillermo.

"Yes, no problems and how about with you?"

"All went well with us," said Mencía. "The three girls are happily reunited with their families."

"Very good."

"Sebastian, Martín, come join us!" said Don Diego happily.

"Thank you, Don Diego, but you have much to talk about tonight and we can talk tomorrow."

"We will see you in the morning, my friends," said Sebastian smiling as he and Martín left.

"Yes, my friends," replied Guillermo.

Walking back into the living room, Guillermo announced, "Father, you would not believe how brave and intrepid your sons Andrés and Agustin were in our adventure. They were magnificent! I believe they have missed their calling. They are men-at-arms, not poets!"

Laughing, Andrés said, "Do not believe it, Father. We were far from it. The experience was, however, most inspiring and agreeable, that is, partaking in the daring rescue of innocent young maidens. I tasted for the first time the sweet sensation of chivalry. It felt most gratifying, would you not say, Agustin?"

"Yes, quite so, Andrés. I found it to be a most unique and agreeable sensation."

"I am proud of you all. It has proved to be a most fortunate event all around, for you have brought us this dear girl Beatriz," said Don Diego, grasping her hand. "In just one week, your mother and I have already become quite attached to her. We hope she will be happy here and decide to stay a while."

"How wonderful, Father. I am very happy for you all."

Going over to Floriana's mother, Mencía took her hand and said, "You are looking well and seem to be much better."

"Yes, thank you. Everyone here is wonderful to us."

"Because we hope to convince you to stay as well," said Don Diego sincerely.

Guillermo and Mencía were then ushered into the dining room to wash up, get some dinner, and tell about their trip. After two hours, Don Diego announced that they should call it a night to let Guillermo and Mencía get some well-deserved rest.

The next morning, Guillermo and Mencía, along with Andrés and Agustin, met with Sebastian and Martín in a happy reunion of compadres. They brought out wine and toasted to the happy success of their venture. Martín told how their return trip giving Seville a wide berth was uneventful and had taken a full day. Upon arrival, they had told no one of the box's contents and had put it in a locked cabinet in Don Diego's study.

Guillermo and Mencía told them about the deliveries of the girls back to their families and the happiness it had brought. Guillermo pulled out the news notice which he had snatched from their apartment lobby and dramatically read to them the words describing the slain trader as one of Seville's sterling citizens, which caused a great deal of disgust and amusement.

After putting away the notice with a final snort of disgust, Guillermo suddenly remembered something.

"And where are the ex-slaves, the man and two women?"

"They are already gone," said Sebastian.

"So fast?" asked Guillermo.

"They understandably wanted to get far away from Seville without delay," said Martín. "After talking together on the carriage ride from Seville, they decided they would travel east to Aragon, which they believed was an area of Spain more hospitable to those of Moorish descent. It sounded like good sense to us."

"We told Andrés and Agustin about the coins in the box and what you said about giving them each a double handful," said Sebastian.

"A box full of gold doubloons. We were quite astonished to hear it," interjected Agustin.

"We were quite surprised ourselves," said Guillermo.

"By the way," added Agustin, "we fully endorse the admirable idea of compensating the victims with portions of it."

"Quite so," seconded Andrés.

"Very good, so they got some coins then," said Guillermo.

"Yes," continued Sebastian, "the next morning, the four of us secluded ourselves in your father's study and made up three sacks of coins in the same manner as you had done in the shack. We later took the three aside and gave them each a sack, telling them that the money was to help them start their new life in Aragon. They happily received it and expressed a desire to leave right away in the morning."

"They told me that they intended to start out on foot and, at the first opportunity, buy two mules for the women to ride," said

Martín. "But I knew Don Hernando has spare mules, so I took the man there. He found two to his liking and bought them with a few of his doubloons. Don Hernando also exchanged two of the man's gold doubloons for silver coins to help them avoid unwanted attention during their travel.

"The three of them got packed up and left the next morning, with the women riding and the man walking in front and leading the mules. Before leaving, they thanked us again most sincerely and asked us to pass their thanks to you both as well."

"I am glad to hear it. So, I suppose we must now decide what to do with the rest of the coins," said Mencía.

That same afternoon, the six of them went into Don Diego's study, closed the doors, opened the box again, and stood looking in amazement at the many gold doubloons they saw. Guillermo suggested they first make equivalent sacks for the remaining victims, who were the girl Beatriz, his mother Floriana, and her mother whose son had been killed by the trader in a duel. They agreed to his suggestion as well as Agustin's suggestion of a reward for the dancer Matias. They made up three sacks and set aside ten coins for Matias.

Looking into the box, Guillermo said, "Now we must decide what to do with the others."

They looked at one another, and Guillermo said half-heartedly, "Well, I guess we could give it all to the church?"

Shaking his head, Agustin said, "You four brave hearts certainly deserve some of them for your daring rescue of the girls, an exploit nobly begun with no expectation of reward."

"Why just us four? You and Andrés were essential to the effort as well," said Mencía in reply.

"I agree," said Sebastian, slapping Agustin on the shoulder.

"And the ones who found my mother in the first place, which precipitated the entire undertaking," added Guillermo.

"I propose that we give ourselves a dozen coins each and then see what is left," suggested Guillermo. It was agreed, and when done, they saw nearly as many remained.

"Half for us and half for charity. That puts a fine unselfish finish to it," commented Guillermo.

"If I may make a suggestion," offered Andrés.

They all turned to Andrés, and he continued, "I, for one, would prefer to savor the enjoyment of our charity, not merely dump it into a church contribution box and be done with it."

"What are you suggesting?" asked Mencía, amused.

"Only that we split up the charity money as well, and then each of us can give it away as we please, such as to injured friends, food for the hungry, rewards for good deeds, or to contribution boxes if you want."

"A marvelous idea, Andrés!" said Agustin. "Getting pleasure from giving charity may sound sinful, but if so, it is a good sin!"

All agreed that Andrés had hit upon a fine idea and clambered to congratulate him. When counted out, each of them got nine more coins. They put the coins in small sacks and poured out wine in toast to their success and good fortune.

"I plan to convert several of my charity gold coins to 4-reales silver coins which I think would be safer for a person in need. A high value gold coin might be dangerous for them and bring them disaster," said Mencía.

"A good point, Mencía," said Agustin. "And 32 people then might benefit from the silver rather than just one from the gold."

"A good notion," agreed Guillermo.

Guillermo and Mencía later presented the sacks of coins to Floriana, her mother, and Beatriz. But Don Diego had been treating them with such kindness and respect, they were content to stay and saw no immediate need for the gold coins to start a new life elsewhere. Floriana wanted someday to visit Alvaro's boyhood friends and the priest in Seville, to thank them personally for their help. She and her mother thought of a headstone for Alvaro's grave. With time and prayers, Beatriz hoped to put the past behind her, find a husband, and start a family. The coins would be of use to her then, but for now, all three of them had no immediate need for the coins and gave the sacks to Don Diego for safekeeping.

Martín also had no plans for his money and would probably give it to Don Hernando for safekeeping. He did, however, ask for one favor of his friends before they left.

They were all together when he told them, "Sebastian said you originally planned to do some hunting here before all this arose. I would like to take you up into our hills for that hunting, which you originally planned. That is the favor I ask."

"Sebastian, Mencía, what do you think? Would you be in favor of a little hunting before returning home?" asked Guillermo, whimsically.

They both nodded their heads, smiling.

"It appears, my friend Martín, that we will be able to do you this favor," Guillermo told him with a smile.

Then to Mencía, he added, "You know, Mencía, I do not ever recall being more willing to do someone a favor."

"Nor I," said Mencía.

Early next morning, they met Martín at Don Hernando's stables and soon were off into the back woods of the estate. The hottest part of summer was over, and the deer were starting to come back down from the higher hills. They found that Martín was an excellent tracker and well acquainted with the usual hiding places of the deer. They were able to surprise a group of them and were back by midday with two good-sized bucks and a doe. They left two at Don Hernando's and brought the other to Don Diego's where the kitchen staff quickly put it to use.

Guillermo had planned to be away two or three weeks on this trip, but they had been away much longer. Needing to get back, they reluctantly decided to leave in the morning.

At their farewell dinner that night, Guillermo, Mencía, and Sebastian were the center of attention. Don Hernando came down with Martín to join in. Guillermo had never seen his father more buoyant and alive as he happily conversed with others and led toast after toast at the festive dinner. Mencía commented to Guillermo on his great affection for his new guests and what appeared to be the makings of his new family. Guillermo smiled and told her it was quite a change from the weak and pale man who he had first seen lying in bed only three months earlier.

He was gratified at the thought that he and his compadres had contributed to his father's great change of fortune. He thanked the new overseer Rodrigo at dinner for his fine work in managing his father's estate. Overall, it looked to be a promising and pleasant future for his father.

When Martín left, he thanked Mencía with great sincerity for including him in the project and for the kind treatment of his morisco kinsmen. He vowed he was forever at her service and ready at a moment's notice if she ever needed his assistance in the future. The three of them said a warm goodbye to their compadre and looked forward to when they might see him again.

Early the next morning, their horses and the extra pack horse were ready and awaiting them in front of the house. They said goodbye to Floriana's mother inside, but everyone else came outside to see them off. Guillermo said an emotional goodbye to his mother and father who stood together waving as they left.

Guillermo felt great affection for his two half-brothers as they did for him. Andrés and Agustin promised to come to see him perhaps in the spring and told him they would take the ten-doubloon reward to Matias on their next trip to Seville.

Since the return of Andrés and Agustin from the exploit with the trader, their father began to see a new side of them. They seemed to have grown a bit and now expressed more interest in events there on the estate. They might still pursue their interest in the arts in Seville, but he began to believe they might someday want to assume responsibility for the family estate when he grew too old. He credited this heartwarming development to Guillermo's influence and example.

Ch.26 Sebastian

AS THEY RODE, Guillermo, Mencía, and Sebastian talked about their recent adventure. Guillermo had only intended to bring punishment to the person who had victimized his mother, but much good had somehow resulted from it. He was not sure what to make of it all.

On their way through one small village, they came upon a weathered woman with two small children sitting by the roadside. She held up a bowl with a pitiful look as they passed. Guillermo continued past, deep in thought, and then stopped his horse. Reaching back, he got several silver coins from his sack and beckoned to the woman who came to him. Reaching down, he gave the coins to the woman who was excited by the generous gift. She blessed him and bowed in appreciation many times as he reined about and rejoined the others.

"I knew you were going to do that," said Mencía, smiling.

"Yes, it must have been obvious. They made me think of my mother and her mother-in-law, of course."

"I am so glad Andrés thought of splitting up the charity money. I felt good watching you help them as you must have felt doing it," said Mencía.

"Yes, much more rewarding than merely dumping gold doubloons into a church contribution box as Andrés put it. And changing a few of them for equivalent silver coins was a good idea too. Several silver coins are much more useful in her case."

Then he mused, "I hope she uses her silver coins for her own needs and does not put them in a collection tray passed at mass. Do not think too ill of me if I say it seems ironic to me that the poor give money to the church and not the other way around."

Sebastian chuckled and said, "Careful, Guillermo, the gift from God and the Wrath of God should not be saying such things."

As they passed through another small town, Sebastian pulled his horse to a stop in front of a shabby cobbler's shop.

He was deep in thought as he stared at the place and then down at his hands on his saddle horn.

Guillermo and Mencía had already ridden past. Looking back, they saw he had stopped and seemed troubled by something.

"Sebastian, what is it?" asked Guillermo, coming back.

He replied with a sad note, "This place reminds me very much of my father's cobbler shop. You see the dilapidated state of it. The cobbler probably lives in the back and barely earns enough to survive. My father was the same way. I was just thinking how he has far greater need of doubloons than me."

With a heavy sigh, he nudged his horse forward again. A few minutes later as they rode beside him, Mencía said, "Sebastian, you have never said much about your father before."

"No, it is not a favorite topic of mine. He has a cobbler shop, like that one, in a town in the desert hills south of the river. He wanted me to be his apprentice when I was young and continue his business. Can you imagine it? Me repairing shoes, groveling to customers, and living as poor as a church mouse for my entire life! I told him 'No thank you,' which caused a big fight and hard feelings. So I left and have never been back."

"No, I cannot imagine you as a cobbler, Sebastian," said Guillermo.

"And what about your mother?" asked Mencía.

"She died when I was small."

"Is this town far from here? Should we pay him a visit?"

"I believe I would like to see him again. It is out of our way, but no more than a day. Would you mind?"

"Not at all."

"I think it is a fine idea, Sebastian," said Mencía.

"Then it is unanimous! And where do we turn to go there, Sebastian?"

"We can turn south and ford the river at Almodóvar del Rio."

"By the castle on the hill," said Guillermo.

"Yes. The river is low this time of the year and should not be difficult to ford there. Then southeast eight or more miles across dry hilly country to the town. We return the same way back to Almodóvar del Rio and then can continue on our way. The dry hilly expanse south of the river is bandit country and we might have to defend ourselves.

"Perhaps we can just scare them off," said Guillermo. "Tell me, Sebastian, does your father live there by himself?"

"Yes, as far as I know."

"And how old is he?"

"I do not know, perhaps fifty."

"Perhaps Pascual could use a cobbler," hinted Mencía.

"I have thought of it," said Sebastian.

"If you are considering bringing him away, we should go first to see Don Carlos and borrow a carriage. He lives only one hour beyond the castle. We will go there first, spend the night, take a carriage to visit your father the next day, and be back with or without him again that night."

"That sounds very sensible. Thank you, my friends."

"There is no need for thanks, my friend. We are glad to do it. Are we not, Mencía?"

"Yes, very much so," Mencía said with a smile.

So it was agreed, and they quickened their pace.

Late the next morning, they saw the castle on the hill. It had originally been built long ago as a Roman fort. Later, it became a magnificent Moorish castle, but now it stood neglected. Still, they admired the impressive structure on the hill as they passed.

An hour later, Don Carlos and Doña Catalina happily welcomed them into their home. While they cleaned up and rested, a rider was sent to tell Don Francisco of their return. Not long thereafter, their neighbors arrived and joined them in an afternoon meal.

They all listened with great interest to their stories of the trip. They were amazed and delighted to hear Guillermo's natural mother had been found alive and brought back to his father's estate. Guillermo was trying to avoid telling all the details, but their questions brought out that she had been victimized and in hiding for years.

The boys knew him too well and asked how he had punished the ones who had victimized her. This brought out the rest of the story of finding the trader and rescuing the girls. Guillermo was only successful in glossing over the grizzly details.

The listeners were all quite enthralled and amazed as he told it. The boys had to periodically stand up in their excitement and give Mencía hugs of admiration. In the end, Don Carlos and his wife expressed their great happiness for their cousin Diego and their interest in possibly visiting him this fall when the weather was cooler.

When Guillermo told them about Sebastian's desire to visit his father, Don Carlos gladly agreed to lend them a horse and carriage for as long as they needed it. The boys wanted to go, but because the trip took them through known bandit country, they were not allowed.

The next morning after breakfast, with Sebastian driving the carriage, they were on their way back to Almodóvar del Rio where they forded the Guadalquivir River with Sebastian leading the carriage horse across by hand. Heading southeast from there, the terrain rapidly became dry, desolate, treeless low hills with an isolated scattering of wheat fields and olive orchards.

Up ahead on the road, they saw a carriage and five riders speeding toward them.

"Those travelers look to be in trouble," said Mencía as the three of them watched the party ahead approach and pull to a stop alongside them in a cloud of dust.

The driver of the carriage called to them, "Go back! Do not continue if you are wise. Bandits are in hiding back where the road runs near the trees along the creek. They normally will not attack a large party such as ours, but a great many of them rushed from the trees and surprised us. We exchanged pistol fire with them and got away, but they wounded one of my men. We must now get him some help."

Guillermo looked at the riders and saw one was leaning forward in his saddle with blood showing on his side.

"How many attacked you, and what weapons have they?" asked Guillermo.

"Nine, ten perhaps, armed with pistols and machetes. Do not continue. There are not enough of you. These bandits are horrid, desperate men."

"We can be horrid and desperate too," replied Guillermo.

"Then be warned and beware. Stay clear of the creek and its trees. We must go. God protect you."

"We thank you for the warning and wish you God's speed," called Guillermo as the carriage and riders started up again.

The three watched as the caravan rolled off in a new cloud of dust.

"What do you think, Sebastian? I am for continuing," asked Guillermo as he turned and looked at Sebastian in the carriage.

"Me too," said Mencía.

"I suppose if we do not bring my father out past these bandits, no one will," he replied.

"It is agreed then. Our arrows have four or five times the accurate range of their pistols. If they are smart, they will stay away," said Guillermo as he urged his horse forward.

After a half hour of travel down the road, they could see the thick growth of trees up ahead along a creek. The road there passed close by them. Guillermo also noted that the bare field along the other side of the road was somewhat flat and not rough. They would be able to leave the road and keep the trees at a distance as they passed.

Before leaving the road, Guillermo and Mencía tethered their horses to the carriage and walked ahead with their bows at the ready. Sebastian, with his bow nearby, coaxed the carriage horse forward off the road and began picking his way through the field. All seemed quiet.

"I can see them there in the trees," said Guillermo calmly.

"Yes, I see them too," added Mencía.

"I do not believe they will listen to any warnings from us, so we shall defend ourselves fully if they attack."

When abreast of the trees, three men on horseback suddenly emerged and rode out to about forty yards in front of their carriage blocking their way. As their horses wheeled about, the riders screamed wildly and brandished their pistols and machetes in the air.

Guillermo and Mencía took aim, and each let fly two arrows in rapid succession at the horsemen. Moments later, their arrows arrived. One arrow struck the upper body of a rider who fell to the ground and a second arrow struck the thigh of another rider. Seconds later, the third arrow whizzed by him. The fourth arrow took off the big straw hat worn by the third rider who looked surprised and unsure what to do.

From the trees, they heard a furious scream, "Now! You dogs! Get them! Attack!"

This set off a tirade of bloodcurdling yells and curses as seven filthy bandits armed with pistols and machetes burst from the trees and dashed madly at them.

Guillermo and Mencía turned their attention to the bloodthirsty fiends charging toward them. They heard a shot and Guillermo felt a bullet whiz past close-by. Surprised by the near miss, he looked and saw a cloud of smoke near the trees where two men with a musket were already beginning to reload.

"Mencía, a bullet just missed me. They are firing at us with a musket! Those two men on the left by the trees. I will take them while you help Sebastian with the ones rushing out."

"I will," she said as she aimed and fired her arrow.

The man with the musket was standing up and using a ramrod to ram wadding down the barrel. The second man, who was assisting in the loading and firing, was beside him, laughing and enjoying the fun. The two musketeers paid little attention to the people so far off at whom they shot. The first man was reaching up to pull the ramrod from the barrel when Guillermo's arrow struck him below his armpit. He slumped over and looked up in pain and surprise as he and his musket fell to the ground. The second man looked wide-eyed at him on the ground and raced for the trees, no longer laughing.

Mencía's first shot had narrowly missed a man who had stumbled in a hole and fallen just before the arrow had arrived. Sebastian was already out of the carriage and had let fly an arrow that struck one of the men in the shoulder. The man screamed and clutched his shoulder as he was whirled about by the impact of the arrow. He fell to the ground, but quickly picked himself up and began staggering back toward the trees.

Arrows from Guillermo and Mencía struck another man in the leg and barely missed a third man who upon noting the skill of the archers had started zigzagging while charging. But the narrow miss had been enough for him. He turned and started running wildly back toward the trees, still zigzagging. The leader of the bandits was furious when he saw the others hesitating as well.

"Attack! I said! Damn you!" he bellowed as he shot down one of his own men running for the trees.

"And he calls them dogs!" said Guillermo with disgust as he raised his bow.

The bandit leader was wheeling about, screaming curses and threats at his men, when an arrow struck him in the gut. He looked down at it in astonishment and started to tug at it. Now enraged, he raised his machete and staggered forward, snarling like a wild animal. He got no more than a half dozen steps before he crumpled and collapsed to the ground.

By now, all the remaining attackers on foot were retreating to the cover of the trees as the three defenders surveyed the scene. None of the rushing attackers had gotten near enough to use their pistols. Only the man with the musket had posed a danger, and he had been quickly dispatched.

"I think they have had enough," said Mencía.

The two remaining attackers on horseback were also headed for the trees with the third riderless horse following.

Still watchful, Guillermo and Mencía continued forward on foot as Sebastian climbed back into the carriage and followed behind them. No one ventured out from the trees to retrieve or use the musket again. As they passed the rider who fell to the ground, they picked up his pistol, found a couple of their arrows, and saw that despite the arrow in the right side of his chest, he was still breathing.

"This one is still alive," said Guillermo.

"We should leave the arrow in him for now. Perhaps his friends can patch him up, and he will learn to give up banditry," said Mencía.

Looking at the trees along the creek, Guillermo said, "I suspect that these bandits have not encountered skilled archers before. They did not seem to appreciate their danger."

Eyeing the man and musket on the ground, Sebastian replied, "I think not. I would like to get that musket away from them, but it is too dangerous to get so close to the trees. With them having a musket, we should take a wider swing past here on the return trip."

Looking around, Guillermo noted, "It looks passable farther out in the field too, so we should be able to do it."

"I agree," said Mencía, "but I suspect they have new respect for our arrows and will not make another attempt at us."

"Maybe not. Well then, we should be on our way," said Sebastian as he urged the horse forward.

In a few minutes, they were back on the road and remounted. When looking back, they saw no further sign of the hapless bandits. The three travelers seemed to be out of danger since the creek was now dry without trees from which they might be ambushed. So they rode on more quickly.

An hour later, Sebastian stood in front of his father's cobbler shop. He looked it over and commented that it had not changed much in ten years. He stepped inside and a small bell on the door announced his entrance. A thin frail man, hearing someone enter, stepped out from a door in the back. It took him a moment for recognition, but then he came forward and hugged his son.

"Sebastian, my son, I hoped you would one day return. I have missed you and am sorry we fought."

"Hello, Father, I am sorry too. It is good to see you again. You look thin as ever. Are you well?"

"I survive. That is all. But look at you, Sebastian. You have grown and are strong and healthy. Apparently, you were right to go, and I was wrong to ask you to stay."

"Father, I have two friends out front. We will bring our horses and carriage around back. Then we can talk more."

Inside the sparsely furnished living room, Sebastian introduced his father.

"Guillermo, Mencía, may I introduce you to my father, Sebastian. Father, these are my very good friends, Guillermo and Mencía."

"A pleasure, Señor," said Guillermo courteously. Then with a look to the younger Sebastian, he added, "Ah, so you are a junior."

"No," said Sebastian, laughing, "I am a sixth or a seventh, I cannot remember."

As Sebastian's father shook hands with Guillermo, he looked down and said, "Oh, you really should take better care of your boots. They are in need of mending. But Mencía, now, she has lovely boots."

"I am sure you are right, Señor. I will see to it at the very next opportunity," replied Guillermo with a look at the younger Sebastian.

The saddlebags were brought inside, and Guillermo pulled out some wine, bread, and sausage. They all managed to find a seat on the sparse furnishings and had a bite to eat. Sebastian's father was not accustomed to so much food and could only nibble at it.

"How is life here for you, Father?"

"Oh, business is good, I suppose."

"Do you have friends here?"

"No, all the old friends have died or left."

"I hate to tell you this, Father, but you are looking old."

"There is no need for you to tell me, my son. I already know it."

"Good. Then you know it is time for you to come live with me as our time-honored Andalusian customs dictate."

"Yes, I suppose it is our custom for a family to take care of its old. I always thought it a good custom. It seems even more so, now that I am the old one. You are indeed a good son, and I will be pleased to join you."

They both rose and embraced.

"Marvelous! Pascual will be pleased to have a cobbler," declared Guillermo as he and Mencía rose to congratulate them.

"How long will it take you to get ready, Father? We can leave today."

"Perhaps two hours. This house is not worth much. I will write a note saying that I donate it to the church. We can then take the note to the priest and, while there, visit your dear mother's grave a last time. I want to take some of my tools and supplies, but there is not much else here to take, just some clothes and a few mementos of your mother."

Two hours later, they were on their way. Sebastian's father was smiling as he sat beside his son in the small open carriage bouncing along the road. The sun was not overly hot and the breeze from their brisk pace felt good to him. It was the first time his father had been beyond the streets of his small town in years.

An hour later, they were at the stretch of the road by the wooded creek where they again steered into the field to keep the trees at a distance. As before, Guillermo and Mencía tied their horses to the carriage and walked with their bows ready. As they made a wider circuit of the trees, they saw the wounded rider was now gone. The musketeer and his musket were also nowhere to be seen. Only the dead body of the bandit leader still laid on the ground with the arrow in his gut. Vultures were already circling above. No bandits could be seen or heard in the trees this time. Guessing that the bandits had retreated to some camp back farther in the hills, Guillermo cautiously went to the dead bandit leader and retrieved his arrow as well as several others nearby. He then rejoined the others, and they continued.

An hour later, they were back again at the river, which they carefully forded without mishap.

When they pulled up in front of Don Carlos' house, Sebastian's father and his things were unloaded and taken into the house. At dinner, the humble cobbler was their guest of honor and quite overwhelmed by all the attention being paid him by these affluent but congenial people, as well as all the food and wine. When Don Carlos said a toast to the good health and happiness of Sebastian and his father, he looked blankly about at them. Sebastian had to tell him he also was to raise his glass and take a drink. He looked at his son and said, "Oh, yes, yes, of course." He then imitated the others, who were greatly touched and amused by his simplicity. For the benefit of his father, they did not stay up late.

After breakfast the next morning, they set out with Sebastian driving the small carriage. They paid their respects to Mateo's in-laws with a short visit to Don Francisco and his family, who were delighted to see that Sebastian had successfully bought his father out. Guillermo was already carrying a number of letters and the plant growing information from Don Carlos' gardener. Now, he was given more letters to take back to Mateo's parents, Luisa, and several others. Without much delay, they were soon on their way to Cordoba to pick up their hats.

Guillermo was pleased with his new hat and put it on right away. Mencía told him with a smile he looked quite dashing. Sebastian agreed with a laugh. That night was spent at Mencía's relations near Cordoba and the next morning they were on the last leg of their journey. They expected to arrive home before the day was out, after being away over four weeks.

When they arrived at Pascual's camp on the way, shouts of "Sebastian! Guillermo! Mencía!" were heard as everyone came out to boisterously welcome them.

"Welcome back, my friends!" said Pascual lustily as he came forward and embraced them.

"It is good to be back, Pascual," said Sebastian happily. "We have been away longer than expected."

"And who is this in the carriage?" asked Pascual.

"My father, who has come to live with me, Pascual," he said helping his father down from the carriage.

"He is a cobbler."

"Excellent! We truly have need of one here, and if you can make shoes as well as repair them, so much the better."

"We are both named Sebastian."

"Well, perhaps we will call him Papa then," said Pascual, shaking his hand.

"An honor, Señor. I am called Pascual."

"An honor, Señor," replied Papa.

"You have a magnificent son and are most welcome here," declared Pascual.

"I thank you very much and will try to be useful," said Papa.

"Very good," replied Pascual respectfully. Then looking at Guillermo, Pascual said, smiling, "So, Guillermo, you now wear a hat like Mencía. It looks good on you."

Tipping his hat with a smile, Guillermo said, "It is indeed good to see you again, Pascual."

"I think he looks quite dashing in it," said Mencía with a smile, which caused Guillermo to turn and frown at her.

"Yes, I suppose he does," said Pascual uncertainly. Then to Mencía, Pascual said, "But, Mencía, my dear, as usual, you look quite becoming in yours."

She smiled and tipped her hat too. Sebastian was laughing at their exchange. Hearing him, Pascual turned and said, "So Sebastian, you have no dashing hat, but tell me, how was the hunting?"

Suddenly remembering all that had happened before getting his father, Sebastian swelled with excitement.

"Pascual, there is so much to tell. You will not *believe* all that has happened. Our simple hunting trip turned into quite an exploit. Should you ever decide to retire, Pascual, I believe we have found your replacement."

Pascual blinked in surprise at this. Turning to Guillermo, still with a look of surprise on his face, he said, "Coming from such a man as Sebastian, I believe that is high praise indeed!"

"Sebastian exaggerates, Pascual," said Guillermo with a smile. "Do not believe him."

"Nevertheless, I look forward to hearing of your adventures, but you, Guillermo and Mencía, you should be on your way. It is happening."

"What is happening?"

"The baby. Mateo and Luisa's baby."

Ch.27 Conclusion

AFTER A MOMENT of stunned silence, Guillermo slapped Sebastian on the shoulder and said quickly, "Sebastian, my friend, thank you again for everything. I will talk with you soon. Pascual, everyone! Goodbye. We must be off."

Sebastian waved in reply as Guillermo and Mencía jumped on their horses, reined around, and galloped off. As he watched them leave, Sebastian said with a look of concern, "God grant it is a healthy baby and mother."

"Things with her have been progressing nicely, and they do not foresee difficulties. Let us hope so for the sake of our good friends," said Pascual.

Guillermo and Mencía rode fast. Less than a half hour later, they galloped up the drive to the main house, past Pedro and Juana's house and several others until the main house came into view. Up ahead, they saw men, women, and children out front kneeling, praying, and crossing themselves periodically. As they neared, someone rushed out excitedly and made a quick announcement, which brought them all to their feet in happiness. Some celebrated jubilantly while others stood rocking back and forth in their fervent prayers of thanks.

The throng of happy people barely noticed as Guillermo and Mencía pulled up, jumped from their horses, and raced past them.

Inside, they saw the housekeeper, who was wringing her hands in prayer, looking upward.

"Rosa! What is the news?" asked Guillermo, clutching her by the arms to get her attention.

Seeing him finally, she looked surprised and then happily said, "Guillermo! Thanks be to God, the news is good. They are all in the back and can tell you."

Already starting to feel happy, he and Mencía rushed back through a hallway. A physician and a midwife were coming from the room wiping their hands with a towel. The door to the bedroom was open, so they went in.

A crowd of people stood around the bed and were all talking at once in their happiness. Guillermo could not see through the crowd yet. Then Mateo's head popped up from the other side and he called, "Guillermo! Mencía! You are back."

At hearing Guillermo's name called out, his smiling parents Miguel and María at the foot of the bed, turned and waved them over.

"Come around by me," called Mateo.

As they came around the bed, they saw through the crowd Luisa propped up in the bed holding the baby. Several in the crowd were saying prayers and crossing themselves. Mateo made room for Guillermo and Mencía to see. There, they saw Luisa happily and proudly holding a beautiful baby. Luisa looked tired and pale but still beautiful. She smiled when she saw them and tilted the baby over so they could see its face.

"It is a beautiful baby, Luisa. Congratulations!" said Guillermo.

"Yes, a darling baby, Luisa. Congratulations," added Mencía.

As Mateo happily embraced Guillermo and then Mencía, he told them, "Luisa and the baby are both fine."

Don Lorenzo on the other side of the bed was focused on his fervent prayers of thanks. Mouthing a final one and crossing himself, he opened his eyes and gazed happily at the baby in front of him. Looking down, he pinched himself on the arm and smiled delightedly.

Glancing at his wife beside him, praying in thanks to God, he hugged her. Opening her eyes, she crossed herself and hugged him back, weeping with tears of joy. Ordinarily, she would have scolded him for interrupting her prayers, but now they happily embraced.

"I have pinched myself, Antonia. I felt it, so this is really happening. It is not a dream," he told her.

She smiled and glanced over at the baby. Seeing Guillermo and Mencía, she gave them a teary wave of recognition.

Noticing her wave, Don Lorenzo looked up too and beamed with happiness when he saw them.

With great emotion and difficulty, he managed to say, "Guillermo, Mencía, can you believe it? It is a boy."

The End

The adventures of Mateo, Guillermo, Mencía, and the others continue in *A Most Unusual Señorita.* Guillermo and Mencía have brought justice to his mother's attackers. Mateo has succeeded in supplying an heir for his family line. However, life in late sixteenth century Spain has more adventures in store for our true friends. JRC

List of Characters

by Mateo's Family (north of Cordoba)

Mateo & Guillermo - The true friends
Don Lorenzo & Doña Antonia - Mateo's father & mother

Miguel - Guillermo's father, Don Lorenzo's overseer
María - Guillermo's mother
Pedro & Juana - Don Lorenzo's gardener and his wife

Mencía - Mateo's date and then true friend
Margarita and Cristina - Mencía's younger sisters

Pascual - Local highwayman, Don Lorenzo's friend
Sebastian - One of Pascual's men, Guillermo's friend
Don Felipe - Don Lorenzo's estranged neighbor and friend
Don Tomás - Don Lorenzo's retired cavalier friend
Father Giraldo - Mateo's priest

by Luisa's Family (West of Cordoba)

Luisa - Mateo's love
Don Francisco & Doña Isabel - Luisa's father & mother
Domingo and Gabriel - Luisa's younger brothers
Don Carlos & Doña Catalina - Mateo's cousin & his wife
Father Benito - Luisa's priest

Don Gaspar & Luis - Rich neighbor & his son
Jorge & Susana – Don Gaspar's spies
Father Esteban - Wayward curate
Nicolas - Don Francisco's overseer
Lucas, Marcos, and Sancho - Don Francisco's stable hands

by Don Diego (Near Seville)

Don Diego - Mateo's uncle
Doña Teresa - Don Diego's deceased wife
Agustin and Andrés - Don Diego's sons

Floriana - Don Diego's love

Salvador - Don Diego's disloyal overseer
Rodrigo - Don Diego's new overseer
Don Hernando - Don Diego's wayward neighbor
Martín - Don Hernando's ranch hand, Mencía's admirer
Alvaro & Matias- Floriana's late husband & his friend
Bartolomé Gómez - rich trader, woman abuser
Beatriz - Rescued girl

Made in the USA
Las Vegas, NV
26 December 2023